Death by
Autopsy

ALSO BY JANE BENNETT MUNRO

Murder under the Microscope
Too Much Blood
Grievous Bodily Harm

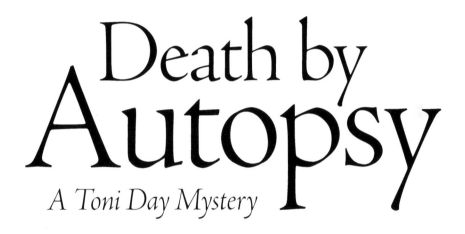

Death by Autopsy

A Toni Day Mystery

JANE BENNETT MUNRO

DEATH BY AUTOPSY
A Toni Day Mystery

iUniverse books may be ordered through booksellers or by contacting:

iUniverse
1663 Liberty Drive
Bloomington, IN 47403
www.iuniverse.com
1-800-Authors (1-800-288-4677)

ISBN: 978-1-4917-4479-6 (sc)
ISBN: 978-1-4917-4480-2 (e)

Library of Congress Control Number: 2014915626

Printed in the United States of America.

iUniverse rev. date: 10/02/2014

For my partners, John, Mike, and Kirk.
May this never happen to them.

Every autopsy I do—which is a very small part of my practice as a pathologist—begins with an external physical exam, starting with the head. Let's see … the patient is normocephalic with no evidence of head trauma. The sclerae of the eyes are not jaundiced. Pupils are round and regular in shape. They are reactive to light …
Whoa.
—posted on *The Straight Dope* web page, October 20, 2009

ACKNOWLEDGMENTS

Occasionally in the course of conversation, the subject of autopsies comes up. During one such conversation, someone said to me, "Eww, you do autopsies? On *dead* people?" To which I replied, "Well, yes, those live ones complain too much." At this point, my BFF, Rhonda Wong, chimed in with, "Besides, it would be death by autopsy." It's become a running joke, and Rhonda has been telling me ever since that I needed to write a book called *Death by Autopsy.*

This is it.

Rhonda reads my drafts and points out all my egregious errors, lets me bounce ideas off her, *ad nauseam*, and comes up with ideas of her own that she lets me use. She was the one who came up with the name Beulah Pritchard. She also knows quite a bit about canals because her father operated draglines for the Northside Canal Company for forty-eight years.

This is a work of fiction; all the characters in it are figments of my imagination, and any resemblance to any real persons is coincidental.

Some things in it are real, such as the Twin Falls Bank and Trust (which closed thirty years ago), the Twin Falls Canal Company, and the Low Line Canal. However, Cascade Perrine Regional Medical Center, Southern Idaho Community College, and the Intermountain Cancer Center are completely fictitious.

Thanks are in order for many people besides Rhonda:

To Dennis Chambers, formerly of the Twin Falls Police and former Twin Falls County coroner, for information on police procedure and for introducing me to the police lab. I'm still using the book he gave me twenty years ago.

To my good friend Marilyn Paul, Twin Falls County public defender, for getting me into the courtroom and giving me essential information on courtroom procedure and points of law.

To Joe Webster and Brian Olmstead of the Twin Falls Canal Company— particularly Joe, who spent countless hours helping me with plotlines involving the canal company and its fictional personnel and actually vetting the chapters pertaining thereto.

To Tom Carter, Twin Falls County sheriff, and Darren Brown, lieutenant in charge of search and rescue, for rescue details.

To Nancy Howell and Kelly Peterson, evidence techs for the Twin Falls sheriff's department, for details on collecting and processing evidence.

To Cathy Powlus, lab employee, for the story of Vern, the dead man who moved on command.

To Charles Smith, MD, radiation oncologist at Mountain States Tumor Institute in Twin Falls, Idaho, for information on radiation therapy of prostate cancer.

To Anne Taylor Pitts, legal counsel for St. Luke's Magic Valley Regional Medical Center in Twin Falls, Idaho, for information on the legal ramifications of death by autopsy.

1

*If it were done when 'tis done,
then 'twere well it were done quickly.*
—SHAKESPEARE, MACBETH

I WAS GOING TO DIE.

I knew it.

The only question was whether I'd drown first or freeze to death first.

I'd had close calls before. I'd been poisoned, trapped in the basement of a burning house, and chased down the Snake River by a gun-toting madwoman. But this was different. Nobody was threatening me this time. It was just my own pigheadedness that had gotten me into this situation.

That's what I got for trying to be a Good Samaritan.

I'd been on my way home from the airport, having picked up Mum and Nigel, and I'd seen the car approaching from the opposite direction, but it wasn't until it was nearly upon us that I became aware that it was going much too fast for the snow and black ice. Moreover, it was weaving all over the road.

"What is that idiot doing?" Mum asked.

"Bloke's obviously in the bag, eh what?" Nigel commented.

Nigel Gray, my stepfather, was a retired Scotland Yard detective. He resembled Doctor Bombay of the old *Bewitched* series, but he was grayer

1

and not nearly as pompous. And he clearly adored my mother, who, even in her sixties, bore a strong resemblance to Susan Hayward. She and I had the same green eyes, but my hair was black and my complexion olive, like my father's had been.

I slowed and pulled to the side of the road. I had no desire to share the bridge over the canal with a drunk driver.

"What are you doing, kitten?" Mum asked.

I had no time to answer her.

The vehicle, a beat-up sedan that looked like it dated back at least to the eighties, crested the rise, swerved, slid off, and disappeared. "Uh-oh," I said.

Mum gasped. "Did you see that?"

I pulled back out onto the road, crossed the bridge, pulled off the road again, and parked on the other side. The car was nowhere to be seen.

I hauled out my cell phone and called 911.

"A car just went off the road into the Low Line Canal," I reported when the dispatcher answered.

"What road are you on?" she asked.

"Washington South," I replied.

"Northbound or southbound?"

"Who, me or the car?" I asked.

"The car. Sorry."

"Southbound."

"Is anyone hurt?"

"I don't know. Want me to look?"

"No. Someone will be there in less than fifteen minutes. Don't try to go into the canal after them," she warned. "We don't want to have to rescue you too. Just stay where you are until we get there."

After asking me for my name and cell phone number, we disconnected. I opened the driver's door and started to get out of the car.

"Where are you going, kitten?" asked Mum.

"I'm just going to look," I said. "Maybe I can help."

"Didn't that lady tell you not to go into the canal?" she said.

I'd used to wish my cell phone were easier to hear. But my new smartphone was so loud and clear that everybody could hear it. "I know," I said, "but I'm a doctor. I have to at least look."

Farmland around Twin Falls, Idaho, is irrigated by a series of canals and coulees. We get about eight inches of precipitation a year here, including snow, and we can't depend on rainfall. Occasionally kids drown in the canals and coulees in the summertime, and rarely an adult. The cool water is tempting, and people don't realize how deep it is or how fast it moves.

The High Line and Low Line canals were big suckers, fifty feet wide from bank to bank and twelve to fifteen feet deep at the points where they ran under the bridges on Blue Lakes Boulevard and Washington Street South. Those were major canals that carried most of the water from Milner Dam, on the Snake River, to this part of the Magic Valley. A lot could be hidden in those canals—like bodies or stolen cars. I'd even heard stories of motor homes that weren't discovered until after the water was turned off in the fall.

I got out of the car, ignoring any further protest from my passengers. I looked both ways, gingerly crossed the icy road, and approached the smashed guardrail. As I made my way to the edge, a concrete abutment blocked my way on the left. A pair of gates, with four-foot-high iron frames, blocked me on the right. Between them, the bank dropped off abruptly. I couldn't see the car at all.

I climbed up on the concrete abutment. From there I could see the car. The back end of it stuck up out of the water. The snow on the bank was deep enough to keep me from sliding into the canal. This gave me the confidence to keep on going until I reached the back bumper of the car. I put my hand on it to help me keep my balance while I made my way down toward the driver's door. Suddenly, the car shifted and slid all the way into the water with a splash. And I went right in after it.

Whereupon every muscle in my body immediately went into overdrive. The breath whooshed out of me. I gasped and whooped, struggling to keep my head above water, and after approximately a century, I realized that I didn't need to struggle after all. My feet actually touched bottom, and the water was not actually over my head. Taking a huge breath, I ducked my head under water and opened my eyes. The water was so murky that I could barely see the car, even though the current had plastered me right up against it.

Well, now it was more imperative than ever that I get the passengers out of that car. With water in the canal, they could drown before anyone could rescue them. What the hell was water doing in the canal in March, anyway? Normally they don't release water into the canals until late April.

I stuck my head up out of the water, took another gasping breath, and put my head back under. My muscles were so cramped with cold that I could barely move. My ears ached. I felt my way down to the driver's door handle and tried to open it, but I had no purchase anywhere. I couldn't get it open. I could see that there was only a driver and no other passengers, but I couldn't make out any details in the murk.

The dispatcher had said that search and rescue would be there in less than fifteen minutes. But I knew that oxygen deprivation could cause brain damage in four minutes. I knew it would take longer in the cold, but I wasn't sure how much longer.

By that time I'd realized that with the current and the pressure of the water against the car door, there was no way in hell that I was ever going to get that door open, no matter how long I struggled with it. Much as it frustrated me to do so, I gave up. I let go of the door handle and pulled myself along the car's length until I reached the side of the canal. Now all I had to do was find a way to climb out and get back into my nice, warm, dry car.

Easier said than done. The sides were straight up and down and reached several feet above my head.

Now that I was standing on the bottom of the canal, I could see that the framework around the gates included a couple of crosspieces between the two sides. They'd make dandy steps for me to climb out of the water, except for one small detail: the lowest crosspiece was at chest level, too high to step up on.

I tried jumping up and grabbing the upper one. Got it! Now what? I'd have to bend myself in half like a jackknife to get a foot onto the lower one. I couldn't do it. I tried kicking to lift myself, grab the frame, and haul myself up out of the water. I couldn't do it. My muscles weren't working. And my boots were full of water. I was well and truly fucked.

I'd thought the water was cold, but that was nothing compared to the air as felt through wet clothes. Had I seriously thought I didn't need to worry about wind chill? If I got out of this water, I'd instantly turn into a five-foot-three ice sculpture. I was going to die of hypothermia whether I stayed in the water or got out in the wind. I could call for help, but Mum and Nigel wouldn't hear me from the car. Then I heard it.

Sirens. Help was on the way.

In Twin Falls County, there aren't that many occasions to rescue people. As a result, people's skills grow rusty, and so do their vehicles. To prevent this, every 911 call results in the dispatch of police cars, fire trucks, and ambulances, whether they're needed or not. That way, everybody's skills stay fresh, and the vehicles are maintained. In this instance, they'd also bring a tow truck and a couple of divers from the sheriff's department's search and rescue team.

I looked up to see Nigel standing by the gates. He reached down and said, "Here, my girl, grab my hand. Fiona, give me a hand here, would you?"

The two of them braced themselves on the gate frame and pulled; but nothing doing. I seemed to have taken root on the bottom of the canal.

Nigel let go of me. "Take off your coat and boots," he said.

"Are you out of your mind?" I asked through chattering teeth.

"No, dash it all," he replied in exasperation. "You're too heavy in your wet clothes. Take off your coat and boots and pass them up here to me."

It took what seemed to be an inordinate length of time just to get the buttons undone with my frozen, uncooperative fingers, but finally I passed my coat up to Nigel, and then my boots, which, luckily, were slip-ons. He poured the water out of them and placed them next to the gate frame. Then he and Mum reached down, took my hands, and hauled me, inch by inch, up out of the water.

Water poured from me as they pulled me steadily upward, and then, as soon as I got my toes on the upper crosspiece, I climbed out the rest of the way myself, hooking my arms around the frame because my hands were useless. Nigel put my soaked boots back on my feet so I wouldn't have to step on the frozen ground in my wet stocking feet.

Oh. My. God. It was so cold. I'd never known such cold. Nigel took off his coat and put it over me, and the two of them got me back to my Subaru just as the rescue vehicles began to arrive. I started to get into the car, but Nigel stopped me. "Take your clothes off," he ordered me. "All of them."

I groaned at the thought of exposing my naked body to the frigid air, not to mention all the police, fire, and sheriff's department representatives that were just arriving, but I knew Nigel was right. If I left my wet clothes on, they would continue to suck heat from my already hypothermic body.

So, somewhat shielded from view by my car and Nigel's coat, I took off all my clothes, underwear and all. Mum fetched the blanket that I kept in the back of the Subaru and wrapped me in it. Nigel tossed my wet clothes and his wet coat into the back. Then he got into the driver's seat and cranked up the heat. Mum got into the backseat and wrapped her beaver coat around both of us to share her body heat while she scolded me.

"Antoinette, really, what on earth were you thinking? You need to go straight home and get into bed, kitten."

"Not yet, more's the pity," said Nigel. "They're going to want to talk to us."

No sooner were those words out of Nigel's mouth than the sheriff himself tapped on the driver's side window. He was a big man, almost as tall as my husband, Hal, but heavier. He wore his badge on a heavily padded brown jacket with the collar turned up around his neck and a bomber hat with earflaps turned up and not doing his ears any good at all. Nigel opened the window but only partway. The blast of cold wind that resulted caused me to moan and shiver convulsively. Nigel glanced back briefly before addressing the sheriff.

"I say, officer, we're trying to keep warm here. I need to keep this window closed."

"I need to talk to you, sir," the sheriff said. He had a deep and resonant voice, and his attitude brooked no refusal.

"Come round and get into the car," Nigel suggested.

The sheriff shook his head. "We'll talk in my car, if you please."

"Very well," Nigel said mildly and rolled the window back up. He got out of the car, causing another blast of cold air, and accompanied the sheriff across the road to his car. The divers, in dry suits, made their way down into the water to hook up the tow chain to the car. After a brief conversation, both men came back across the road. Nigel got back in the car, and the sheriff came around to the passenger side and got in, closing the door behind him. He took off the bomber hat to reveal a bald head rimmed with graying brown hair. I noted the lack of a comb-over with approval. He also had a thick brown moustache that rivaled Nigel's gray one and kind brown eyes.

"Bob Barton," he said. "Twin Falls County sheriff."

"Toni Day," I told him. "I'm a pathologist at the hospital. This is my mother, Fiona Gray."

I'd had lots of contact with the police and fire departments, but so far I hadn't been involved with anything in the sheriff's jurisdiction.

"Heck, I know who you are," he said. "I bowl with Pete Vincent. He talks about you all the time."

"I hope it's good," I said, "seeing as how I'm his mother-in-law."

Pete Vincent, a police detective lieutenant, was married to Hal's daughter, Bambi, a police evidence tech.

"Was it you who called this in?" the sheriff asked.

I nodded.

He looked at me and frowned. "Did you go into the canal?" he asked.

I nodded. "I'm a doctor. I had to try to help," I told him.

"How about you tell me what happened? Just in your own words, of course."

He must have been an aficionado of courtroom drama. I wondered whose words he thought I might use instead.

The tow truck seemed to have encountered a problem. Men congregated around it. The divers had climbed out of the water. I wondered how. I hadn't been able to manage it, and I hadn't been wearing a dry-suit. A deputy came over to the car and tapped on the window. Nigel opened it partway and said, "The sheriff's over here," and closed it again. The deputy came around to the passenger side and opened the door, which let in another blast of cold air. He might as well have stayed on Nigel's side of the car and talked to the sheriff through the window.

"What's up?" the sheriff asked.

"Guess they're gonna have to get an excavator over here. That car needs to be pulled straight up, and the tow truck can't do it."

Mum said, "Do you have any more questions? Because we really need to get Antoinette home. She's frozen, and her husband will be frantic."

"No, Mum," I objected. "I didn't go through all that just to leave without seeing how this ends. Hal will be okay. Don't you want to see the rescue?"

"Not especially," my mother said. "How long is this going to take, do you think?"

"Not too long," the sheriff said. "There's the excavator now." He got out of the car and headed back across the road to where a truck pulling a trailer had just pulled over and parked. On the trailer sat a large yellow vehicle on tank treads with a huge apparatus sticking straight up in the air. It was folded double, with a large scoop hanging from the end. The driver ran around to the back of the trailer and let down a ramp. As he began to back the excavator down it, the other rescuers hastily relocated their vehicles to allow the excavator access to the submerged car.

With fascination I watched as the driver skillfully positioned the excavator and began to extend the arm with the scoop out over the water. As he lowered the scoop toward the water, I noticed that the scoop had an opposing jaw. By the time the scoop hit the water, the jaws were wide open.

With excruciating slowness, the scoop sank into the water and came up holding the car. Water ran from it as the arm lifted it high, swiveled around, and placed it on the ground. Rescuers pulled open the driver's door and began to extract the driver, a short plump woman with sodden blonde hair that obscured her face.

I extricated myself from Mum's coat and reached into the cargo compartment for Nigel's coat and my boots.

"Antoinette, what do you think you're doing?" my mother demanded.

"I need to get a closer look," I said as I struggled into Nigel's coat.

"You'll do no such thing, young lady."

I pulled my wet boots back on my feet, gritting my teeth as I did so. "I have to, Mum." I got out of the Subaru and ran across the street. Paramedics had the body on a gurney and had begun to administer CPR. Cold wind hit my bare legs, making me shudder. "Any idea who she is?" I inquired through chattering teeth.

The sheriff held out an open wallet in which the driver's license was clearly visible. The name on it was Beulah Mae Pritchard.

Oh my God.

I knew Beulah. I'd known her for years. Furthermore, I knew her well enough to know that there were a number of people who would be glad to have her out of their lives for good.

Could one of them have had anything to do with this?

"You want to make sure that car wasn't tampered with," I told the sheriff. "This may not be an accident."

He stared at me in disbelief. "You mean ..."

"Yes. She could have been murdered."

2

'Tis because stiffish cocktail, taken in time
Is better for a bruise than arnica.
—ROBERT BROWNING

BY THE TIME WE GOT home, I was warm enough to have stopped shivering, but the barelegged sprint from the car to the house wrapped in Nigel's coat started me up again. Killer and Geraldine, our dogs, circled me, sniffing. Killer was a big German shepherd who was beginning to go a little gray around the muzzle, and Geraldine was a diminutive terrier mix, black with brown markings that made her look like a tiny Rottweiler. They were the best of friends.

Geraldine sneezed and looked disgusted.

Hal looked at me, aghast. "What the hell—" he began.

"Run upstairs and change, kitten," Mum urged.

"Will someone," Hal thundered, "please tell me what's going on?"

My husband, Hal Shapiro, towered over me by a foot and outweighed me by nearly a hundred pounds, so when he thundered, he could be quite intimidating. With his blond hair, blue eyes, and ruddy complexion, he looked like a Viking, but in actuality he was a mild-mannered college professor. Throwing his hands in the air and shouting *"Oy gevalt!"* to the ceiling was about as violent as he ever got.

I slipped past him and ran upstairs. Spook, my black cat, ran ahead of me and fell over right in front of me on the landing, no doubt expecting me to stop on a dime and rub his belly. I sidestepped him. *Not today, cat.*

"I daresay we could all use a little libation, eh what?" I heard Nigel say. "Brandy all around? For medicinal purposes, of course."

"Make it scotch," I yelled from the head of the stairs. "I don't like brandy."

"I believe I'll have some brandy," my mother said in a shaky voice. She sounded as if she was about to cry—reaction setting in, no doubt. But no worries. Nigel would wrap her in his arms and fix all that. A very comforting sort of bloke, our Nigel, in spite of all his British bluster.

By the time I'd taken a hot shower, washed my hair, and come back downstairs all snug in my favorite old black sweats, everyone was settled in with their libation of choice. Hal handed me a large scotch. I took a huge swig and nearly choked myself on the fumes.

"Hey, take it easy!" Hal said. "You don't have to drink it all at once. Your mother's told me all about what happened." He drew me over to the couch and sat next to me with his arm around me. He kissed the top of my head.

"Did she tell you who it was?" I asked.

Hal shook his head.

"Beulah Pritchard."

"Beulah Pritchard, really? Good riddance," Hal said. "Couldn't have happened to a nicer person."

"Who's Beulah Pritchard?" asked Mum.

"She's a nurse at the hospital," I said.

When I first came to Twin Falls seventeen years ago, Beulah Pritchard, RN, had already been at Perrine Memorial for ten years. At the time, she'd been office nurse to an elderly family physician who has long since retired, and she had been office nurse for several different doctors since.

Beulah, a short, plump, blonde with washed-out blue eyes behind smudgy spectacles, had a pug nose and round, red cheeks, and she always gave the impression that she was a warm and friendly person. That is, until she opened her mouth. She reminded me of a dog that wagged its tail and smiled at you until you got close enough for it to bite you.

At the time of our move to the new hospital earlier this year, some of the office nurses had retired or quit because Cascade didn't pay office nurses as much as Perrine Memorial had. Some of them had said openly that they couldn't afford to keep their present jobs. Beulah had been in her late fifties by then, and I'd hoped she would be among those who quit—but no such luck.

Instead, she had been promoted to nursing administration. Perhaps it was because of her outstanding people skills, but I doubted it. I thought it was in spite of them.

It was the Peter Principle at work.

Instead of patients, Beulah would deal with nurses, pharmacists, the microbiology lab, and doctors. She would be the Chairman of Infection Control.

At Perrine Memorial, that had been me.

At Cascade Perrine Regional Medical Center, it was Beulah, a newly promoted nurse administrator with a chip on her shoulder. Beulah took delight in informing people that she was now doing the same job that I had previously done, intimating that she would do it better than I had.

I forbore to point out that infection control was her full-time job, whereas for me it had been just one of many jobs, and she had assistants that I hadn't had. It wouldn't have made any difference.

"Did you know her well?" Nigel asked.

"I've known her a long time," I said, "but I wouldn't say I know her well. She was a swizzle stick. She liked to stir up trouble. She went around starting rumors. She started a rumor that I was having an affair with one of the doctors, and his wife found out about it and threatened to divorce him. She also went around saying that Hal and I were having trouble and might get divorced."

Hal interrupted me. "You didn't tell me about that," he said. "Why would she say such things? What did you ever do to her?"

"More to the point, what did Russ Jensen ever do to her?" I returned.

"Russ Jensen?" my mother asked.

"The doctor in question," I said. "Anyway, neither of those rumors is true. I'm sure she spread lots of rumors like that about other people, because that's what she does. Did. But I don't pay any attention to gossip—it's not my thing—and that's hardly a reason to kill a person, anyway."

"*Oy vey*," Hal muttered.

Nigel interjected, "That would depend on what the rumor was and whom it was about, eh what?"

"You took an awful chance, you know," Hal said.

"I know that," I said. "Are you telling me that I shouldn't have even tried to save her? That I should have just stood by and waited for search and rescue to show up?"

"That's what most people would have done."

I threw up my hands. "I may as well have done just that, for all the good I did."

Hal's arm tightened around me. "Calm down, sweetie. I'm proud of you for what you tried to do. But that doesn't change the fact that two people drowned in the canals last year."

"Really." I looked at him narrowly. "So how come you're all up on the drowning statistics for the canals?"

Hal reached over and picked up a newspaper from the coffee table. "Because," he said smugly, "there's an article in today's paper that says the Bureau of Reclamations is releasing water early this year because they expect more spring runoff from the snowmelt than the reservoirs can hold. It says here that they can predict how much runoff to expect, and they know how much water is in the reservoirs from the year before, and if there's too much, they release it."

"Well, that explains why there's water in the canal in March," I said. "And by the way, I didn't intend to go in. I fell in."

"Was the current as fast as they say?" Hal asked.

"I'd say so. If that car hadn't been there, I'd be halfway to Buhl by now."

"If that car hadn't been there," Nigel said, "you wouldn't have been in the canal, eh what? And speaking of which, what about those canals? I mean to say, this isn't Venice."

"The canals were built for irrigation," I said. "This is a desert."

"They were the brainchild of one Ira Burton Perrine," Hal said, "who came to this valley in 1883 and decided that it would make prime farmland if only it had water."

"The bloke your hospital's named after," Nigel said.

"So that's how the Twin Falls Canal Company was born," I said.

"Right," Hal said. "Perrine got a bunch of investors together, and they formed the Twin Falls Land and Water Company, the parent company of the Twin Falls Canal Company. They hired engineers and laborers, and when the canals were first opened to let the water out onto the land, it bloomed. Like magic."

"Which is why this area is called the Magic Valley," I said.

"I say," Nigel said. "I was wondering about that too. Toni, my girl, another scotch?"

"Why not," I said. "Mike's on call this weekend."

"Righto," Nigel said and headed for the kitchen.

The phone rang.

"Dr. Day, it's Natalie. We've got an autopsy."

"But I'm not on call," I told her. "Mike is."

Mike Leonard, MD, was my partner. Originally from Texas, he grew up in a family of five brothers and a pathologist father. His perpetually sunny disposition never failed to make me feel better about practically everything. Mike had come to Perrine Memorial almost by accident seven years earlier. His father-in-law, Nicholas Schroeder, MD, a pathologist, had done a *locum tenens* for me; that is, he substituted for me while I dealt with my role as chief suspect for the murder of Dr. Sally Shore, the itinerant surgeon who had tried to short-circuit my career back in 2005. Her body had been found in my office, and I'd been the prime suspect. Because of Dr. Schroeder's insistence that one person could not possibly handle the workload that I'd handled solo for the previous ten years, the medical staff had agreed to recruit a second pathologist, and Mike had just happened to be finishing his residency without a job prospect in sight. He'd won my heart from the first time he'd stuck his hand out and said, "Hey."

"I called Dr. Mike," Natalie said. "He's got the stomach flu."

Crap. "Okay. I'll be there as soon as I get dressed." I hung up. Nigel returned with my scotch. I shook my head at it. "I guess I don't get to have this yet. Mike's got the stomach flu, so I have to go do this autopsy."

My mother had come downstairs while I was on the phone. "Antoinette, darling, that is simply out of the question. You need to be tucked up in bed."

I turned my palms up. "Mum, I don't have a choice. Mike's sick."

"You'll catch your death," she warned me. "You mark my words."

No matter how often I explain to my mother that colds are caused by a virus and not from being cold, she always says that.

On the other hand, who knew what nasty little critters might have been floating around in the Low Line Canal this morning?

3

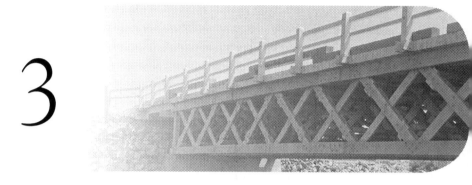

It ain't over till it's over.
—Yogi Berra

"THE BODY IS THAT OF a fifty-eight-year-old, well-nourished, well-developed, unembalmed white female, sixty-two inches in height and weighing approximately ... oh, what would you say, Natalie? One eighty? Two hundred?"

Natalie Scott was one of my two histotechs, whom I was training to be an autopsy assistant. Natalie, already ASCP-registered in both medical and histologic technology, had come to work for me during the Sally Shore affair. Actually, she was Sally Shore's daughter, a gorgeous girl with long, black hair and blue eyes. She had been brought into the hospital by her mother when Lucille Harper, my other histotech, was severely injured and required months of therapy before returning to work. By that time, I'd acquired a partner, and we needed two histotechs. Sally Shore was long gone, but Natalie was still here, happily married to one of my med techs.

We'd begun the autopsy at five o'clock, about an hour after Natalie had called me. When I arrived at the morgue, she had everything set up and ready to go, and the coroner, Roland Perkins, was waiting for me.

"Hello there, young lady," he greeted me.

Roland Perkins was the proprietor of Parkside Funeral Home, which was just across the park from where Perrine Memorial used to be. I'd used his establishment as my morgue for the last ten years or so. Now that we had our own morgue, I kind of missed Rollie's avuncular presence. Rollie always referred to himself as "this fat little mortician," and that was a pretty apt description. His eyes twinkled behind wire-rimmed spectacles, and he was nearly always smiling, but his sepulchral voice, so appropriate for an undertaker, belied his jolly fat-man persona.

"Hi, Rollie," I greeted him. "Have you come to sign the consent?"

"I guess I have to," he rumbled. "Your son-in-law tells me they haven't yet located a next of kin."

"They haven't found her husband yet?"

"Not so far." Rollie signed the consent with a flourish, and I slipped the top copy into the patient's chart, which had accompanied her to the morgue. Then he left.

Now Natalie squinted critically down her nose at Beulah's body. "I'd say she's at least two hundred," she said disdainfully. Of course, Natalie herself weighed about as much as my left leg, so maybe she was less forgiving of the exogenous obesity of others than I was.

Beulah's short, round body threatened to spill over the sides of the autopsy table. There was barely room for her arms. Water that ran from the hose at her head threatened to back up on either side of her and run over the sides, because her arms impeded the flow back to the drain at the foot of the table. I kept having to lift them up out of the gutters to allow the water to flow. Finally, I shoved a couple of headrests under them to keep them up out of the water, and then her fingers kept catching on my apron as I walked back and forth.

I had my shoes protected by surgical booties; what I needed were galoshes—or waders. The rest of me was encased in a plasticized paper jumpsuit that would have accommodated two of me. My hair was protected by a surgical cap and my face by a splash shield. Natalie was similarly clad. Over it all, I wore a plastic apron that reached to the floor and had ties long enough to go all the way around me and tie in front. That's what Beulah's fingers kept catching on.

Beulah's body, when I touched it, was icy cold. She had apparently gone directly from the canal to the emergency room, where she'd been pronounced dead, and then to the morgue, where she had been stored in the cooler ever since. As I circled the table, palpating her abdomen for fluid or enlarged organs, her breasts for lumps, her armpits and groins for enlarged lymph nodes, my gloved fingers grew as cold as she was.

She had a hell of a shiner on the right side of her face. Below it, a wide, reddish mark suggested that she'd been slapped really hard. You could practically see the imprint of each finger. I pulled back her eyelids. Her pupils were fixed and dilated, measuring at least six millimeters. The sclera, or white, of the right eye was hemorrhagic, and the eye was deviated upward. I palpated the edge of the orbit; it gave slightly, and I felt sharp edges. Her orbital bone had been fractured. Her nose had been fractured too. It was deviated to the left and had been bleeding.

Her wispy blonde hair was full of blood. I palpated her scalp gingerly, parting the hair to look for the responsible injury, and I found it on the left side of the back of her head—a jagged laceration about ten centimeters long, or about four inches.

When I moved on to the rest of the body, I found more bruises on her lower chest and abdomen, arms and legs. Her left little finger had been fractured. Several of her fingernails were broken and bloody. Was it her blood—or someone else's? Perhaps she'd fought back. Whoever she'd been fighting with would have deep scratches on his face.

Somebody should have bagged her hands, I thought.

It would have taken more than one blow to fracture both her orbital bone and her nose. Perhaps her head had hit the steering wheel on impact. Was it possible to hit one's head that hard on the steering wheel while restrained by a seat belt? Had she been restrained by a seat belt? Maybe she had hit the windshield instead. Could the seat belt have inflicted those lower chest and abdominal bruises? Again, that was assuming that she'd been wearing one.

No way had she gotten all those injuries from going into the canal. For one thing, if she'd banged her head on the steering wheel or windshield, or had sustained bruises from the seat belt, would she have bruised that much after going into the canal? Wouldn't the cold water have prevented that? And where had the injury on the back of the head come from? Not from hitting the windshield, surely. That would have left a bruise on the front of her head, which she didn't have.

I pointed out all these injuries to Natalie as she was laying out my instruments for me.

She sucked air through her teeth. "Did she get all that from her accident?" she wondered aloud.

"I think not," I told her. "I think she was severely beaten before she drove into the canal."

"By her husband, I suppose," Natalie said darkly, which reminded me that when she had first come to work for me seven years ago, she had been on the run from an abusive ex-fiancé.

"I don't know," I said. "It's anybody's guess. Whoever it was, she fought back. We need to bag her hands."

"How did she manage to drive with a broken finger?"

"God knows," I said. "Besides that, if she got that orbital fracture before she went into the canal, she'd have been driving with only one working eye."

"Oh my God," Natalie said. "What about the head laceration?"

"I'm thinking that whoever punched her in the right eye hard enough to break her orbital bone knocked her over so that she hit her head when she fell," I said. "The blow would turn her head to the left, so that would be where it hit whatever caused the laceration."

The bell rang just then, and Natalie ran to see who was there. I pulled the sheet hastily over Beulah's body. Natalie returned with Sheriff Bob Barton and another man I didn't recognize. "Hi, Doc," the sheriff greeted me. "This here's Randy Schofield from the Twin Falls Canal Company. He's the manager, and he drove the excavator that got the car out of the canal."

Then, of course, I recognized him. Randy Schofield was as tall as the sheriff and about the same age but much thinner. He had sandy hair and blue eyes, and he reminded me of my son-in-law, Pete Vincent. "Hi, Randy," I said, holding my gloved hands up. "Pardon me if I don't shake hands. I was just about to start an autopsy here."

"Glad to meet you, Doc," he said. "I heard you went into the water to try to save her. You were lucky you didn't drown."

"I know," I said. "Can I ask a stupid question? What keeps the excavator from tipping over when you extend that arm out over the water?"

"Counterweights," Randy said. "Those things won't tip over unless some idiot drives one down the bank. So, what'd she die of? Drowning or hypothermia?"

"I don't think she drowned," the sheriff said. "The divers said there was an air bubble, and her head was out of the water."

"Where do they take the car?" I asked him. "To the police station?"

"There's an impound lot that we use," he said. "It's a secure facility where our evidence techs can go over it. Normally, they'd do that right at the scene, but under the circumstances, we decided to do it at the impound lot."

I hoped for their sakes that the impound lot was more shielded from the icy wind than the canal was.

"Was she wearing a seat belt?" I asked.

"Yes," the sheriff said. "That was the only thing keeping her head out of the water. I went out to her house to notify her husband, but he wasn't home. There was a pickup in the driveway. I ran the plates, and it's registered to Dwayne and Beulah Pritchard. The car we pulled out of the canal is registered to them too."

"Where do they live?" I asked, curious.

"In South Park," he said.

South Park was the southern end of Twin Falls, a mixture of residential and commercial. Low-income housing and apartment buildings made up most of the residential portion. We'd passed through South Park on our way home from the airport.

"Well, in that case," I said, "I think somebody beat her up pretty badly before she ever got into that car."

"Really?" the sheriff asked. "How do you figure?"

A picture is worth a thousand words. I whipped the sheet off Beulah's body. Both men gasped and recoiled. Randy put his hand over his mouth and turned a delicate shade of chartreuse. "Excuse me," he mumbled and quickly left the room.

"Looks like she fought back too," the sheriff continued. "Look at those fingernails! Didn't anyone think to bag her hands?"

Like who? I thought. I refrained from reminding him that he or his deputy could have done that at the scene. I'd warned him at the scene that I didn't think this was just an accident. Maybe he hadn't believed it at the time. I bet he did now, though. "We could do that now," I suggested, "if you brought your evidence kit."

He produced a plastic cooler. "Got the stuff right here."

So we cleaned under Beulah's fingernails and put the material into evidence bags. With teeth gritted, I did the rape kit, which I really hate doing. One has to swab all body orifices, pits, and groins, and it's really disgusting. The sheriff took photographs. "Did you notice that welt on her right cheek?" he murmured as he leaned in close for another shot of it. "You can almost see the individual fingers. Maybe I can lift some fingerprints from that."

While he did that, I drew as much blood as I could from the heart with a cardiac needle. It flowed freely, and I filled one of every kind of tube the lab had. "I know we did a blood alcohol already," I said, "but it wouldn't hurt to test for drugs as well. And maybe I'll find something else we should test for." I gave the tubes to Natalie. Her job was to label them and find a safe place in the lab refrigerator to put them until they were needed. Then I did a suprapubic puncture to get urine from the bladder and gave that to Natalie as well. "The lab can run a tox screen on that."

The sheriff said, "Wait," and handed her a plastic envelope with a chain-of-evidence form attached to it. "Put everything in that, and sign it, and make sure everybody who touches it signs it too."

"Okay," she said and departed.

The sheriff put the other items in the cooler. "Okay if I stay and watch this?" he asked.

"Of course, Sheriff," I said.

"How about you call me Bob," he suggested. "No need to be so formal."

"Okay, Bob," I agreed. "Then you can call me Toni."

"Let me go check on Randy," he said. "I'll be right back."

He left. Natalie came back. "They're starting the tox screen now," she reported.

"Good," I said. "Let's get started." I reached to pick up my scalpel, but something held me back. I looked down. Beulah's fingers were tangled in my apron strings. "What the hell?" I muttered as I put the scalpel back on the tray.

"What's wrong?" Natalie asked, moving closer to me.

"Beulah's got hold of my apron strings," I told her with a nervous laugh. I tried to untangle them, but Beulah seemed to have a death grip on them. "Beulah! Let go of me!" I said, half-jokingly.

Beulah let go.

Huh? "Oh my God!" I exclaimed. "Did you see that? She let go!"

Natalie gasped.

During my residency, I'd heard a story from a longtime lab employee about a dead guy named Vern who'd moved his legs on the gurney while being transferred from the ER to the cooler, which had freaked everybody out, including the pathologist. But the excitement had been short-lived. Vern had not come back to life. Luckily, an autopsy hadn't been requested.

So I figured that Beulah was doing the same thing. Maybe it had something to do with warming up.

Bob came back. "How's Randy?" I asked.

"He's pretty shook up," the sheriff said. "He's gone back to the canal company. What's going on? You two look like you've seen a ghost."

"I'm not so sure we haven't," I said, and I told him what had happened.

He looked skeptical. "You're kidding, right?"

"Watch this." I wasn't at all sure I'd really seen what I thought I'd seen—or that anything would happen when I gave Beulah a command, but I tried anyway. "Beulah! Squeeze my hand."

Beulah obediently squeezed my hand—hard.

"I don't see anything," Bob said.

"Okay, then, watch this," I said. "Beulah! Let go of my hand!"

Beulah did so. I looked at Bob while trying to get some feeling back into my fingers. He merely shook his head and folded his arms across his chest. "You're just messin' with me, aren't you?" he asked.

Natalie said, "Did she let go?"

"She did," I said, "and the sheriff doesn't believe it. How about this?" I said to him. "You take her hand, and I'll tell her to squeeze it."

He demurred. "I'm not touching her without gloves," he said.

"Okay, put some gloves on," I challenged. "There are some large ones over there in the wall dispenser. Go ahead; do it."

Bob sighed, but he put on gloves and reluctantly took Beulah's hand. I said, "Beulah! Squeeze Bob's hand!"

Beulah did so. Bob gasped and tried to pull away, but nothing doing. Beulah didn't let go—until I said, "Beulah! Let go!," and then she did.

Bob's brown eyes were wide, and he looked pale.

"Now do you believe me?" I demanded, but I didn't really need to ask, because clearly he did.

"Her eyes are open too," Natalie remarked.

We looked. They were. And they were looking straight at me.

"This has gone on long enough," I said. "Natalie, hand me that penlight, would you?"

Natalie did so. I shone it in Beulah's right eye and then her left. Both pupils reacted.

Whoa.

"I've heard that dead people can move," Bob ventured in a shaky voice.

"On command?" I asked skeptically. "I don't think so."

"What do you think, then?" Bob asked.

I moved over to the counter, stripped off my gloves, and picked up the phone. "I don't think she's dead."

Bob looked as if he was about to faint. He was pale, and his forehead was sweaty. I told him to go back out and sit in the waiting room, and then I called the emergency room.

"I need a doctor and a crash cart in the morgue," I told the receptionist.

"Is this some kind of a joke?" she asked me. "Who is this, anyway?"

Don't argue with me, you officious little twit. "This is Dr. Day," I said with monumental patience, "and this body on my autopsy table isn't dead."

I heard the phone clatter to the counter, but not the thud of the little twit's body hitting the floor, so I figured she'd actually gone to get whatever doc was on duty, and with luck, might actually succeed.

The next voice I heard was Dr. Dave Martin. "Toni? Did I hear that right? She's not dead?"

"Yes, Dave, that's what I said. You need to come see for yourself. And bring the crash cart."

"Okay," he said, "I'm on my way."

Dave Martin and I go way back. His specialty is family medicine, and he does a lot of emergency room call. It was Dave who had admitted Hal when he'd had hantavirus pneumonia a few years back, and it was Dave who had admitted me for my various run-ins with deadly poisons. Dave had picked brick fragments out of Hal's head and rocks out of my back.

In short, Dave had seen and dealt with all the medical results of my involvement with murder and mayhem, but he was about to get in on the ground floor with this one. I was sure that there was more to this than met the eye.

I dithered over whether we should begin CPR or not, and I decided not. I suspected that when Beulah warmed up enough, she'd start breathing on her own and would have a pulse. In the meantime, CPR would do no good, and it might possibly do harm. We might break a rib. For that matter, the paramedics might have already broken one. Or maybe there were broken ribs under those bruises on the lower chest. We could puncture a lung. And we didn't have any drugs or oxygen or IV fluids to give her. Besides, I hadn't run a code blue since I was an intern twenty-two years earlier. Things had to have changed since then.

Of course, Beulah also had that head injury. There was always the possibility of a subdural hematoma, and when she warmed up, that would bleed more. Her other injuries would bleed too. There was no telling how much brain damage she'd have just from lack of oxygen. Maybe bringing her back to life wasn't such a good idea, at least not down here in the morgue. She should be up in ICU on a ventilator, with monitors and central lines, IV fluids, antibiotics, vasopressors, and the like. She might need emergency neurosurgery if she had a subdural hematoma. For that, she'd have to be life-flighted to Boise, and she might not survive the trip.

The bell rang within about five minutes, and Natalie admitted Dave, along with a nurse and an emergency room orderly. They'd brought a crash cart, which contained all the drugs and paraphernalia needed to manage a cardiac arrest. During the five minutes we'd waited for him, we'd covered

Beulah back up with the sheet, except for her head, and turned off the running water. There would be no autopsy here today.

Dave stopped short when he came around the curtain and saw Beulah. He was a few years younger than I, and of medium height and build. He had light brown hair and hazel eyes and a wry sense of humor, but he wasn't laughing now. "She still looks dead," he said flatly.

I was just about to drag him over to the side of the table and have Beulah squeeze his hand, when Beulah took a breath. Just one. Just one long, rattling breath that made us all jump. The nurse and the orderly gasped in unison.

"Jeez," Dave said, "maybe we should have kept her in the ER longer. But her temp was ninety-five, apparently, and depending on where you look it up, hypothermia is anything less than ninety-four or ninety-five."

"'Apparently'?" I asked, curious. "What do you mean, 'apparently'?"

"I wrote orders that she be released when her temp was ninety-five and she still had no vitals, and she got released, so I assume—"

"Did you use a low-temp thermometer?" I asked him. "Because regular clinical thermometers aren't accurate below ninety-four."

"I don't think we have one," Dave said. "I've never seen one."

"Well," I said, rummaging through a drawer, "I've got one here somewhere. Aha! Here it is. Let's just see what her temperature is."

With Natalie's help, I managed to stick the tip into Beulah's rectum. After a minute or so, I pulled it out. "Her temperature right now is eighty-six."

"Holy shit," Dave said. "We need to get her upstairs, pronto. She's gonna need internal warming at that temperature."

"I'll call transport," the nurse said, and she hauled out her cell phone. Then she and Dave sprang into action. By the time transport arrived, Beulah had been intubated, and a central IV line had been started. The orderly had attached an Ambu bag to the endotracheal tube and had begun bagging her, and Ringer's lactate was running into her IV. Dave had tried to find a pulse but hadn't been able to. Even with his stethoscope, he wasn't altogether sure he could hear a heartbeat. The sooner Beulah got hooked up to a monitor, the sooner we'd know what was going on with her.

After transport had taken Beulah away, and Dave and company had left, Natalie and I busied ourselves cleaning and straightening up the morgue. Because we hadn't actually done an autopsy, there really wasn't much to clean up. I personally cleaned off the low-temp thermometer and stuck it in the pocket of my lab coat. If the ER didn't have one, maybe ICU didn't either. It was hard to believe, but maybe we didn't get hypothermia cases all that often. That seemed hard to believe too, given the climate.

The sheriff came back in. "I'm okay now," he said.

"Good," I said. "We're done here. Just cleaning up. They took Beulah up to ICU."

Bob's cell phone rang, and he answered it. "You've got to be kidding," he said, and then, "Okay, I'll let her know."

"Let who know?" I asked, fearing the worst.

"They found her husband," he said.

"Where was he?"

"In the trunk of her car."

4

Certainly nothing is unnatural that is not physically impossible.
—RICHARD BRINSLEY SHERIDAN

CHRIST ON A CRUTCH—WHAT WAS going on here? "I hope you're not going to tell me that's an accident too," I said.

The sheriff shook his head. "I wouldn't even try."

"I suppose that means another autopsy?"

"I'm afraid so," Bob said. "If you're not going to do her today, can you do him?"

"I don't think so," I told him. "It's already after six, and I got pulled out of the canal today too, if you remember." *And if Mike's over his stomach flu by tomorrow, he can do it,* I thought.

The sheriff left after extracting a promise that I'd keep him posted.

"When we get done here, I want to go check on Beulah," I told Natalie.

"You go ahead," she said. "I can finish up here."

"Let me know if you hear anything about that other autopsy," I said.

By the time I got up to ICU, Beulah was comfortably ensconced in her cubicle, attached to a ventilator and a heart monitor. Her heart rate was thirty-four beats per minute, but other than that, the tracing looked pretty good—which shows how much pathologists know about reading heart tracings.

She was wrapped in a Bair Hugger and had begun to look less blue.

But maybe that was a trick of the light. After all, nobody looks good in the morgue.

Dave stood by the bed, reading an EKG strip. "Look at this," he said to me. "See that? The ST segment? See that elevation?" He sounded excited, and I fell right into it.

"ST segment elevation?" I asked. "Does she have an acute MI?" Myocardial infarction is the medical term for a heart attack.

"No," Dave said. "That's not your garden-variety ST segment elevation. That's an Osborn J-wave. It's diagnostic of hypothermia."

"Wow," I said, impressed. "You've done your homework."

"I kind of panicked when I saw it," Dave admitted. "Last thing I need to do is miss an MI. So I Googled 'hypothermia' and found it." He held up his smartphone. The screen showed a Wikipedia illustration of an Osborn J-wave. It looked just like Beulah's EKG.

"Has her temp come up any?" I asked.

"I don't know," Dave said. "They don't have a low-temp thermometer up here either."

I pulled mine out of my pocket. "Here. Take mine. I can get another one."

Jack Allen came around the curtain with a chart in his hand. Short, dark, and impatient, Jack was an internist with a subspecialty in pulmonary medicine. He was chief of staff more often than not because he was so good at it. He had dragged Hal back from the brink of death when he'd had hantavirus pneumonia, and me when I'd been poisoned with succinylcholine. He was the perfect person to take care of Beulah. He'd known her even longer than I had, although I didn't think she'd ever actually worked for him.

"Those blood gases back yet?" he demanded. Then he saw the thermometer in Dave's hand. "What's that?"

"A low-temperature thermometer," Dave replied. "For hypothermia."

"She's not that hypothermic," Jack snapped. "Her temp's ninety-four."

"It was eighty-six in the morgue," I put in. "Twenty minutes ago."

Jack turned his head and saw me for the first time. "Toni? What are you doing here?"

"Not doing an autopsy on Beulah," I said, "seeing as she wasn't quite dead enough."

A nurse poked her head around the curtain. "Here are those blood gases you wanted, Doctor." She handed Jack a printout.

Jack looked quickly at them and handed them back to her. "Okay, good," he said. "She doesn't need to be on 100 percent O2 anymore. We can cut it down to 60 percent."

"Yes, Doctor." She disappeared.

"Okay," Jack said. "Let me get this straight. She came into the emergency room at what time?"

"Around one or two o'clock," Dave said. "Her car went into the canal, and search and rescue got her out, and the paramedics brought her in, doing CPR. But she had no pulse and no respirations when they stopped."

"How long was she in the water?"

"I don't know. Toni, do you know?"

Jack snapped his head around to look at me as if to say, "What would you know about it?" but I didn't give him a chance.

"Well, I picked Mum and Nigel up at the airport at 12:20, and I saw her car go into the canal when we were coming back, so that would be maybe 12:40, and then—"

"You saw her go in?" Jack demanded.

"Well, yes, I was the one who called 911."

"You called." Jack seemed to be having a problem assimilating all this.

"And then I went into the canal after her, but I couldn't get the car door open, so ..."

Now Dave looked startled. "Toni, you mean you went into that cold water and—"

"Doctor?" the nurse said. "This thing says her temperature's eighty-eight degrees. It was ninety-four fifteen minutes ago. What's going on here?"

"Your thermometer isn't accurate below ninety-four degrees," I told her. "This is actually good. She's warmed up two whole degrees since she was in the morgue."

"If that's the case," Jack said to Dave, "perhaps her temperature wasn't ninety-five when you released the body to the morgue either."

That sounded accusatory, and the last thing I wanted to do right then was participate in a medical dogfight. Jack had his hands full with Beulah's acute medical problems, which would only worsen as she warmed up, and I didn't think this was the time to discuss how Beulah had ended up in the cooler when she had. Besides that, I was exhausted.

So I left Jack and Dave to duke it out and went home.

Mum and Hal were busy fixing dinner when I got home, while Nigel was watching football on TV. It had to be a rerun. Football season was over. I hung up my coat in the closet and went to the bar to fix myself a scotch.

"How are you feeling, kitten?" asked my mother.

"How was the autopsy?" asked Hal at the same time.

Nigel stomped into the kitchen before I had a chance to answer either one of them and said huffily, "Dash it all, I've been in this country three years now, and I don't understand American football any better than I did when I got here."

"I'm feeling fine," I said, "and there wasn't any autopsy. She wasn't dead."

They all stopped talking and stared at me in disbelief. I waited, enjoying their discomfiture.

Hal said, "What do you mean she wasn't dead yet? I thought she was dead when they pulled her out of the canal."

"So what happened?" asked Mum. "Was it like that episode of *NCIS* where Ducky was about to cut into the body and it sat up?"

"Not quite that dramatic," I said and told them what had happened. Nigel recoiled. "Blimey!"

"Is she going to recover, do you think?" Mum asked.

"I doubt it," I said. "Somebody beat her up pretty badly before she went into the canal. When she warms up, all of that's going to bleed. I think this autopsy has just been postponed."

"Have they found her husband yet?" Hal wanted to know.

"Oh, yes, and you're not going to believe it. He was in the trunk of the car."

"Does that mean you have two autopsies, then?" asked Mum.

"Only if Mike's not over his stomach flu," I said.

"One can always hope," she said crisply. "Now, shall we eat?"

We suspended discussion of the nonautopsy during dinner in deference to my mother, who had very definite views on what was and was not table talk. Countless times during my medical school, internship, and residency days, Mum would put a stop to shoptalk at meals by drawing herself up and intoning in her iciest British, "Antoinette, really, must we have bowels at dinner?"

But the hiatus was short-lived.

"How low does one's temperature have to be to be hypothermic?" Mum inquired after we'd finished eating and gone back to the living room.

"Below ninety-five degrees," I said.

"So what was Beulah's temperature?" Hal asked.

"Well, that seems to be a bit of a problem," I said. "It seems that our emergency room doesn't have a low-temperature thermometer, and neither does ICU."

"But you do," Hal said. "Don't you? I thought you got one online a while back."

"I did," I said. "I saw one on Amazon.com and thought it might be a cool thing to have in my autopsy kit."

"'Cool' being the operative word," said Nigel.

"So, in the emergency room, her temperature was ninety-four, according to the thermometer they had. Dave had left orders for someone to take Beulah's vitals every fifteen minutes and release the body when her temp was ninety-five, if she still didn't have any vital signs. So that was what they did. But with my thermometer, her temp was eighty-six when she came out of the cooler after being in there for an hour and a half."

"So that temperature of ninety-five was meaningless," Hal said.

"True, but the temp of eighty-six was meaningless too, since she'd been in the cooler. And even at that temperature, she should still have been conscious."

"P'r'aps not with bleeding in the brain," Nigel put in.

"She was conscious enough to drive a car," I argued, "and once she was in the water, bleeding would have stopped because of the hypothermia."

"But she wouldn't have been hypothermic right away," Mum said. "How long would it take for her body temperature to drop to hypothermic levels?"

"Well, body temperature drops about one degree per hour after death," I said, "but that depends on ambient temperature. In that cold water, it could have dropped much faster—say, two degrees per hour? Or more?"

"Even at that," Hal said, "a drop from 98.6 to eighty-six would take six hours."

"True," I conceded, "and she was only in the water for about two hours, then in the ER for about an hour, and then in the cooler for an hour and a half, and during all that time, nobody knows what her temperature really was. All we know is that it was eighty-six when she came out of the cooler. So there's no way to know how much bleeding she's done."

"How serious is a temperature that low?" Mum asked.

"A temperature of eighty-six is considered moderate hypothermia," I said. "Severe hypothermia is below eighty-two. At that temperature, the heart rate decreases to somewhere in the thirties. But Beulah had a heart rate of thirty-four when I was there in ICU, with a temperature of eighty-eight."

"Which means," Hal said, "that despite Beulah's temperature being in the moderate range, her clinical picture was more consistent with severe hypothermia."

"Right," I said. "She actually had undergone clinical death. But in severe hypothermia, the body will actually take longer to undergo brain death.'"

"That's what happened on that episode of *NCIS*," Mum said.

"I suspect it will happen to Beulah too," Nigel said.

"Dave showed me an Osborn J wave on her EKG, which is a classic finding in hypothermia and looks very similar to the acute ST elevation that you see in an acute MI," I said. "It's important not to be fooled by it and give thrombolytic agents, or clot-busters, because hypothermia itself causes a coagulopathy."

"In other words," Hal translated, "it would make Beulah bleed worse than she was going to do in any case. That would have landed Dave in a malpractice suit."

"Assuming there was anyone available to file one. It won't be her husband, that's for sure."

"Does that mean another autopsy?"

"Yep. I'm doing it tomorrow."

"You'd better hope that Beulah doesn't die during the night," Hal grumbled, "or you'll have two."

Well, duh. Hal didn't need to tell me what to hope for. "You know, the American Heart Association recommends taking at least thirty to forty-five seconds to verify the absence of a pulse before starting CPR. I don't think the paramedics did that. They started CPR the minute they got her on the gurney. Luckily, Dave knows better than to declare someone dead before they're warm and dead."

"And that's what would land Dave in a malpractice suit, if anything did," Hal pointed out. "Even if he didn't personally release Beulah's body to the morgue, he was ultimately responsible for whoever did."

"It might have landed me in one too," I said. "Do you know how close I came to cutting open the body of a living person? I would have entered the chest cavity. I actually had the scalpel in my hand. The Stryker saw was plugged in and ready to go. That alone would have killed her. Even if I discovered my mistake in time to get her on the vent and enlist the help of a surgeon, it would have been a hell of an operation to put the rib cage back where it belonged and make it airtight again."

"But how would you have known, even then?" Hal argued. "She wasn't breathing, and she didn't have a pulse."

"On that episode of *NCIS*," Mum began.

"Fiona, will you give over?" Nigel turned to me. "She loves that show, God knows why."

"She thinks Leroy Jethro Gibbs is a hunk," I said.

Nigel harrumphed. Mum blushed. "Antoinette, really."

I continued my rant, undeterred. "I didn't know until after the fact that the emergency room didn't have a low-temperature thermometer. I believed that Beulah's temperature had been ninety-five in the emergency room, because otherwise she wouldn't have been there."

"Even though she felt cold?" Hal asked.

"She'd been in the cooler," I countered. "It wouldn't have occurred to me to take her temperature before beginning the autopsy, and even if it had, it would have been meaningless."

"You dodged a bullet," Hal said.

"No kidding," I returned. "If Beulah survives this and returns to her previous mental state, she'll never let me live it down."

5

THE PHONE RANG AT MIDNIGHT.

Hal cursed and reached for it. I knew it was for me, and I knew why. With Mum and Nigel right here in the house, it pretty much had to be about the other autopsy.

Hal handed me the handset. "It's for you," he growled.

I took it. "Hello?"

"Hello there, young lady," Rollie Perkins intoned. "We've got another autopsy for you."

"Beulah's husband?"

"That's the one. Name's Dwayne Pritchard. When do you think you can do it, Doctor?"

"Here's the deal, Rollie," I said. "I'm actually not on call this weekend. Dr. Leonard is. Now, I know he was suffering from the stomach flu yesterday, which is why I was there to do Beulah. But he might be able to do this one. So you need to call him, and you need to wait until morning so that he can get a good night's sleep. Then, if he still can't do it, let me know, and we'll talk about it then. Okay?"

"Sounds good," Rollie said, and we disconnected.

"You know perfectly well you're going to do that autopsy tomorrow,"

Hal said. "There's no way you're going to let go of this case when it's just getting interesting."

"I know," I grumbled. "Mikey is going to owe me a weekend on call after this."

Beulah's battered body lay on my autopsy table, covered only by a sheet. Her blonde hair was clotted with blood. The entire right side of her face was purple, her nose broken, and her eyes swollen shut. Although I knew her, she was virtually unrecognizable now. It was my opinion that her own mother would have had trouble recognizing her.

I removed the sheet. Slowly, I circled the table, pointing out large purple ecchymoses on her left upper chest and right lower flank, while Natalie noted them on the body diagram sheet. Underneath them were broken ribs. I palpated armpits, neck, and groins for swollen lymph nodes, and her breasts for masses, not finding any. I ran my fingers through her hair and located a lump with a four-inch laceration on the back of her head.

I picked up a scalpel and handed it to Natalie. "Go ahead," I said. "Do the Y-shaped incision."

This would be Natalie's first Y-shaped incision. With trembling hand and excruciating slowness, she executed it. "Dr. Day? Is there usually this much blood?"

There did seem to be somewhat more of it than usual. "No, not usually." I took the scalpel from her, but I waited before proceeding with the dissection to see what would happen. Sometimes unembalmed bodies ooze quite a bit, especially if there's terminal congestion. The other possibility would be that the body was still alive. But that was unthinkable. Surely there would have been some reaction to the incision if that were the case, but this body hadn't moved a muscle.

The blood flow slowed, and I quickly dissected the chest muscles away from the ribs. It was still pretty messy, though, so I rinsed the area with the hose before cutting through the ribs with the Stryker saw. I lifted up the breast plate and dissected it free of the diaphragm.

Natalie stared wide-eyed into the chest cavity, which was rapidly filling with blood. "Dr. Day? I thought I saw something move in there."

I reached into the chest cavity and put my gloved hand on the heart, beneath the pericardium. I felt it beat.

Once.

Twice.

Oh, my God.

I stared into Natalie's eyes, trying not to panic.

"Did you feel it?" she whispered.

I nodded slowly.

"What do we do now?" she asked.

"I haven't the faintest idea," I replied, my voice trembling as panic overcame me.

"You haven't the faintest idea about what?" asked Hal, at which point I awoke, shaking and drenched in sweat, my heart threatening to jump right out of my chest. The clock radio on my bedside table said it was 4:00 a.m. Too scared to go back to sleep and risk going right back into the same dream—which always seems to happen when they're bad—I lay awake, clinging to Hal, until the sky began to lighten beyond the bedroom windows.

I was guzzling coffee and still trying to shake the residual horror of that nightmare when Rollie called me at nine Sunday morning to tell me that Mike was still under the weather.

"If you can take that body over to the hospital and put it on the table," I told him, "I'll get to it in a couple of hours."

I thought that would allow us to have a leisurely breakfast, but I'd reckoned without phone calls from Sheriff Bob Barton; my son-in-law, Pete; and his partner, Bernie Kincaid. The case had become multijurisdictional, because Beulah's husband had already been in the trunk of the car when it went into the canal, and even though the Pritchards lived in South

Park, they were still within the city limits. Evidence found at their house indicated that Dwayne Pritchard had most likely been killed there.

So this was shaping up to be quite a party. I figured I may as well include Bambi. Maybe she could get extra credit for her college classes. I was sure Mum and Hal would just love to babysit Little Toni for a while.

I went to my office before going to the morgue, booted up my computer, and checked on Beulah. She was still alive but hadn't regained consciousness. The progress note mentioned that the EEG had registered some brain activity but not much. Her vital signs and blood gases looked okay, but then, she was still on the vent. Other lab work indicated ongoing deterioration of liver and kidney function.

Since Dwayne Pritchard hadn't died in the hospital, there was no hospital chart to review. I looked him up in the computer anyway, just in case he'd been a patient in the past, but there was no record of him in our database.

In the morgue, Natalie, already clad in protective clothing, was going through the paperwork with Rollie Perkins and Sheriff Bob Barton. She'd already set out my instruments and specimen containers, my protective gear, and my camera.

The bell rang, and Natalie went to answer the door. My son-in-law, Pete Vincent, came in, followed by his partner, Bernie Kincaid.

Pete and Bernie were the "Mutt and Jeff" of the Twin Falls Police Department. Sandy-haired and blue eyed, Pete stood well over six feet and was as burly as Hal. He'd played football at Twin Falls High School. Bernie, on the other hand, had probably just barely made the height and weight requirements. He was not much taller than me, and he was dark haired, dark eyed, and wiry like Jack Allen. They could have been brothers.

Pete wasn't the least bit squeamish when it came to autopsies. Hal and I had known him since he was a student at the community college where Hal taught. He'd seen me do several autopsies during that time, and he'd put gloves on and gotten his hands right in there with mine.

His partner, Bernie, also a detective lieutenant, was not so lucky. I knew from personal experience that Bernie had never yet made it through an entire autopsy. In fact, I had done him in with a gangrenous bowel the first time we'd met, and I still wasn't sure he'd forgiven me.

Bernie had come to Twin Falls about seven years earlier from California. He'd been going through an ugly divorce at the time, which may have turned him off to women completely. In any case, he'd taken an instant dislike to me, and he had been only too happy to arrest me for the murder of Dr. Sally Shore. Then, after I'd proved my innocence by solving the case, he'd done a complete volte-face and decided he wanted to have an affair with me. Go figure.

We hadn't done it, though, and after all these years, we'd finally established what I hoped was a platonic friendship—although sometimes I wasn't sure that Bernie saw it that way. Once in a while, I'd catch him looking at me with an intensity that should have burned a hole in my back, and I'd hastily look away so as not to meet his eyes with mine and give him the wrong idea.

Bambi, her waist-length blonde hair tied back in a braid, arrived just as I was climbing into the plasticized paper jumpsuit. Those things are "one size fits all," large enough to fit men as tall and husky as Hal and Pete. I'm five foot three, Natalie's five five, and Bambi's six feet, but we all had an awful lot of extra jumpsuit to fold and tuck. Then we all put on head covers, shoe covers, and plastic aprons. For Natalie and me, it was like déjà vu all over again.

I handed out clear plastic face shields to Bambi and Natalie, and put one on myself, and all three of us donned gloves.

"You going to be okay, Bernie?" I asked him now. "Maybe you'd better stand near the door to the waiting room in case you need to leave suddenly."

"Give it up, Toni," he returned. "You're not gonna get rid of me that easily."

"Yeah, right, you say that now," I teased. "Anybody want to start a pool on how long he's going to last?"

I heard chuckles and whispering from Rollie, Pete, and Bob, and I saw money changing hands. Bernie turned and glared at them.

"Thanks a lot, Toni," he grumbled, turning back to me.

"Always happy to help," I replied.

Bernie snorted.

While I'd been talking, I'd started examining the body for skin lesions, scars, bruises, cuts, palpable lymph nodes, and abdominal masses. Natalie made note of their locations on an autopsy form depicting the human body, front and back. Beulah's husband had quite a few bruises all over him. He'd apparently been in one hell of a fight. He also had a long surgical scar down the middle of his back.

Dwayne Pritchard measured six foot two and probably weighed less than I did. His arms and legs were corded with stringy muscles that were probably a lot stronger than they looked. I wondered if his face had looked as cadaverous in life as it did now.

There were deep scratches all over his face, and a nostril had been torn. If Beulah had done that, she clearly hadn't gone down without a fight. His eyes and cheeks were sunken, and his chin looked scruffy. After death, the skin retracts away from the hairs, making them look longer, giving rise to tall tales of hair growing after death.

I peeled back his eyelids. His pupils were fixed and dilated. Although I felt silly doing it, I shone my penlight into them just to be on the safe side. They didn't budge. The sclerae, or whites of his eyes, looked jaundiced.

Experimentally, I pressed on the bloody area on the side of the head. The bone gave. Dwayne had a depressed skull fracture. I called attention to it. "Anybody want to feel this?" I asked of the company in attendance. "This is the working cause of death at this moment."

Bambi gingerly palpated the area with her gloved fingers. Nobody else volunteered.

Pete said, "We found a cast-iron skillet on the floor in the kitchen. It had blood and hair on it. Could that have been the murder weapon?"

"Sure," I said. "Assuming the blood and hair are his. It could be Beulah's. She's got a head wound too."

"We also found blood and tissue on the fender around the oil stove—with blonde hair in it," Pete said. "That could be Beulah's. We'll know tomorrow."

Dwayne's abdomen, in stark contrast to the rest of him, was distended. His liver felt nodular and firm. I was pretty sure there was a fluid wave too.

If there was fluid in the belly, we might have a geyser when the abdominal cavity was opened.

I stepped back. "I suppose we'd better do a rape kit and clean his fingernails and draw some blood before I go any further. Pete, did you bring the stuff?"

Pete produced the cooler. With Bambi's assistance, we did all the necessary swabs, removed the bags from the hands, and cleaned under his fingernails, putting the material in evidence bags. Then, with a cardiac needle, I aspirated blood from the heart, the same as I'd done with Beulah, and filled a quantity of tubes. I aspirated urine through a suprapubic puncture. It was much darker than it should have been. Then I sampled the peritoneal fluid with an abdominal puncture, and it was also dark colored. It wasn't obviously bloody, although I couldn't tell if it was blood or bile or both making the color as dark as it was.

"Uh-oh," Bambi said. "What does that mean?"

"Any number of things," I told her. "He's obviously jaundiced. Maybe he's also got a ruptured spleen or a lacerated liver. Or maybe there's a cancer in there." I handed Natalie a scalpel. "All yours," I said. "Careful with the belly."

Gingerly, Natalie began the Y-shaped incision that would open the body. She did it a lot more slowly than I would have, but I was trying to make an autopsy assistant out of her, and she needed to practice these things. Everything was fine until she punctured the peritoneum, and the fluid erupted like a fountain, filling the gutters of the autopsy table and splattering on the floor.

Everybody jumped back. Efficiently, Bambi threw towels on the floor and pushed them around with her feet. When she'd soaked up all the fluid on the floor, she kicked the towels into the corner and began to suck the fluid out of the abdomen with the hose.

Meanwhile, I began dissecting the fat and muscle off the ribcage so I could use the Stryker saw to remove the breast plate and expose the chest organs. The diaphragm was elevated, compressing the lungs. The heart looked enlarged. There was no fluid in the chest cavity. I carefully cut the diaphragm away from the chest wall, exposing the liver, which was extremely nodular and obviously cirrhotic but showed no lacerations. I reached up under the diaphragm on the left side and pulled out the spleen, still attached and intact.

"Natalie? Want to run the bowel?"

"Sure," she said and reached for a clean scalpel. I'd shown her on a previous occasion how to hold the blade at an angle so it would cut fat and not the bowel as it separated the bowel from its mesentery. She severed the small bowel at the ligament of Treitz, which separates the jejunum from the duodenum, just as I'd shown her, and then proceeded to remove it. She did a fairly good job of it too, with only a few small nicks.

When she got to the colon, however, I took over, because that was much more technically difficult, a subject for another occasion. She put the bowel in the sink and slit it along its length with scissors, rinsing away stool, which was grayish rather than brown. Aside from a few colon polyps, the bowel was clean. Dwayne hadn't been body-packing drugs either, which removed one potential contributing cause of death.

This was the point at which we usually lost Bernie, but evidently the ventilation in our new morgue was better than it had ever been in Rollie's embalming room, where I'd always done autopsies until now. When I looked up, Bernie was still standing, and didn't even have his hand over his mouth.

While Natalie opened the bowel, I freed up the diaphragm, the great vessels, and the pelvic organs. That made it possible for me to haul the entire organ block up out of the body and lay it face down on the cutting board. Then I could open the esophagus, the trachea, the aorta, and the vena cava from the back.

Dwayne had clearly suffered from obstructive jaundice, which accounted for the color of his eyes, his urine, and his stool. The reason was obvious. Innumerable scars and nodules had replaced his liver, which was no doubt the reason for his truly impressive esophageal varices. A cirrhotic liver compresses the portal vein, which drains the bowel, resulting in blood backup and enlargement of the venous circulation—rather like varicose veins in the legs but in the GI tract instead. It's also the cause of fluid building up in the abdominal cavity.

To my surprise, I found no blood in the esophagus. Usually those puppies bleed like stink, especially in patients whose livers aren't producing all the coagulation factors they should, owing to being severely cirrhotic. People had been known to bleed out and die from a single esophageal variceal bleed.

The only thing that didn't fit was that instead of being small and shrunken like most cirrhotic livers, Dwayne's was enlarged, and some of the nodules had a yellowish tinge. The reason was obvious when I sliced into it and found several yellow nodules, the largest of which was necrotic in the center.

Dwayne had hepatocellular carcinoma. It had grown into the hepatic vein and into the superior vena cava, from which it could have broken off and sent tumor emboli all over the body—even into the heart and pulmonary artery to cause instant death.

"Could this have killed him?" Rollie asked.

"It could have," I agreed, "if someone hadn't hit him over the head first."

After that, the head was almost an anticlimax. Almost. The depressed skull fracture was more dramatic from the inside than it had been from the outside, with bone fragments poking into the brain, and there was a large subdural hematoma compressing the left parietal lobe. This was, as I'd thought, the definitive cause of death. It would have caused death even if he hadn't been stuffed into a car trunk and run into the canal to drown.

And he hadn't drowned. There was no water in the airways or the lungs. He'd been dead when the car went into the canal. Had Beulah known he was in her trunk? Had she put him there? Unless she regained consciousness, we'd never know.

Pete and Bambi took numerous photographs throughout the autopsy, Bambi using my camera. When we were done, Pete packed up his cooler. Everybody seemed satisfied with the results, and Bernie Kincaid had, for the first time ever, made it all the way through an autopsy.

"Damn!" Pete said. "I didn't think he could do it."

"Me neither," said Rollie.

"Repent, O ye of little faith," Bob said, brandishing three twenty-dollar bills.

"Don't spend it all in one place," I advised as I divested myself of bloodstained protective garb. Bambi kept hers on and helped Natalie clean up after the three men had gotten the body back into the body bag on Rollie's gurney.

I gathered up all the papers I needed and went back to my office to dictate the gross description and the provisional gross anatomic diagnoses. Then I fired up the computer and checked on Beulah again.

She was still alive. The lab work looked a little worse than it had that morning. There was a note indicating that the EEG brain waves were decreasing and that Jack planned to pull the plug once brain activity ceased.

There was also a procedure note indicating that a pericardiocentesis had been done. That is to say, bloody fluid had been aspirated from the sac around the heart—grossly bloody fluid, the note said, two liters of it—which had caused cardiac tamponade, meaning that the pressure of the fluid on the heart interfered with its ability to beat.

Where the hell had that come from? Had a broken rib penetrated the heart during CPR?

Or had I done it with my cardiac needle?

Yikes. Which would kill her first?

That bullet I thought I'd dodged was back with a vengeance and aimed straight at me.

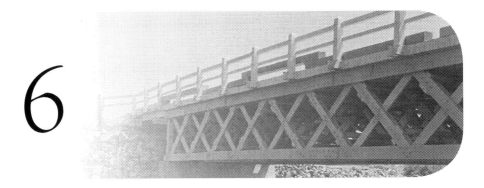

6

The law is a sort of hocus-pocus science, that smiles in yer face while it picks yer pocket; and the glorious uncertainty of it is of mair use to the professors than the justice of it.
—Charles Macklin

I KNEW I WOULDN'T REST until I found out more about this, so I called ICU and asked for Dr. Allen, figuring that if he'd been the one on call the day before, he'd be on call for the whole weekend.

The nurse who answered informed me that Dr. Allen was indeed on call, but he was not in the unit right at that moment. Did I want her to page him? I most certainly did, and I thanked her very much. I waited in trepidation for the eternity it took Jack to call me back, which was really probably only a couple of minutes, and I dived for the phone the instant it rang. I picked up the receiver with a shaking hand. "Jack?"

"Yes, what's up, Toni?"

"I see you had to do a pericardiocentesis on Beulah," I began. "Just how bloody was that fluid?"

"Basically, it was blood," Jack said. "I figured maybe a broken rib had lacerated the heart during CPR, or something. She's bleeding quite a lot in there. We're going to have to aspirate her again pretty soon, and we might have to transfuse her again too, although I'd rather not when she's going to be brain-dead soon, but I also don't want to hasten brain death by letting her bleed out. Why? Is there something I should know?"

Honesty is the best policy. "When I had her in the morgue yesterday, I drew blood from the heart by cardiac puncture. I'm worried that I might have caused the injury to the heart that's causing the bleeding."

"I doubt it," Jack said. "How big a needle did you use?"

"I used a cardiac needle," I said. "The same size we use to give intracardiac epinephrine during a code."

"That shouldn't cause significant bleeding," Jack said. "Do you usually do that at autopsy?"

"I usually try," I told him. "Sometimes I don't get enough blood on the first try, and then I have to draw it from the heart or the great vessels after I open the body and can see what I'm doing. But this time I got blood right away on the first try."

"Good," Jack said. "Even better. I can't see that it's a problem."

"But these circumstances aren't the usual," I went on. "Usually the body is dead when I puncture the heart. It doesn't come back to life and bleed afterward."

"But when we give intracardiac epinephrine during a code, with any luck the body does come back to life," Jack objected.

"That's true," I admitted. "But in a code the heart isn't beating when the needle punctures it. That's why you give epi in the first place, to get it started."

"Right," Jack agreed. "So what's your point?"

"My point is that if one did a cardiac puncture on a beating heart, couldn't it cause injury? I mean, there's the needle and the heart beating against it—couldn't that lacerate the myocardium?"

"Wouldn't the needle move with the heartbeat in that case?"

"Maybe," I said. "I didn't feel it move when I did it."

"Then you don't have anything to worry about. Is there anything else?" Jack seemed anxious to end this conversation and get back to whatever he'd been doing.

"Yes," I said and thought I heard a faint groan. "The coagulopathy caused by hypothermia. Wouldn't that cause significant bleeding from a relatively small injury?"

Jack sighed. "Possibly. Her coag studies are abnormal, and we've given her fresh-frozen plasma to counteract that. I don't know what else we could do, unless you happen to have any ideas." His sarcastic tone indicated how unlikely he thought that would be.

I didn't disappoint him. "No, I don't."

"All right then." He hung up.

Maybe Jack was right, and I didn't have to worry. But where was the sense of relief that should have accompanied that thought?

Wait a minute. If Jack was right, and a broken rib had pierced the heart, why hadn't it also pierced the pericardium?

It would have to go through the pericardium to get to the heart.

And if it had, Beulah would be bleeding into her pleural space, not her pericardium, and there would be no cardiac tamponade.

But there was cardiac tamponade.

Therefore, a broken rib couldn't be the problem.

Damn.

I was back to square one.

Oh well. There was nothing more I could do, so I went home.

***

Hal looked up from his newspaper when I walked into the living room. "How'd it go?"

"The autopsy went fine," I said, "but I may need a lawyer."

Mum and Nigel looked up from their respective reading material with inquiring expressions on their faces. "Whatever for, kitten?" Mum inquired.

"Let me call Elliott and make sure he's home," I said, "and then I'll tell you all about it." I went straight for the phone and dialed. I knew the number by heart, because Elliott and Jodi Maynard were our next-door neighbors and best friends.

Elliott was a lawyer, who just happened to be the legal counsel for the hospital, which also might get sued if I got charged with the wrongful death of a patient. I didn't stop to think about what an anomalous position I'd be putting him in if I needed him to defend me for accidentally murdering somebody during an autopsy.

Jodi owned a beauty salon and was given to wearing her bright-red hair in the latest way-out hairstyles and dressing in psychedelic clothing and big, chunky jewelry. Elliott was as tall and thin as Jodi was short and stocky. He favored three-piece suits and looked like a rabbi with his bushy, black hair and beard—salt-and-pepper now, actually.

Jodi answered the phone. "Hey, I was just thinking about you guys. What are you doing for dinner? I thought we could get together and order in pizza or something."

"You know Mum and Nigel are here," I said.

"They are? That's even better."

"Hang on." I covered the receiver with my hand. "Jodi wants to know if we want to go over and have pizza with them."

"Okay with me," Hal said. "Nigel? Fiona?"

"I quite like pizza," Mum said.

"Do you know, I've never had it," Nigel said. "But always willing to try something new, eh what?"

"You've never had pizza?" I asked in amazement.

Nigel shrugged. "Fiona doesn't prepare it at home," he said, a trifle defensively.

I laughed. "Nobody does," I told him. "They order it in from a pizza place."

"Tell Jodi okay," Hal said. "Unless she's gotten tired of waiting and hung up on you."

She hadn't. "Come over any time," she said. "We can have a drink while we're waiting for the pizza."

"What did you need Elliott for?" Hal wanted to know after I'd hung up the phone.

"He might have to defend me for murdering a patient," I told him.

"What?" said Nigel, astounded.

"Antoinette, you can't be serious," Mum added.

"Who are you supposed to have murdered?" Hal asked.

"Beulah," I said.

"Oh, come on," Hal snorted. "How could you have done that?"

"Has she died, kitten?" Mum asked.

"Not yet," I said. "I looked her up on the computer before I came home. She had a pericardiocentesis."

"What's that, when it's at home?" Nigel inquired.

I explained and then added, "I'm afraid that I might have caused that."

"How?" Hal demanded. "Didn't she have broken ribs that could have done that?"

"That's what Jack said," I said.

"You didn't even open her up, kitten," Mum argued.

"No, I didn't," I agreed. "But I aspirated blood from her heart for lab work. I suppose it's possible that I could have caused a small leak that could have filled the pericardium over the last twenty-four hours."

"Toni, you've done it again," Hal said, almost admiringly. "You've come up with a worst-case scenario that rivals all your other worst-case scenarios. How could you possibly expect to be accused of murdering Beulah when she has five hundred other injuries that are going to kill her first?"

"This would have killed her first if they hadn't done the pericardiocentesis," I argued. "And she would have died because of that little leak I possibly caused."

"So, if she hadn't had that 'little leak,' she would have lived?" Hal argued back. "What about her head injury? You think she's gonna survive that?"

"Probably not," I admitted grudgingly. "The chart said her EEG brain waves were decreasing and that Jack was going to pull the plug when they ceased."

Hal threw up his hands. "There, you see? They're gonna pull the plug. Your 'little leak' won't matter. She'll be brain-dead, regardless."

"Maybe," I said grudgingly. "But I still want to talk to Elliott about it."

❧

"Don't be so freakin' quick to dismiss that out of hand," Elliott advised Hal after we'd eaten our fill of Maxie's pizza. Maxie's had been in Twin Falls since 1956 and had the best pizza in town, to our thinking. I'd filled Jodi and Elliott in on the current crisis.

"There are several legal ramifications here," Elliott continued. "Toni could conceivably be charged with murder if the district attorney wanted to charge her. Then there's the malpractice consideration. The next of kin could file a malpractice suit against her. A wrongful death suit."

"There is no next of kin," Hal said. "Her husband's dead too."

"Really?" Elliott asked. "What about children? Brothers or sisters? Aunts and uncles? Cousins? Are Beulah's parents still living?"

Hal and I looked at each other. We didn't know.

"So, you see what I mean by not dismissing it out of hand," Elliott said. "Then there's the hospital liability. There could also be peer review. Toni could lose her privileges. That's reportable to the State Board of Medicine, even if a family member doesn't file a complaint with them first."

"So I could lose my license to practice medicine," I said. "This is worse than I thought."

"It is, however, the worst case scenario," Elliott said. "Chances are, none of that will happen. For example, if nobody wants to charge you or the hospital with any crime, none of it will happen. But people being what they are, the minute they get a whiff of anything that's not quite kosher, they'll descend like freakin' vultures."

"Then I guess we'd better not talk about this to anybody else," Hal said.

"You may have to," Nigel said. "Somebody did try to murder the poor woman, otherwise Toni wouldn't be involved in the first place, eh what?"

"And her husband too," my mother chimed in. "Somebody's going to be charged with murder, and Antoinette and her partner are going to be right in the middle of it. They'll ask her all sorts of questions. They'll want a copy of the autopsy report. It'll all be in there, won't it?"

"Not if Toni doesn't put anything in about the 'little leak,'" Hal suggested.

"I can't do that," I objected. "They already know something's leaking in there, because they had to aspirate it. They'll want to know about it specifically. Plus, it would be dishonest. If Beulah's next of kin decides to sue me for malpractice or report me to the board of medicine or have me charged with murder, that would make me look even guiltier than I already am. Trying to cover stuff up would practically guarantee a guilty verdict."

"You don't have to put it in as a freakin' cause of death," Elliott said.

"I don't plan to. I'll put it in as a contributing factor, along with all her other trauma. The head injury is probably the cause of death, unless she's also got a belly full of blood from a lacerated liver or something."

"It's a good job the poor woman has all those other injuries," Mum said. "Otherwise, it would be …." She hesitated.

Hal didn't. "It would be death by autopsy," he finished.

7

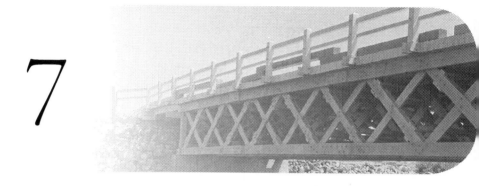

Who shall decide when doctors disagree,
And soundest casuists doubt, like you and me?
—SAMUEL POPE

SUNDAY NIGHT, WE FINALLY GOT around to discussing the reason Mum and Nigel had come to visit at this particular time. Usually they visited at Christmas and in the summer.

Nigel handed me an envelope from Long Beach Memorial Hospital, from a doctor whose name I recognized. He'd been one of my classmates in medical school. I opened it. Inside was a plastic slide container wrapped in a folded piece of paper and fastened with a rubber band.

I removed and unfolded the paper. It was a pathology report.

"GRAY, NIGEL HENRY. AGE 68."

My eyes flew to the diagnosis.

Prostate cancer.

I needed more information. I read the microscopic description in detail. Nigel's cancer was focal, limited to one lobe. It was Gleason grade three, score six.

Prostate cancers are graded by identifying growth patterns, which were first labeled long ago in order of worsening prognosis by a pathologist named Gleason as grades one through five. Adding together the two predominant patterns gave a Gleason score. A score of six was intermediate grade.

I heaved an internal sigh of relief. A Gleason six prostate cancer was unlikely to have metastasized to lymph nodes, although I supposed a PET scan would settle that question, if it hadn't already been done in Long Beach. If Nigel's nodes were negative and his cancer focal, he might be a good candidate for radioactive implants—like Mike Leonard's father, who'd also had prostate cancer—and wouldn't have to have a radical prostatectomy and lymph node dissection with the attendant complications, like postoperative wound infection or impotence.

I wanted to reassure Mum and Nigel that his diagnosis wasn't life-threatening, but that would have to wait until I looked at the slides myself. My job would be to review the slides and dictate a consultation report, in which I'd either agree or disagree with the Long Beach Memorial Hospital pathologist. Most of the time, we agreed with outside pathologists, and the consult was merely a formality to allow the local practitioners to treat the patient, knowing that the local pathologist agreed with the outside pathologist's diagnosis. Occasionally, however, the local pathologist would disagree, and it would alter the patient's treatment.

So I kept my counsel and promised that I'd look at the slides in the morning.

Beulah's chart was on my desk Monday morning when I got to work. Mike was over his stomach flu by then, but since he'd been officially on call during the weekend, I was officially on call for Monday. So Beulah's autopsy fell to me anyway.

Mike suggested that because of the possible liability issues, perhaps he should do the autopsy instead of me. I pointed out that if he did that, he'd be facing the liability alone instead of me. So we decided to do it together.

Nigel's appointment with his oncologist was at nine o'clock, and I fully expected him and Mum to drop in to my office afterward to find out what all the medical folderol—as Nigel put it—actually meant, so we postponed the autopsy until after that. Besides, I had to hurry up and review Nigel's slides and talk to his radiation oncologist, since there was no way in hell that either Mike or I could dictate a consultation, have Arlene type it, and sign it out in the computer by nine o'clock.

What I ought to have done was to pass the case to Mike and be done with it. But oh, no, I had to look.

I skimmed over the sections from Nigel's prostate needle biopsies, feeling a sensation not unlike that of a child who unwittingly witnesses his parents having sex. I felt like I was invading Mum and Nigel's privacy just by looking at these slides. I imagined that Nigel might also feel uncomfortable with me looking at his prostate, the same as he would if I were to see him naked. But that was silly. I should be thinking of Nigel as any other patient, not my mother's husband, and get a grip. So I did, and I started looking more carefully at the tissue in the slides. That was when I saw it: a focus of Gleason grade four.

That upped the ante. That changed the score to seven, and between Gleason scores six and seven was a major breakpoint in the prognosis. Gleason seven cancers did significantly worse than did Gleason six.

On another slide, I found a focus of perineural invasion. This was another bad prognostic sign, because prostate cancer spreads by growing along the nerves. This finding had not been mentioned in the original pathology report either. It increased the likelihood that Nigel's cancer had metastasized to lymph nodes or beyond. I showed the slides to Mike, and he agreed with me. "Y'all want to sign those out, or shall I?" he asked me. "Bein' that it's my day to sign out anyway."

"It might be better if you did," I said.

I guessed I wasn't going to be relieving anybody's mind anytime soon.

On the contrary, Mum might blame me for making Nigel's prognosis worse. People sometimes did, even though it made no sense; I merely reported what I saw. Mum ordinarily was more sensible than that, but this wasn't just any patient. This was Nigel.

Damn.

Before I gave Mike the case, just out of curiosity, I glanced at the section of the path report labeled Clinical Information to see if Nigel's prostate-specific antigen was mentioned, since an elevated PSA was the usual reason for prostate biopsies in the first place; and wished I hadn't.

Nigel's PSA was fourteen. That was pretty high; normal was less than four. PSAs that high usually indicated that the disease had spread beyond the confines of the prostate—another bad prognostic sign.

Double damn.

Of course, PSAs that high could also be seen in men who had enlarged prostates. But men who had prostate cancer hardly ever had enlarged prostates, in my experience.

I called the oncologist and told him the bad news. Then I went into histology and grossed in the surgical specimens from the weekend—mostly appendixes and gallbladders—to save time later in the afternoon when I'd have to gross in today's surgicals. Any frozen sections that came down from surgery would slow everything down that much more. As it was, I'd probably be working past six o'clock, long after all the histology personnel had gone home.

After I got that done, I reviewed Beulah's chart. It was awfully thick for just one and a half days' stay, but ICU is like that. A lot goes on there, and every little thing must be documented, every form filled out.

Beulah's official time of death was Sunday night at 10:30. She'd never regained consciousness, and she'd been on the ventilator the whole time she was in ICU, until the plug was pulled. She'd been pronounced brain-dead by EEG prior to that. Her body temperature had come up to the normal 98.6 by then.

She was truly warm and dead.

Of course, after spending the night in the cooler, she wouldn't be, but that didn't matter anymore.

By lunchtime, I'd finished signing out the abnormal Pap smears, and I'd reviewed the cases Mike had signed out the Friday before. Mum and Nigel showed up right at twelve and wanted to take me to lunch.

Because I was on call, we went to the hospital cafeteria, where Mum and I were holy and ate only salads, and Nigel had a cheeseburger with fries. "I can't believe how good these are," he said between bites. "In England, only the tourists eat them. The rest of us know better."

"So, what did Dr. Nichols have to say?" I asked. Guy Nichols was one of the two radiation oncologists at the Intermountain Cancer Center with whom Nigel had had his appointment.

Mum threw up her hands. "What *didn't* he say, would be the question," she said. "So much information! Really, I'm quite overwhelmed by it all."

Nigel twirled a French fry through the puddle of fry sauce on his plate. "Well, first thing tomorrow morning, I'm scheduled for something called a PET scan. What the devil is that, exactly?"

I was only too happy to demonstrate my knowledge to my stepfather, who up till now had never seen me in the medical setting. I explained that he'd be given radioactive glucose solution intravenously, and that because cancer cells take up more glucose than normal tissue, any cancer would show up as a "hot spot" on a CT scan.

"But that's not all," Nigel said. "Then he started talking about things called EBRT and HDR. It's like bloody Scrabble, all these letters."

I was perplexed. "Didn't he say anything about what those were?"

Nigel shrugged. "He probably did, but I couldn't understand any of it. All I know is, it's some kind of radiation, and he said one of them was done in the operating room, but I can't remember which one."

I explained what I knew about the relative merits of HDR and EBRT. HDR is high-dose brachytherapy, where radioactive seeds are placed inside the prostate where the cancer is, are left there to kill the cancer, and are then removed. EBRT is external beam radiotherapy, where a linear accelerator is used to concentrate the beam on the prostate without damaging the bowel or bladder.

Simply put, one is radiation from the inside, and the other is radiation from the outside.

Mum looked as if she wanted to come out with her "bowels at dinner" comment, but she didn't. "Tell me, kitten," she said. "None of this has anything to do with your specialty. How do you know all this?"

"I hear all kinds of things at Tumor Board," I said. "That's a weekly meeting where surgeons present their cancer cases, and the oncologists—the cancer docs—discuss how they'd treat them. They always have a radiologist there to discuss all the imaging studies and a pathologist to discuss the pathological findings—what the tumor markers show, whether the margins are clear or not, whether lymph nodes are involved. They also present patients who've been treated before and the cancer came back—what options they have. Stuff like that."

"Will they discuss Nigel?" Mum asked.

"Probably not," I said. "They concentrate on cases that are unusual or problematic. Nigel's case is pretty routine, so far."

"Well, that's a relief," Mum said.

When we got back to my office, Mum said that she needed to use the ladies' room. "Come with me, kitten," she urged.

Nigel snorted. "Women. Can't go to the loo by themselves, I ask you."

Mum ignored him. "We'll be right back, dear."

In the ladies' room, Mum said, "I didn't want to talk about this in front of Nigel. It embarrasses him. What about impotence?"

"Do you mean to tell me that Guy Nichols didn't address that?" I demanded. "It's the one thing that's on everybody's mind."

"Nigel didn't want to ask," Mum said, "and if he couldn't ask, I couldn't either, do you see?"

I saw. It's a sensitive subject. "In Tumor Board once," I said, "I heard that radiation carries a 30 percent risk of impotence, and surgery, 70 percent."

"Then radiation it is," Mum said. "And about the risks of surgery, do they apply to that HDR thing as well?"

"Maybe a little," I said, "but it's a much shorter procedure and much less invasive than a radical prostatectomy."

"But that other kind of radiation, the external one, would have no surgical risk at all," Mum said.

"But HDR," I told her, "is a one-time thing. With external beam, he'd have to come back every week for two months for another treatment. You'd have to do it in Long Beach, unless you're planning to stay here for that long. Are you?"

"I don't know. There's so much to think about. But we don't want to put you out, kitten."

If it were Hal in the same circumstances, I'd choose HDR in a heartbeat. But it wasn't Hal. It was Nigel, and he and my mother had to make that decision together. They didn't need me throwing roadblocks in their path by telling them they couldn't stay that long.

"You can stay as long as you need to," I said.

❧

While I'd been at lunch, Mike and Dale, Natalie's husband, had moved Beulah out of the cooler and put her on the autopsy table. Rollie had already signed the consent and left. Pete, Bernie, and Bob waited for me in the waiting room.

I felt extremely nervous about what I might find in Beulah's pericardium, and I tried to cover it up by making small talk. "Where's Bambi?" I asked.

"She's got a class," Pete said. "Otherwise she'd be here. Fiona said she'd be glad to babysit, but Bambi didn't want to upset Little Toni's routine, so she's at her usual babysitter's. By the way, the blood and tissue under Beulah's fingernails matches her husband."

"Well, that explains those scratches. Whose blood was on the skillet?"

"That was his too."

"What about fingerprints on the handle?"

"Well, that's the thing," Pete said. "There weren't any. Not any that we could retrieve. They were all smudged."

"How's that possible? It should have had Beulah's on it, at the very least. His too. I mean, it's their kitchen."

"Obviously, whoever hit him with it wore gloves."

"You think that Beulah, in the middle of a knock-down, drag-out fight, took time out to grab some oven mitts so she wouldn't leave her prints on her own skillet when she hit Dwayne with it?" I asked. "Or are you saying someone from outside the house came in and beaned him with his own skillet? If so, that person would have to be wearing gloves too."

"That could be," Pete said. "It was really cold that morning."

"It sure was," I said, remembering. "Especially in wet clothes."

❧

Beulah looked a hell of a lot worse than she had Saturday afternoon.

The shiner now covered the entire side of her face. Her eye was swollen shut. Her pupils were probably not reactive to light anymore, but I couldn't get her puffy eyelids apart enough to tell. Her nose had been set and bandaged. A nasogastric tube ran from one nostril, and an endotracheal tube protruded from her mouth. The head laceration had been sutured, but her blonde hair was still clotted with blood. Her fractured little finger had been taped to the ring finger next to it. Everything else was covered by a hospital gown, which Mike and I removed.

Pete, Bernie, and Bob gasped.

Beulah's entire right flank had turned dark purple. Her left upper chest didn't look much better. The paramedics had obviously broken some ribs doing CPR. The mark from my cardiac puncture didn't even show on the skin. I sent up a silent prayer that it wouldn't show on the heart either.

Pete started taking pictures. Natalie did too, with my camera.

Then Mike and I removed the ET and NG tubes, as well as the central venous line and the intra-arterial line from her arm, and the Foley catheter from her bladder. The urine in the bag was bloody. I recalled uneasily that I'd done a suprapubic puncture as well. The tox screen on that specimen had been negative.

We did our external exam, Mike on one side and me on the other, looking for scars, swollen lymph nodes, bruises, and any other marks, while Natalie noted them on the body sheet.

Then we both stepped back. "All yours, Natalie," Mike said.

Natalie did the Y-shaped incision a little faster than she had the day before, while I watched and tried not to think about my nightmare. The incision stayed dry. She opened the belly gingerly, but there was no geyser this time. Mike and I dissected the skin, fat, and muscle off the rib cage. Hemorrhages over the breastbone and ribs told the story. I grabbed the camera and photographed them.

"Fractured sixth, seventh, eighth, and ninth ribs on the right," I said.

Natalie made a note on the body sheet.

"Fractured sternum," Mike chimed in, "and fractured third, fourth, and fifth ribs on the left."

Natalie made another note.

"I don't suppose any of those are poking a hole in the heart?" I ventured.

"The sternum might be," Mike said. "Whoever was doing chest compressions must have been a frustrated linebacker."

"How often does that happen?" Bernie asked.

"Broken ribs happen about a third of the time," I said. "Broken sternums occur in about 4 percent."

"Thing is," Mike said, "if y'all don't push hard enough to break bones, you're not compressing the heart enough to do any good."

I began to remove the breast plate with the Stryker saw. As I cut the diaphragm away from it, we all saw it at the same time.

A swollen, purple pericardium the size of a basketball, with dark-red and purple patches on it from which blood had oozed, forming an adherent clot. More clots floated in the pleural space around the lung. So the pericardium had been punctured, I thought, feeling a little better about the whole thing. It had been punctured and had clotted off, while the heart had continued to leak inside it. The trouble was, none of the rib fractures corresponded to the injury, which left the sternal fracture as the only possible alternative. That didn't exactly correspond with the site of the injury either, but it was closer than any of the rib fractures.

"Is that her heart?" Pete asked in awe, snapping pictures.

"It's in there somewhere," I told him. "Natalie, get a picture of that, would you?"

Bernie peered over my shoulder. "What is that?"

"The medical term is *hemopericardium*," I said. "The pericardium is full of blood, and it's leaking into the pleural space."

"Why?" asked Bob.

"Probably trauma," I said evasively, unwilling to bring up the subject of my cardiac puncture here in a roomful of law enforcement officers. They'd find out soon enough, and I still hoped that something else would turn up and let me off the hook, although I couldn't imagine what it would be.

Beulah's lungs looked nearly as purple as her pericardium. She must have hemorrhaged into them as well. If all this bleeding was caused

60

by hypothermia-induced coagulopathy, maybe my premortem cardiac puncture wasn't the only reason for Beulah's pericardial hemorrhage.

I took a syringe and aspirated fluid from the pericardium. It was gross blood. I estimated that there were at least two more liters in there, or about half a gallon. With another syringe, I sampled the pleural fluid before instructing Natalie to suction it out. Then I cut the pericardium open, avoiding the bruised area.

The fluid spilled into the thoracic cavity, revealing more clots. Natalie suctioned that out too, but she kept having to remove clots from the suction tip. Removal of a large clot covering the anterior surface of the heart revealed bruising corresponding to the location of the pericardial bruising, which was only to be expected. But right in the middle of it was a jagged laceration about two centimeters long. It hadn't been obvious at first. The area looked like raw hamburger.

My heart sank. Did the fractured sternum make that laceration, or did I? There were no other marks on the myocardium, so my needle puncture had to be somewhere in that bruised area.

"What's that?" Pete asked.

I took a deep breath and tried to appear calm. "It appears to be a laceration of the left ventricle."

"Is that where the bleeding came from?"

"More than likely." My voice trembled. "Photograph it. Just in case."

"Just in case what?" Mike asked.

Damn. I so didn't want to mention this here, and then I had to go and shoot off my big mouth. "Just in case I did that with my cardiac puncture."

"Come on. Cardiac puncture?" Mike said. "Y'all gotta be kidding. That's a hell of a big hole for a cardiac needle, I tell you what."

"Which would tend to implicate the fractured sternum rather than a skinny little cardiac needle, wouldn't it?" I said for the benefit of law enforcement. If any legal action resulted from this, and the cops were asked to testify, it might be handy to have that concept already implanted in their brains. Mike caught on and allowed as how it certainly would.

I had Natalie photograph the underside of the sternal fracture too, and then I put the breast plate back in place on the body. I pushed down on it experimentally as if I were doing CPR and tried to see exactly where it hit the heart in relation to the bruised left ventricle, but it was difficult with the ribs in the way. I had the impression that the fracture didn't correspond exactly to the bruise but merely grazed the area.

"Natalie? Do we have any India ink down here?"

"No, but I could call Lucille and have her bring some."

When the ink arrived, I coated the underside of the fractured area of the sternum and then repeated the maneuver. Now the bruised area on the heart was partially coated in black. Good. I sprayed it with vinegar to fix the ink in place. Then I stood looking at the fractured sternum, undecided—for long enough that Mike commented on it. "Y'all waitin' for Christmas, or what?"

I turned the breast plate over and laid it upside down on the cutting board. "What I really want to do is cut this area out and save it."

"Well, why can't you? Here, I'll hold it steady for you." He handed me the Stryker saw.

With Mike's help, I cut out the fractured area, wrapped it in a paper towel, and tossed it into the formalin bucket.

After exploring the pulmonary artery for emboli and not finding any, I removed the heart and rinsed it off. The fat on the surface of the heart looked red and inflamed, with patches of yellowish-white fibrinous exudate on it. Similar exudate coated the inside of the pericardium as well.

"What caused this?" Mike wondered.

"Good question," I said. "This looks more like some kind of inflammatory process. That fibrinous exudate suggests uremic pericarditis."

"Had she been sick recently?" Mike asked.

"I don't know," I said.

"We need to go into her medical records," Mike said. "Maybe she's got some kind of chronic illness we need to know about. Who was her doctor?"

We stared at each other. I realized that neither of us knew anything about Beulah's past medical history. All I'd looked at was her hospital record for the current admission.

We moved on to the abdomen, where we found that Beulah had

neither a ruptured spleen nor a lacerated liver, but she did have a badly bruised liver and right kidney. A bruised kidney could account for the blood in her urine. The kidneys were otherwise pale, small, and pitted. Maybe she had been chronically uremic prior to her immersion in the canal.

When we opened the head, we found a huge subdural hematoma that had caused her left parietal lobe to herniate under the falx cerebri, the membrane that separates the right and left cerebral hemispheres. The brainstem and cerebellum had been pushed backward into the foramen magnum, the opening leading into the spinal canal, which was way too small for it. This much of a brainstem herniation should have caused her to stop breathing even before brain activity ceased. But since she was on the vent, nobody would have noticed.

But could it have caused death before the cardiac tamponade would have?

Probably not. And even if it did, was there any way to prove it?

I couldn't think of one.

"Well?" the sheriff asked.

"This is one cause of death," I said, "but I can't rule out the injury to the heart. They did have to drain the pericardium at least once, maybe twice, to keep her heart beating."

"Could that have killed her before brain death occurred?" the sheriff asked.

"I can't rule it out," I said.

Death by autopsy. I couldn't rule it out.

Damn.

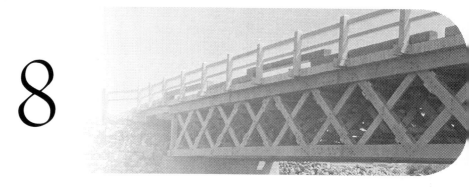

8

A lady of "a certain age" which means
Certainly aged.
—LORD BYRON

BACK IN MY OFFICE, I fired up the computer and looked up Beulah's medical record.

She had indeed had a second pericardiocentesis, during which another 1,500 cc's of blood had been aspirated. I found the lab reports, which described both specimens as "grossly bloody" but with way too many white blood cells to be just peripheral blood. Something else was going on here, like maybe an infection—but from what?

Maybe she was infected with something she'd picked up in the canal. But I would have thought it more likely to manifest itself as pneumonia, not a pericardial effusion, and definitely not pericardial hemorrhage. Of course, I hadn't yet seen what her lungs looked like under the microscope. They'd been edematous and congested, but there could have been pneumonia there too.

She'd had pleural effusions also, fluid around her lungs, more on the left than the right, owing to the leakage from the pericardium where the broken sternum had injured it. They'd withdrawn a total of 3,500 cc's, about seven pints, from her pericardium. There had been at least four more pints present at autopsy, which had accumulated in twelve hours' time, making a total of about eleven pints—nearly equal to the total blood volume of the human body, not to mention roughly 1,500 cc's, or three pints, more in the left pleural space. If they hadn't done the pericardiocentesis and replaced the blood volume with transfusions of packed cells and fresh frozen plasma, she definitely would have died from cardiac tamponade—not to mention hypovolemic shock and anemia—before brain death occurred. Actually, those things would have hastened brain death.

But that didn't explain the inflammation. Could it be something that had ailed her before she went into the canal? Myocarditis? Pericarditis? Bacterial? Viral? Autoimmune? Uremic? How long had it been going on? How could Beulah have recovered consciousness and have had the strength to drag her husband's body out of the house, get it into the trunk of the car, and drive to where she went into the canal, with all that going on?

More to the point, how the hell had she managed to drag her ass out of bed to go to work every day with all that going on?

Beulah became more of a mystery with everything I found out about her.

I called the lab and ordered cultures and cytology on the pleural and pericardial fluid. The cultures would detect bacterial infection, not viral infection, but the cytology might show viral cytopathic changes in the cells.

I had to go back to her medical history prior to this hospital admission. I went all the way back to 2005, which was when we'd gone live with our present computer system, and found out what I needed to know.

It didn't get me off the hook, but it did introduce a modicum of reasonable doubt.

∞

I sank onto the couch, scotch in hand, put my feet up, and prepared to regale my family with the results of my research. "Lupus," I said.

"Lupus?" echoed Hal.

"What's that, dear?" Mum asked. "Is that what was wrong with Beulah?"

"Among other things," I said. "She's had it for about twenty years. It's an autoimmune disease where the body forms antibodies and attacks itself. Any organ can be affected. With lupus, it's usually the skin and kidneys, but it can affect heart, lungs, brain, liver—you name it. It's a chronic condition that requires corticosteroids at the least. Stronger immunosuppressive drugs are frequently used, but they come with their own set of side effects. Beulah's been on prednisone for most of the time, with occasional flare-ups requiring something stronger."

"And nobody knew?" Mum asked.

"Well," I said, "her doctors knew, but Beulah probably never talked about it. She preferred to talk about other people instead. It explains a lot."

"Like what?" asked Nigel.

"Corticosteroids, like prednisone, cause puffy cheeks, a buffalo hump, centripetal obesity, cataracts, osteoporosis, and personality change. They also suppress the immune system, so she would have been more susceptible to infections."

"That explains what Beulah looked like," Hal said. "But personality change?"

"Yeah. I thought maybe she was such a piece of work because she felt like crap all the time, but maybe it was because of the prednisone. Or both. But that's not the most important thing."

"What's that, kitten?" Mum asked.

"Lupus can cause pericarditis."

"Pericarditis?" said Hal. "Is that why the pericardium was full of blood and they had to do a pericardiocentesis?"

"I don't know," I admitted. "I know lupus can cause pericardial effusions, but I don't think it causes pericardial hemorrhage. She's had pericardiocentesis before, but according to the lab reports, the fluid wasn't bloody, and this time it was."

"But didn't you say that hypothermia causes bleeding?" Mum asked.

"I did. I suppose it's possible that the bleeding was from the area of bruising from the sternal fracture, complicated by the hypothermia-induced coagulopathy."

"Right-o," Nigel remarked. "Nothing like a little hypothermia to bugger things up, eh what?"

"She also had fibrinous pericarditis, which is usually caused by uremia. According to her records, she'd been in chronic renal failure for the last couple of years due to advanced lupus nephritis, which explains why she was uremic. She was looking at going on hemodialysis in the near future."

"So, she had two reasons to have a pericardial effusion," Hal said.

"Three, actually," I said, "but she still has that laceration. That might have been caused by the sternal fracture too, but I can't rule out my cardiac puncture. The other two things are what they call 'confounding factors.'"

"So you're still on the hook," Hal said. "You'd better let Elliott know."

"I'll call him right now," I said and did so.

Pete and Bambi came over after dinner, carrying a somnolent Little Toni in a Snugli and a huge diaper bag. "You guys planning to stay a month, or what?" Hal joked as he went to the kitchen to get beers out of the refrigerator. Mum gently took the baby from Bambi and settled herself in a corner of the couch.

Little Toni woke up enough to utter a single "Gah!," looked up into Mum's face, and held her arms out. Mum lifted her up on her shoulder, and Little Toni wound her tiny arms around Mum's neck.

"Hush, little one," Mum crooned softly. "Grammy loves you."

Mum was Grammy. I was Bubbe, which is the Yiddish word for grandmother. Little Toni, at nine months, had achieved "Gah" for Grammy and "Bah" for me, so far. Grandfather Hal was Zayde, but Little Toni called him "Bah" too.

The prodigy gurgled and went right back to sleep. Nigel brought scotches from the bar for himself and me.

I suppose it was inevitable that my grandchild would look nothing like me. She had inherited her blonde, blue-eyed looks from Pete, Bambi, Hal, and Hal's first wife, Shawna. Even at only nine months, her tow-colored hair was thick and curly, like a halo.

She'd inherited my name, though, sort of. She'd had been named Toni Amanda, not Antoinette, like me. Amanda was Bambi's middle name.

I suppose it was also inevitable that we'd end up talking about the case. It was on all of our minds for different reasons. Maybe if it could be proved that Beulah was murdered, it would get people's attention away from the autopsy findings, away from me and my cardiac puncture as the cause of Beulah's death.

"Here's what we know so far," Pete said. "The blood and hair on the fender of the oil stove is Beulah's. The blood under Beulah's fingernails is her husband's, according to the sheriff. The blood on the bottom of the skillet is his too."

"And the fingerprints on her face where she was slapped?" I asked. "The sheriff lifted them on Saturday."

"They're her husband's," Pete said.

"So that means that Beulah hit her head on the fender and scratched her husband, and somebody, possibly Beulah, hit him with the skillet," I said. "Somebody else may be involved, but we don't know who."

"It's really hard to get fingerprints off cast iron," said Bambi in her evidence tech persona. "It's such a rough surface."

"So you deduce from that," Nigel said, "that someone wearing gloves used the skillet to kill her husband. I say, does the bloke have a name?"

"Dwayne," Pete said.

"It had to be someone other than Beulah," I said.

"Why?" Hal asked. "How do you figure?"

"Well, is Dwayne going to stop in the middle of a knock-down, drag-out fight to let Beulah put on gloves?" I argued. "Besides, he broke her little finger."

"Maybe he hadn't done that yet," Hal said. "But you're right. He's not gonna just stand by while she grabs the skillet, gloves or no gloves."

"Everything that Dwayne did to Beulah," I said, "had to be done before he got hit with the skillet, because that's what killed him."

"What if he didn't die right away?" Hal argued. "Don't people with fatal head injuries sometimes wake up and walk away and then die someplace else? How do you know Dwayne didn't do that?"

"If he did, he didn't get far," Bambi said. "Just as far as the trunk of Beulah's car."

"Surely he didn't unlock the trunk and climb in," my mother said. Little Toni squirmed and whimpered. "Shh," Mum said. "Go back to sleep, sweetheart."

"She's really a good baby," Bambi said. "I don't know how we got so lucky."

"Isn't it usually the second baby that's colicky and never sleeps?" Hal asked. "My mother always says that I was a good baby and my brother Harvey was impossible."

"I've heard that too," Pete said. "Maybe we'd better stop right here."

"In your dreams, bub," Bambi said good-naturedly.

"So, to sum things up," I said, "someone slapped Beulah's face, punched her hard enough to break her orbital bone, broke her nose, fractured a finger, knocked her down so that she lacerated her scalp on the fender of the oil stove and was rendered unconscious, and punched or kicked her in the right side, hard enough to break four ribs—but not necessarily in that order."

"What side did he slap her on?" Pete asked. "Which eye did he punch her in?"

"Right, for both."

"Then whoever hit Beulah was most likely left-handed. Was Dwayne left-handed?"

"Somebody at the canal company should know," I suggested.

Pete said, "Bernie said that the next-door neighbors heard Beulah and Dwayne fighting almost every night, but they didn't hear them fighting that morning."

"Maybe it was too early," Hal said. "Maybe they were still asleep."

"Did Beulah ever fight back?" I asked.

"Bernie said, and I quote, 'Beulah gave as good as she got,'" Pete said. "So maybe her scratching him and ripping his nostril was not unusual behavior on her part."

"I wonder if kicking her in the side hard enough to break ribs was usual behavior for him."

"Jeez, Toni, I don't know," Pete complained. "Bernie didn't go into that much detail."

"Beulah had lupus," Hal said. "Didn't you say that the prednisone causes osteoporosis? Maybe it didn't take much effort to break Beulah's ribs."

"He must not have done that very often," I remarked, "or she'd never show up for work."

"Or maybe he did it so much that she got used to it," Hal said.

"Come on, Hal," I objected. "Get used to having broken ribs? Get real."

"Okay, you two," Pete said. "Toni, please don't kick him in the ribs just to prove a point. We've got our hands full already with this case."

"Spoilsport," I said.

"I'd guess that hitting Dwayne upside the head with a cast-iron skillet wouldn't be normal behavior for Beulah either, assuming that she did that," Hal said. "That would suggest that she was extra pissed off at him."

"Well, kicking her in the ribs suggests that he was extra pissed off too," I said.

"What in the world would make two people so mad that they'd do that to each other?" Mum wondered. "It certainly doesn't sound like the usual kinds of fights married people have."

"That's easy," Hal said. "One of them was having an affair, and the other found out about it."

"Somehow, I can't picture Beulah having an affair," I said. "She wouldn't want to do anything that would give anybody else something to gossip about. She'd never put herself in that position."

"So maybe it was Dwayne who was having the affair," Pete said.

"Yuck." Bambi wrinkled her nose. "I can't see anybody having an affair with him either."

"He probably didn't always look like that," I pointed out. "He had a rapidly growing cancer. He might have looked much better a few months ago."

"Who could he be having an affair with?" Mum wondered.

"It's usually someone in the workplace," Pete said. "We'll be checking that out."

"What I can't figure out is this," I said. "If Dwayne knocked Beulah down so that she was knocked unconscious, who hit Dwayne with the skillet? On the other hand, if Beulah hit Dwayne with the skillet, who knocked her down?"

"What if Dwayne got up and knocked Beulah down?" Hal asked.

"If he could do that, then Beulah could get up and hit him with the skillet," I said. "But I don't believe it. I mean, I've had a concussion. I've been knocked unconscious. I know how crappy it feels to regain consciousness afterward. I couldn't even move my head without throwing up. Was there vomit at the scene?"

Pete shook his head.

"Unbelievable. So unless Beulah was Superwoman," I continued, "she'd be in no condition to go after Dwayne with a skillet. Likewise, if Beulah had beaned Dwayne with the skillet, he'd be in no shape to knock Beulah out and kick her. He'd be dead."

"So if Beulah killed Dwayne," Pete said, "who knocked Beulah out?"

"If Dwayne knocked Beulah out," Nigel put in, "who killed Dwayne, what?"

Hal and I looked at each other. "There's no way around it," he said.

"No, there isn't," I said. "Somebody else had to be there."

Little Toni opened her blue eyes and looked straight at me. "Bah!"

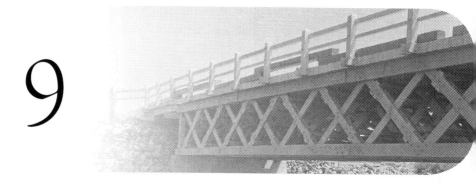

9

To know anything well involves a profound sensation of ignorance.
—John Ruskin

TUESDAY I "SHOULD OF STOOD in bed," as the late Joe Gould is rumored to have said about the San Francisco Giants of yesteryear. Or maybe it was Joe Jacobs about the 1935 World Series.

At breakfast I spilled coffee on my shirt and had to change it. Geraldine was sick underneath the dining-room table, and I had to clean it up. Hal was in a bad mood and snapped my head off. The phone was already ringing when I got to the office at 7:30, and that was just the beginning.

To top it off, I felt like I was coming down with a cold.

At least I hoped it was a cold and not some exotic, incurable, and possibly fatal malady from being immersed in canal water.

Rollie called about both cases. "Rollie, for heaven's sake," I protested, "I just got here. I haven't even had a chance to cut in the tissues yet."

"Don't you have provisional gross diagnoses yet?"

"Dictated but not typed. Come on, Rollie. It's 7:30 in the morning. I just did Beulah yesterday. Arlene isn't even here yet."

Commander Ray Harris, Pete and Bernie's boss, called next. He was just now getting into the story, having been off duty all weekend. "Hey there, Doc. Heard you went for a little swim."

"Not on purpose," I declared and sneezed.

"Is it too soon to ask what you found?"

"I don't know anything that Pete and Bernie don't."

I heard the snap of a toothpick breaking. At least I assumed it was a toothpick. Ever since he quit smoking, the Commander's always had a toothpick in his mouth. Except when he was breaking them. That was what he did when he neared the end of his patience. Perhaps he was having as bad a morning as I was. "Well, that's just it, Doc. They were on duty all weekend, so they're off today. So how about filling me in?"

My throat was sore. I didn't want to talk. But I knew the next thing he'd say was that I could tell him on the phone or tell him at the station, so I swallowed my irritation and told him what I'd found and that he'd have a report as soon as I could get it to him. It took up twenty minutes that I didn't have to spare, but when I was finished he said, "Thanks, Doc. You're a lot smarter than they said you were."

It made me smile right out loud, and I said, "You're not so bad yourself, Commander." I hung up feeling a little bit better, which was always a good thing—especially since the next call was from Jack Allen.

I knew that Jack would be even more impatient than the Commander had been, so without protest I ran through the litany of gross diagnoses—the subdural hematoma and resultant brainstem herniation, which was the cause of death, the pleural effusions, the pulmonary edema, the fractured ribs, the fractured sternum, the bruise and laceration on the heart, and the pericardial hemorrhage with the fibrinous exudate covering the heart—at which point Jack interrupted.

"What caused that?" he demanded.

"Uremia," I said.

"That doesn't make sense," Jack objected. "She had terminal multiorgan failure, not just renal failure. That wouldn't cause fibrinous pericarditis. For that she'd need to have chronic renal failure."

"She did," I told him. "From lupus nephritis."

"Lupus?" Jack said. "She had lupus?"

"For the last twenty years. And she'd had pericardial effusions before."

"But lupus doesn't cause hemorrhagic effusions," Jack said.

"I didn't think so. But with the bruising from the broken sternum and hypothermia-associated coagulopathy, maybe this time it did."

"What about the laceration?" Jack asked. "Do you think the sternal fracture caused that?"

"I suppose it could have," I said.

"It was a hell of a big hemorrhage," Jack said, "for a skinny little cardiac needle. We gave her practically an exchange transfusion, for God's sake. She had to be bleeding from a much bigger hole than a needle could cause. A needle puncture would clot off right away."

"Makes sense to me," I said, stifling the urge to argue that maybe hypothermia-induced coagulopathy could prevent even a needle puncture from clotting off in a timely manner. Should I end up being sued for this, Jack could repeat that in court.

After a bit more speculation, Jack let me go. Another twenty minutes had passed, and Lucille and Natalie had been piling tray after tray of surgical slides on the corner of my desk. I looked at them with dread. Was I ever going to get off the phone so I could attack that pile, or was I going to be buried and slowly crushed to death by the sheer weight of them?

The next call was from a gastroenterologist in Boise, who wanted to know if I'd done an autopsy on his patient, Dwayne Pritchard, and if so, what I'd found.

I told him.

"Hepatocellular carcinoma?" he said. "I'm not surprised."

"Was he an alcoholic?" I asked.

"I doubt that he drank," he said. "He wasn't supposed to. He had chronic hepatitis."

"From what?"

"Not sure," he said. "His viral markers were negative—at least I think they were—and so were his autoimmune markers. I suspect it was drug induced. When he was younger, he used anabolic steroids. He really went downhill fast in the last few months, and I suspected that he might have developed hepatocellular carcinoma. So I guess it was a toss-up what got him first, that or drowning."

"He didn't drown," I said. "He was already dead when he went into the water."

"Already dead?"

"Yes. He was murdered. The cause of death was a depressed skull fracture with cerebral hemorrhage."

Well, after that, the gastroenterologist didn't have much to say, which was a blessing, because maybe now I could finally get at those surgical slides. But first ...

"How did you know he'd died?" I asked.

"I saw the article in the paper."

"In the *Statesman?*"

"Yes."

Oh. Wow. We'd made the Boise papers. Whoopee.

After that, the phone just kept right on ringing.

Once the autopsy calls began to let up, the calls about the surgical slides I hadn't yet had a chance to look at started, and by then I was feeling truly lousy. The first day of a cold is the worst. You feel like shit but sound completely normal, so nobody feels sorry for you. And you're as contagious as hell.

By then, Arlene had typed my gross dictations and provisional diagnoses into the computer. I signed out the latter so that she could distribute them.

Most people think that once someone opens up a body and looks inside, the autopsy is done. Nothing could be farther from the truth. Samples of the organs removed at autopsy had to be cut into sections small enough to put in cassettes and run through the tissue processor so the histotechs could prepare slides—the same as with the surgicals. Blood and other bodily fluids removed at autopsy had to be analyzed. All the findings had to be correlated with the clinical history and the evidence from the police and sheriff's department crime labs.

They don't show all that on TV. All they show is the body with blood on it, or a suitably gory wound, or the Y-shaped incision, already neatly sewn up. They show detectives wandering around the crime scene, wearing gloves and occasionally putting something in an evidence bag. Or sometimes people walk around touching things without gloves on, which makes me crazy.

After that, the real work begins, the work that takes so much time. On TV, fingerprints are run through AFIS, facial recognition gets done, and DNA gets matched in a matter of minutes. But it's not that way in real life, not even in big cities, let alone in small towns like Twin Falls. That's the reason everybody involved is reluctant to come right out and make definitive statements about the cause of death, or who did it, or why it was done—not because they're trying to cover something up, as some may think.

Of course, they may hold back certain information from the public, something only the killer would know—something they wouldn't even tell me about.

All this was complicated by the fact that neither the Twin Falls Police Department nor the Twin Falls County Sheriff's Department had a proper lab. All they could do was collect evidence, process it, and send it to Boise. Even Boise's lab was limited and had to send certain things to other labs, so nothing got processed right away. There was a tremendous backlog, especially for such things as DNA testing, due to a shortage of qualified personnel to do it.

The murders of Beulah and her husband made no sense. Clearly, I needed to know more about both of them before any of it made sense. I needed to talk to people who had known Beulah better than I had. But where could I start?

Charlie Nelson. Where else?

Charlie had been assistant administrator at Perrine Memorial. But with the new hospital, Cascade had transformed little old Perrine Memorial from a community hospital into a tertiary care center for patients too sick for the smaller hospitals, and a bright, shiny, new administrative staff had been provided to run it. Charlie was the only administrator carried over from the old hospital. He was almost as big a gossip as Beulah, but unlike her, he wasn't malicious. I used him as a substitute for my recently retired former lab manager, Margo Winters, to keep me up to date on all the goings-on.

If Charlie didn't know about Beulah's background, nobody did. Accordingly, I sought him out and told him my troubles.

Charlie was only too happy to oblige. Plump, jolly, and fiftyish, he favored three-piece suits with a pocket watch on a chain. His blue eyes twinkled behind wire-rimmed spectacles, and he loved nothing better than to sit around and chew the fat. Like Margo, Charlie kept his finger on the pulse of everything that went on in our hospital. He wasn't spiteful like Beulah, but you didn't tell Charlie anything you wanted kept secret. The man had a mouth like a sieve, but the best part was that he actually had information to give.

"Oh, heck, yeah, I went to school with Beulah. We graduated high school together," Charlie told me. He leaned back in his chair, lacing his fingers over an expansive midsection. "She was Beulah Mae Gibson then. She was really smart too—straight As. And now that I think about it, she wanted to be a doctor. She used to talk about it. Until our senior year, she talked about it all the time."

"What happened in your senior year?"

Charlie looked away and shrugged. "She just quit mentioning it."

Well, now, that was odd, I thought, because Charlie was the type of person who knew everything and told everybody. How come he didn't know this? Or did he know it but just not want to talk about it? And why wouldn't he want to talk about it? Was Charlie hiding something? All in all, it was most un-Charlie-like behavior, but I decided not to press the issue just then, because I figured I'd get more information out of him if I didn't piss him off.

What he said about Beulah reminded me of something that had happened to me at the beginning of my senior year in high school in Long Beach. My counselor called me into his office one day after school and told me that it was time for me to stop "crapping around" and decide what I really wanted to do with my life, because becoming a doctor just wasn't going to cut it. I'd never be able to live a normal life, get married, have a family, et cetera—something he would never have said to a male student.

I didn't argue with him, because it would have been pointless. Even way back then, I knew that male chauvinist pigs could not be changed.

They just had to die off, one by one. But I'd told Mum, who had been outraged. She went to see the head counselor, who reprimanded my counselor, who in turn reprimanded me for ratting him out. He claimed I'd misunderstood him. But I hadn't. I'd understood him all too well. It didn't matter, though, because the head counselor, a woman, took me over and counseled me for the remainder of my senior year.

In my second year of residency, I had occasion to do a bone marrow on my former counselor, by then retired. Although bone marrows are reputed to be very painful, I made sure his wasn't. I wanted him to know that I had not only become a doctor but that I had become a damn good one, by God. Being able to tell him that I was also happily married was just the frosting on the cake.

Maybe something like that had happened to Beulah, and maybe she hadn't been lucky enough to have a kick-ass mother like mine, or a sympathetic head counselor.

"What was she like back then?" I asked. "Was she a gossip then too?"

"Not that I remember," Charlie said. "She was one of those studious types—didn't talk to people much. I was one of the few she did talk to, because I was kind of like that too, and we were in a lot of the same classes."

"So, were you her boyfriend?"

"Oh, no, it wasn't anything like that. We were just friends."

"Did she go on dates, have a boyfriend, anything like that?"

"Not that I knew of, at least not in school. But she married some guy right after she got out of school, some guy a lot older than she was."

"Did they have kids?"

"One, but he died when he was a toddler. It broke up their marriage. Then she married somebody else."

"Dwayne," I said.

"Right. Far as I know, they didn't have any kids. He may have some from a previous marriage, but I don't know that either."

There wasn't much more that Charlie could tell me, but after talking to him, I had a better picture of what had made Beulah tick. Obviously, something had happened in high school that had dashed her hopes of becoming a doctor, so she'd had to settle for being a nurse, which was bound to cause resentment. Perhaps that was the root of the reason she gossiped about doctors: to take them down a peg or two by letting everybody know that they were only human like the rest of the employees. This was especially true of the female doctors, and for many years, I'd been one of only two female physicians on the medical staff, so I was one of her favorite targets.

And none of this took into consideration the pain of having lost a child. Being childless myself, I couldn't even imagine how bad that could be.

I wondered if there was anyone else at the hospital who knew Beulah better than Charlie did. He'd only known her in high school and as a hospital employee. Maybe Donna Foster, one of the older office nurses, had been friendly with Beulah. They were about the same age, were both office nurses, and might also have been friends.

When I had a chance, I called Donna. She just happened to have a few minutes to talk to me, so I went up to the second floor of the new medical plaza where she worked.

"Beulah and I graduated from nursing school together," she told me. "She used to be one of my best friends—until she married that husband of hers. What a jerk. She met him in a bar, of all places. I suspect he was an alcoholic, although she never actually told me that."

"Charlie told me that Beulah wanted to be a doctor when she was in high school," I said. "Do you know what happened to change her mind?"

"I didn't know her in high school," Donna said, "and she never told me that."

"Did you know her first husband?"

"No. I didn't know her then either. But I know they had a child who died."

"Charlie mentioned that," I said.

"He drowned in the coulee in back of their house," Donna said. "They didn't have a fence."

"Oh, how awful," I said. "Was Beulah home at the time?"

"She said she just took her eyes off him for a minute, and he was gone," Donna said. "They found him miles downstream, and he was already dead."

Oh, the guilt, I thought. "She must have been devastated," I said.

"You have no idea," Donna said. "The hell of it was that her husband worked for the canal company. Come to think of it, the jerk does too—did, I mean. Anyway, he blamed her completely for being so careless. Their marriage broke up over it."

"Charlie told me that too. Why don't people put up fences, for heaven's sake?"

"Some do," Donna said, shrugging. "Others can't afford it. Fences are expensive."

By the time I finished talking to Donna and got the rest of my surgicals signed out, it was five o'clock, and I was more than ready to go home. But the day wasn't over yet.

Natalie came to my office just as I was leaving, looking very upset. My heart sank.

"This can't wait till tomorrow, can it?" I said, observing her red-rimmed eyes and trembling lips.

"Oh, I suppose it could," she said, her blue eyes pleading.

"Natalie. Out with it!"

She showed me a bandaged finger. "This," she said.

"Do you want me to look at it and see if you need stitches?"

"It's not that." She unwrapped the bandage and showed me a cut about half an inch long. It wasn't bleeding, though. In fact it looked a couple of days old.

"How'd you get that?" I asked, although I suspected I knew. Judging from her demeanor and the apparent age of the cut, she had to have gotten it from …

"I cut myself doing the autopsy."

Damn. "Which one?"

"Dwayne Pritchard's."

"And you're just telling me now because …"

"I was scared," Natalie said. "But Lucille said I had to report it. She said if I got sick from it, workmen's comp wouldn't pay my bills unless I reported it."

Lucille, a large, loud, bleached blonde about my own age, watched out for her younger colleague like a mother hen. She'd been at Perrine Memorial nearly as long as Margo, so she'd been with me from the beginning.

"Lucille's right," I said. "Come see me tomorrow, and we'll fill out the paperwork. You'll need to be tested for HIV and hepatitis B and C, and so will Dwayne. We should have enough serum in the refrigerator to do that. Now go home and quit worrying."

I said that, even though I knew there was no way she could do that. Neither could I. Dwayne's gastroenterologist had told me that he thought his viral hepatitis markers were negative, and I prayed that they still were. HIV was another matter entirely.

"But what about Dale?" Natalie asked with a sob. "If I've got HIV ..."

"We'll get those tests done on Dwayne's blood tomorrow, and then you'll know," I told her. "In the meantime, don't borrow trouble."

"Should I tell Dale?"

"You haven't told him yet?"

"No, because—"

"You were scared, I know," I said. "But you need to tell him the truth. He has a right to know."

Natalie nodded and wiped her eyes. "Thanks, Dr. Day. I feel better now."

I was glad I could make her feel better, but jeez. What next?

◦≪≫◦

I stopped at the post office on my way home from work to mail a package. There was only one clerk on duty and a long line of customers that extended back into the area where the post office boxes were located. Whom should I see there but Randy Schofield, the manager of the canal company, retrieving the contents of box 367. There seemed to be quite a lot of mail in it—wedged into it, judging by the way he struggled to pry it loose.

"Hey, Randy," I greeted him.

He seemed startled to see me there. "Dr. Day. What are you doing here?"

I opened my mouth to answer, but just at that moment, the entire pile of mail he was juggling slid out of his hands onto the floor. "Here, let me help," I said and squatted down to help him pick it all up. He protested, saying, "Never mind, I'll get it," but not before I'd seen that the top one was addressed to S & P Pipe Company with a Twin Falls Canal Company return address.

"What's S & P Pipe Company?" I asked.

"It's where the canal company gets its pipe," he said.

"Then how come you're getting mail for them?" I asked innocently.

"I'm just picking up their mail for them," he said. "This is their box."

"Because it's on your way to work?"

"Yeah. So what?"

"Then why are you picking it up on your way home? Didn't you pick it up this morning?"

He glared at me. "What's with all the questions?"

I shrugged. "Nothing. I just wondered why you didn't wait till you were actually on your way to work, that's all."

He shoved the pile of mail under one arm. "Are we done here?" he demanded.

"I certainly am," I said, trying not to act intimidated by his rudeness. He sketched a wave and stomped out.

I stared after him, wondering why he'd overreacted to such a simple question.

When I got home, I looked up S & P Pipe Company in the phone book.

I couldn't find it.

I Googled it on the Internet. I found S & P Coil Company, which made heated coils and gutters. I found Northwest Pipe Company. I found tons of references to the Standard & Poor stock index. I did not find S & P Pipe Company.

I called Information and asked for the number for S & P Pipe Company in Twin Falls, Idaho. The disembodied voice asked me for the address. I told her I didn't have it. She said she couldn't help me, since they were obviously unlisted.

Mum said, "What are you doing, kitten?"

"Looking for S & P Pipe Company," I said.

"S & P Pipe Company? What's that, dear?"

"I ran into Randy Schofield at the post office," I said, and I told her what had happened. "So I'm trying to look up S & P Pipe Company, and I can't find them. They're not in the phone book. They're not on the Internet. Information doesn't have a listing for them. How the hell do they expect to sell pipe if they're unlisted?"

"How indeed?" Hal said. He picked up the phone and handed it to me. "Why don't you ask Pete to check them out?"

"On what grounds?" Nigel asked. "He'd need a warrant, eh what?"

But I was already on the phone. "Pete," I said when he answered, "have you ever heard of S & P Pipe Company?"

"No," he said. "Is it here in Twin?"

"I don't know. I can't find them. They're not in the phone book or on the Internet, and Information doesn't have a number for them."

"Why do you want to know about them?"

I told him. "If Twin Falls Canal Company gets pipe from them, they've got to be somewhere," I argued.

"Granted," Pete said, "but what business is that of ours?"

"Why would Randy be picking up mail for a company that doesn't exist?"

"Oh. Do you think he's up to no good?"

"What other reason can you think of for him to be involved in a nonexistent company?"

"Okay," Pete capitulated. "I'll see what I can do."

∞

I knew it would take time for Pete to get a warrant, assuming a judge would even issue one, so on Wednesday morning I called the canal company from my office.

"Twin Falls Canal Company, this is Carole. How can I help you?"

"Hi, Carole. This is Toni Day. I was the one who saw Beulah Pritchard's car go into the canal Saturday morning and called 911."

"Oh, yes," Carole said, and her voice trembled. "Our dispatcher was killed in that accident."

"Your dispatcher? Dwayne Pritchard was your dispatcher?"

"Yes," she said with a muffled sob.

"I'm so sorry for your loss," I said. "That isn't what I called about, though. I wanted to know about S & P Pipe Company. Is that where you get your pipe from?"

"S & P Pipe Company? I've never heard of it. We get our pipe from Pipeco on Washington. Whatever made you think we get it from S & P Pipe Company?"

I told her.

"Oh, I know," Carole said. "That's who Randy used to work for before he started working here. When he was in college. In Pocatello."

"He went to Idaho State?"

"Right."

"Okay. Thank you. And I'm real sorry about your dispatcher."

"Thank you."

We rang off, and I called Pete. "Any luck?"

"Have a heart, Toni. I just got here."

"Well, I've got a news flash for you. I just called Carole at the canal company, and she says they get their pipe from Pipeco on Washington."

"Toni—"

"She said that S & P Pipe Company is the place Randy used to work when he was in college in Pocatello."

"He went to ISU?"

"Apparently," I said. "But here's the thing, Pete. At the post office, Randy told me the canal company gets pipe from them, and he was picking up their mail because S & P Pipe Company was on his way to work. Pocatello's not on his way to work. Somebody's lying. Why? What's the point?"

"I'll check it out. And Toni ..."

"Yes?"

"Let us take it from here. Stay out of it. I mean it."

"Okay," I said meekly, fingers crossed behind my back. "It's all yours."

"Good," he said. "And thanks for the tip."

I really always meant to stay out of it, but things had a way of pulling me back in, if experience was any guide.

And the fact that either Randy or Carole had lied to me was a giant red flag.

10

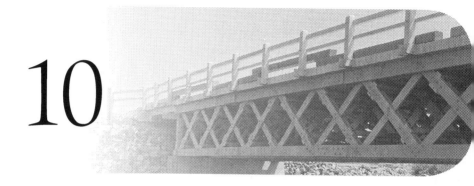

Litigious terms, fat contentions, and flowing fees.
—John Milton

"IS DR. DAY HERE?"

The voice was unfamiliar. My ears pricked up. I heard Arlene answer in the affirmative and ask the visitor what he wanted to see me about. Next, she called me and said that Mr. Clark Dane wanted to see me. Should she send him in?

That was a nicety she'd probably learned in secretarial school, and it might have worked in a huge firm with many offices that were remote from the secretarial pool; but here in our tiny office complex, the stranger stood practically right outside my open door and could clearly hear our conversation, so what else could I do but say, "Please, send him in."

Mr. Clark Dane stood roughly six feet tall, had a full head of silver hair, and wore a three-piece gray suit. He looked fit and tanned. He carried a black attaché case that looked like alligator. I could see reflections in the shine on his shoes.

He had "lawyer" written all over him.

My heart sank. What had I done now?

He held out his hand. "Dr. Antoinette Day? Clark Dane."

I shook it. "Please, have a seat. What can I do for you?"

He sat, placed his expensive-looking attaché case on his knees, and removed a legal pad. "I represent the estate of one Beulah Mae Pritchard."

"She has an estate?" I asked. "Her estate hired you? How does that work?"

"Actually it was her sister and brother-in-law who retained me," he said reprovingly, a slight emphasis on the word *retained*, as if to remind me that lawyers are not merely hired, they are *retained*. "Brenda and Mortimer Duke."

"I didn't know Beulah had a sister," I said. "Nobody's ever mentioned her."

"They had been estranged for some time," Mr. Dane said stiffly.

"How come?"

"I'm afraid I can't divulge that information. Client-attorney privilege, you know."

Hmm. Perhaps an estranged sister had nothing to do with Beulah's death, but then, perhaps it did. In any case, it was something else to check out—or to have Pete check out, or to ask Charlie about.

"So, why is an estranged sister hiring—excuse me, retaining—a lawyer to represent Beulah's estate?"

"She alleges that the autopsy you performed on her sister while she was still alive was responsible for her death."

Death by autopsy.

Suddenly I couldn't seem to get enough air into my lungs. I felt as if someone had punched me in the solar plexus. "That's insane. I didn't perform an autopsy while Beulah was still alive."

"She claims you did."

"Well, I didn't."

"Nonetheless, that is the claim."

"Nonetheless," I mimicked him, "I didn't."

Did not, did too. This was clearly getting us nowhere. Mr. Dane shifted gears. "The Dukes have retained me to sue you, your department, and the hospital for wrongful death."

I stood up, endeavoring not to hyperventilate. Never let 'em see you sweat. "In that case, Mr. Dane, I have nothing more to say until I consult my own legal team."

He raised his eyebrows. I interpreted that as surprise. Did he really expect me to roll over and play dead? No way. He didn't have to know that my "legal team" consisted of Elliott Maynard, my next-door neighbor.

He stood up too. We shook hands. I had to restrain myself from wiping my hand on my lab coat.

"In that case, Dr. Day," he said, "I shall see you in court."

He handed me a card as he left. Katz, Klein, Rabinowitz, and Dane, Attorneys at Law, Boise, Idaho. The big guns.

I was in so much trouble.

⚬⚬

I didn't know if Mr. Clark Dane would visit Administration next, or if he'd already done that before he came to see me, so I decided to pay Charlie a visit and sound him out about the pending lawsuit. Besides, I hadn't known that Beulah had a sister. Charlie hadn't mentioned her when I'd talked to him, but that didn't mean he didn't know about her.

Charlie was on the phone when I got to his office. He held up a finger to indicate that he'd be done in one minute, so I plunked myself into one of his visitors' chairs and waited.

He hung up and swiveled his chair around to face me. "What's up, Doc?"

I got right to the point. "You didn't tell me Beulah had a sister."

"I didn't?"

"No, you didn't. Why not?"

He raised an eyebrow. "What does Beulah's sister have to do with you?"

Why was Charlie being so evasive, I wondered. It wasn't like him. I slapped the card down on his desk. "She's suing us, that's what."

That did it. Charlie sat up straight and paid attention. "She's what?"

"You heard me."

"What for?"

"For wrongful death. She claims that I did Beulah's autopsy while she was still alive and killed her."

I watched the blood drain from Charlie's normally ruddy face. He picked up the card and looked at it. "Oh, I know these guys," he said.

"We've dealt with them before." He handed the card back to me. "If they're suing you and Dr. Leonard, they're probably suing the hospital too."

"They are," I said.

"I hate to even ask this, Doc, but is there any truth to their claim?"

"No," I said. "When I had her in the morgue on Saturday afternoon, she showed signs of life. So I called Dr. Martin in the ER, and he admitted her. She died Sunday night, and Mike and I did the autopsy Monday afternoon."

Charlie sat back in his chair and folded his hands across his expansive middle. "I suppose you can prove all that."

"Certainly. The sheriff was there Saturday afternoon. Natalie was there to assist me. The sheriff took pictures of the body. Then there were Dr. Martin and Dr. Allen and various and sundry nurses and other personnel. Tons of people can attest that Beulah hadn't had an autopsy done on her when she arrived up in ICU."

"Okay, good," Charlie said. "I'll contact the hospital counsel and get him up to speed on this." He picked up the phone.

"Not so fast," I said, holding up a hand to stop him. "That doesn't mean there isn't a problem."

He put the phone down. "What?"

"Beulah was bleeding into her pericardium," I told him. "She lost eight or nine units of blood. They aspirated it twice and removed four or five units each time."

Charlie, no longer relaxed, sat up straight and leaned forward on the desk. "What was the cause of that?"

"She had a badly bruised area on her left ventricle with a laceration in it. I don't know if it was transmural or not ... I mean, whether it went all the way through the myocardium, but it bled buckets just the same."

"I don't understand," Charlie said. "What's that got to do with a lawsuit against us?"

"I drew blood from the heart on Saturday."

"You drew ...," Charlie repeated. "I thought you said you didn't open her up on Saturday."

"I didn't. I put the needle into the heart through the chest wall."

"Is that what caused the bleeding?"

"That's just it," I said. "I couldn't see a needle mark on the heart. My needle had to have gone right through the bruised area."

"Do you think your needle caused the bruising and the laceration?"

"Not the bruising," I said. "Her sternum was fractured. I think that's what caused the bruising."

"From CPR?"

"Yes."

"How often does that happen?" Charlie said. "I know CPR breaks ribs sometimes, but the sternum?"

"It happens," I said. "Not as often as ribs, but Beulah probably had osteoporosis because she's been on prednisone for about twenty years for lupus. So her bones would break more easily than most people's."

"Seems to me a broken sternum would damage the heart a whole lot more than your needle," Charlie said.

"It seems that way to me too," I said, "but can I be sure the needle didn't have something to do with it? No, I can't."

"Will you be able to show what caused the laceration after you look at the heart under the microscope?"

I shook my head. "I'll put in lots of sections from that area," I said. "I'll put the whole thing in. But all it'll show is a lot of hemorrhage. I can't imagine anything that would show it was one thing or the other that caused it."

"Okay, I think I get it," Charlie said. "Now I'll call our lawyer and get him up to speed."

"Not until you tell me about Beulah's sister."

"What about her?"

"How come you didn't mention her?" I asked. "Did you know her? Was she older or younger than Beulah? What was she like?"

He took his glasses off and wiped them with a handkerchief. "You're not going to let this go, are you?"

"No," I said, "especially since you seem so reluctant to talk about her."

He sighed. "All right. Yes, I knew Brenda. She and Beulah were twins. Fraternal, not identical. Brenda was a party girl, a knockout. Every guy in

90

school had the hots for her. Hell, I even asked her out once, but she just laughed at me. Then she went around telling everybody about it, like it was this big joke. Everybody teased me about it for weeks. It was humiliating. That's why I didn't want to talk about her. Okay? You satisfied?"

"Charlie, that was years ago," I protested. "Why are you still embarrassed about that now?"

"Easy for you to say, Doc," he returned. "You probably never had anything like that happen to you."

"Sure I did," I said. "Everybody does. You don't have to let it affect your life. Look at you now. You're a hospital administrator."

"Assistant administrator," he corrected me. "Probably always will be."

"Come on, Charlie. Do you honestly think that if Brenda hadn't turned you down for a date back in high school that you'd be a CEO now?"

He looked sheepish. "Not really. Guess I just wasn't her type."

"What was her type?"

"Hard to say. There were so many of them."

"Did she have a steady boyfriend?"

"Strangely enough, she didn't. She dated a lot of guys, but never went steady with any of them."

"Did she put out?"

"Beulah said she did. She used to claim she could have boys too if she slept around like her sister."

"Was there any truth to that, or was Beulah just jealous?"

"Hard to say, with Beulah. You know as well as I do what a gossip she was. That may be where it started, in high school. I never heard any of the boys say it, though. Just the girls."

Girls can be so cruel. "Mr. Clark Dane said that Beulah and Brenda were estranged," I said. "Do you know anything about that?"

"I wouldn't blame Beulah for being jealous of Brenda," he said. "Their parents doted on Brenda—gave her piano lessons, dancing lessons, singing lessons, the works. They pretty much ignored Beulah, at least to hear Beulah tell it."

"I get that," I said, "but was there anything specific that happened between them in high school?"

Charlie sighed. "Beulah got caught with a copy of one of the final exams in her locker. She swore she didn't take it, that she didn't know how it got there. Maybe Brenda stole it and stashed it in Beulah's locker so she'd get blamed. I don't know. All I know is that our final exam was postponed because they had to make up a new one."

"When did that happen?"

"Senior year. It was at the end of the first semester."

"What happened to Beulah? Did she get punished?"

"She got an F. Had to repeat the semester. She didn't graduate with the rest of the class."

"No wonder she stopped talking about becoming a doctor," I said. "Wow. Cheating on exams? Maybe that put a black mark on her record that prevented her from getting scholarships or getting into a good college, let alone getting into medical school. If Brenda really did that to her sister, it would be a dandy reason for them to be estranged."

"It sure would," Charlie agreed. "It essentially ruined Beulah's life."

"So what happened to Brenda?"

"She ran off to Hollywood to become an actress, and that's the last I've heard about her until now. Everybody was sure she'd be somebody someday."

"Sounds like she was a real piece of work."

"She certainly was," Charlie said. "And I'm betting she still is."

I turned to leave, and then I had a thought. "Charlie? Could I look at your high school yearbooks?"

"Sure, but I don't have them here. I could bring them in tomorrow, if I can find them. Is that okay? What are you looking for?"

"Clues," I told him, and I went back to my office.

By that time, it was nearly eleven and time to start the morning gross. I asked Natalie to fetch Beulah's autopsy bucket from the morgue so that I could cut in the tissues after I finished grossing. Unless you rinse autopsy tissues in running water for a while, the fumes from the formalin can take the top of your head right off—even if your nasal passages aren't already raw from a cold. It wasn't just that I wanted to get Beulah's autopsy completed, but I had an idea for the way I wanted to process the heart and was anxious to try it out.

I put in sections of the entire bruised and lacerated area of the heart, hoping that something, anything, would show up that would exonerate me. Lucille volunteered to help by labeling cassettes for me, from which I deduced that she really just wanted to talk. She'd known Beulah longer than I had, after all, and Beulah had never been satisfied to simply call the lab to relay orders or get results when a visit would be so much more fun—especially when she could get off one of her little left-handed zingers at somebody else's expense.

"It wasn't just us," Lucille said. "She did it to everybody. You have no idea how mean she could be. She could make people cry."

Lucille was wrong there—about me having no idea how mean Beulah could be, that is. Back in the day, right out of residency, when my self-confidence had been as fragile as a tiny seedling trying to break through the soil to reach the sun and grow, Beulah's remarks had been like a giant foot stomping it right back into the ground. Back then, the rest of the medical staff—all male—had tended to think of me as a glorified tech rather than a physician and a peer, and being female hadn't helped. Their attitude had probably rubbed off on the office nurses, most of whom had been too polite to take advantage.

But not Beulah. For her purposes, I was the best thing since sliced bread, an absolute gift. "Dr. Day," she'd said, "I'm so glad to meet you. It's such a pleasure to have you here. All the doctors are really excited, because maybe now the lab will start doing its job." "Dr. Day, I met your handsome husband the other day. What does he do? Teach? Is that all?"

Sometimes she'd waylay me in the parking lot on the way into the hospital in the mornings to make sure my day started properly. "Dr. Jones said he thinks you overcall Pap smears too much, because the biopsies never show anything."

My mother had always taught me that if I couldn't say anything nice I shouldn't say anything at all. If Beulah's mom had ever taught her that, she'd obviously chosen to ignore it. She was an artist at saying something complimentary—only to spoil it in the next sentence.

Beulah's little barbs had always seemed to be about my competence as a pathologist, things that really didn't need to be said. I mean, no physician had ever mentioned them to me, and I'd never been subjected to peer review for any of them. But they all found their mark in my basic insecurity.

I was sure I wasn't the only physician who felt that way at times. We all strive for perfection in patient care, and it continues to elude us, because every patient is different, and they don't all respond the same way to the same treatment for the same disease. So, just because I thought I was doing okay didn't necessarily mean I was.

It didn't necessarily mean I wasn't, either.

What I should have done was to investigate every time Beulah told me that some doctor had put something uncomplimentary in a chart, to see if she was telling the truth. She may have been making things up just to get my goat. Then, if I'd found out that she was telling the truth, I should have contacted the doctor in question and confronted him about the comment—as an exercise in quality improvement. But I didn't have the stomach for it.

I had thought those doctors were taking a terrible chance, though, putting derogatory comments about another doctor in a chart. Even if there was never a lawsuit involving that patient, things like that have a way of coming back to bite one in the butt.

As long as I heard nothing from other physicians about the results of my diagnoses, I assumed that they were accurate. Besides that, Mike and I always reviewed each other's cases from the previous day. If a physician were to question the diagnosis, we would review the case again, or send it to an expert, or do something to resolve the discrepancy. But this was a fairly rare occurrence, and it happened to Mike as often as it happened to me.

Perhaps if I'd just ripped her ass a new one the first time she did that, it would have solved the whole problem. On the other hand, it might have just made it worse. A man could do that with impunity, but if a woman did it, it would just be ignored and put down to general female bitchiness.

But Beulah wouldn't have ignored it; she'd have used it. It would have been just one more weapon in her arsenal. I could just hear her: "I really admire you for making it through medical school as a woman. How did you manage it if you can't control your emotions any better than that?"

"Thank you, Beulah," I'd say, pretending to ignore whatever she'd said to me. "You have a nice day too."

But that was then, and this was now, seventeen years later.

"Lucille," I said, "how well did you really know Beulah?"

"Better than I wanted to," she said. "She used to ask me things like, was it true that my husband was having an affair with so-and-so—and half the time he was. Or was it true that my daughter Traci was pregnant? The thing was, she asked other people the same questions, so I was always hearing stuff from other people that heard it first from Beulah."

I reflected that Beulah's technique prevented anyone from being able to say that Beulah had actually told them anything at all. She had simply asked if something was true, the implication being that she had heard it from somebody else and didn't know whether to believe it or not.

"Did she ever say who she heard those things from?" I asked her.

"I didn't ask," Lucille said. "What I did was go home and ask the bastard to tell me himself if it was true and to kick his sorry ass out of my house."

I didn't have to ask which of her husbands Lucille was referring to. She'd had four of them and had divorced them all. It could have been any one of them—or all four of them. And Traci had been pregnant, more than once, the first time while she was still in high school.

"But," I persisted, "do you know of anyone she might have done that to that might want her dead?"

"I didn't kill her, if that's what you're getting at," Lucille retorted. "She mighta busted up a coupla my marriages, but they needed busting up, you wanna know the truth. She did me a favor. But I can tell you one thing. That husband of hers, Dwayne, was having an affair with someone at work."

"Oh, really?" I said. Now we were getting somewhere. "Did you go up to her and ask her if it was true?"

"Yeah, right," said Lucille with a laugh. "No, I didn't have to. Kenny bowls with Dwayne. Bowled, I mean. It's true all right."

Kenny was Lucille's current live-in boyfriend, and he had been for nearly ten years—longer than any of her marriages.

"How does Kenny know Dwayne?" I asked.

"They bowl in the canal company league," Lucille said.

"How did Kenny get on the canal company league?"

"Kenny's a ditch rider," Lucille said. "Didn't you know that?"

I shook my head. "What's a ditch rider?"

"They're the guys that the dispatcher sends out to check out problems. Then they report to the maintenance supervisor, and he sends out the excavators."

"Oh. So did Kenny know who Dwayne was having an affair with?"

"Yeah," said Lucille. "The manager's wife, Carole."

No wonder Carole had sounded so teary when I'd talked to her about Dwayne.

"Wow. Did Beulah know?"

"I don't know," Lucille said. "Hey, ya wanna know about Beulah, ya know who you should talk to? Margo. She knows Beulah a lot better than I do."

Margo, my former lab manager, could be a veritable treasure trove of information, and I couldn't imagine why she hadn't occurred to me before now. Besides, her tenure at Perrine Memorial predated mine by at least fifteen years, and maybe she'd known Beulah even before that. After I finished what I was doing and got back to my office, I called her.

Margo was in her late sixties and had worked at Perrine Memorial since she'd graduated from med-tech training. What she hadn't known about the goings-on at the hospital really hadn't been worth knowing. I hoped that was still the case, even though she'd retired.

She seemed delighted to hear from me. "Dr. Day! I thought maybe you'd all forgotten all about me."

"No way, Margo. Now that you're not around, I'm having a hell of a time keeping up on all the gossip around here."

"So am I," she said. "It's like I dropped off the face of the earth or something. If I didn't go to church, I'd never talk to anybody."

Margo and her husband, Lionel, had always been active in their church, although I never could remember which one it was. There were an awful lot of churches in Twin Falls.

I debated how to go about asking her about Beulah, but couldn't think of any way other than to just come right out and ask. "How well did you know Beulah Pritchard?"

Margo's reaction caught me off guard. "Why? What's she done now?"

"What do you mean, 'what's she done now'?"

Margo answered my question with a question. "Why do you want to know about her?"

"Because she and her husband were both murdered, and I did the autopsies."

Margo laughed shortly. "I'm not surprised. Beulah pissed people off. She could never say anything good about anybody without adding something bad to it. She was a master of the left-handed compliment."

"Did you know that she'd been promoted to a nurse administrator? She was in charge of infection control."

"I did hear that," Margo said. "That's what you used to do, along with everything else."

"Beulah never failed to point out," I said, "that she was doing a better job at it than I ever did."

"That sounds like Beulah," Margo said.

"Did she ever tell you that I was having an affair with Dr. Jensen?"

Margo laughed. "She told that one to anybody who'd listen."

"Did anyone listen?"

"They did, but nobody believed it."

"Or that Hal and I were getting a divorce?"

"That too. You're not, are you?"

"Oh heavens, no. Did you know that Beulah wanted to be a doctor when she was in high school?"

"Really? What stopped her?"

I told her what Charlie had told me.

Margo fell silent, and I asked, "Are you still there?"

"Yes, I'm here. I was just debating how much to tell you."

"I'm not interested in gossiping, Margo. But somebody killed her— and killed her husband too. I'm just trying to make sense out of it."

I heard her take a deep breath. "Here's the thing. Did you know that Beulah had a child who died?"

"Yes, I heard that," I said, trying to mask my disappointment. Was this just going to be a rehash of what Charlie and Donna had already told me? "And that her marriage broke up because of it."

"No," Margo said. "That's not why their marriage broke up."

"What was it?"

Margo sighed. "Beulah's first husband was Marlin Schofield. Do you know who that is?"

"No," I said. "Should I?"

"He was the general manager of the canal company for years and years. He's actually descended from one of the original investors in the Twin Falls Canal Company. His grandfather, I think. He married his first wife as soon as he got back from his mission ..."

"Was he Randy Schofield's dad?" I asked.

"Yes," Margo said. "How'd you know? Do you know Randy?"

"The sheriff brought him to Beulah's autopsy," I told her, without mentioning the gory details.

"Oh, dear," Margo said. "What a mean thing to do."

"Randy drove the excavator that got Beulah's car out of the canal," I said. "I just assumed he wanted to be there."

"Whatever," Margo said. "Anyway, Marlin's wife died in childbirth. He didn't marry again for a long time."

"A broken heart," I said.

"You may say so," Margo said. "Rumor has it that he didn't lack female companions. But that doesn't matter. When he was in his fifties, he married Beulah. Met her at a square dance or something."

"So he was a lot older than she was."

"He was," Margo said. "And therein lies the problem. Marlin was a lot older than Beulah, and maybe they didn't have much of a sex life. Anyway, Beulah began flirting with Randy, who was just about her age, and they had an affair. Then she got pregnant."

"Oh, no," I said. "You're going to tell me that Beulah's child was by Randy."

"That was the scuttlebutt," Margo said. "When Bobby drowned in the coulee, Marlin divorced Beulah."

"How old was Bobby?" I asked.

"About a year and a half," Margo said. "Just old enough to wander off and fall in."

"That's so sad," I said. "A double whammy. No wonder Beulah was the way she was."

"Don't waste your sympathy," Margo advised. "She brought a lot of it on herself. She really wasn't a nice person, you know."

"Surely Bobby's drowning was an accident," I objected.

"Maybe," Margo said. "And then again, maybe not."

She said this last bit with an air of finality that made me think she had more to say but didn't want to say it.

"What do you mean, 'maybe not'?"

Margo didn't answer.

"Are you saying that Bobby was *murdered?*"

11

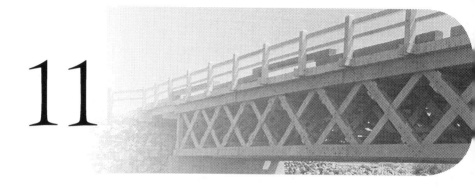

I cannot tell how the truth may be;
I say the tale as 'twas said to me.
—Sir Walter Scott

OVER THE PHONE I HEARD a door slam somewhere in Margo's house. "Oh, there's Lionel," Margo said. "I've got to go. Bye, Doctor."

"Margo? Margo!"

But it was no use. She'd hung up.

At least now I knew why Randy'd had such a violent reaction to my whipping the sheet off Beulah in the morgue. Knowing what their relationship had once been, it must have been quite a shock.

On the other hand, hadn't he recognized the car when he'd hauled it out of the canal?

Or had he been expecting Dwayne to have been the driver?

And if it had been Dwayne, so what?

The questions just kept on coming.

My conversation with Charlie made me think that perhaps Beulah had learned how to spread rumors around by watching her more socially adept sister. That in turn reminded me of the rumor Beulah had circulated about me having an affair with Russ Jensen. He and I had never talked about that, preferring to just ignore it until it went away. But it never did go away. It was still out there, just as bright and shiny as ever—and maybe now would be a good time to get his thoughts on why Beulah would start such a rumor.

I mean, I knew Beulah didn't like me, but what could she possibly have against Russ Jensen? He was truly a nice guy, a "right darling," as Mum would have said. If Beulah wanted to impugn another doctor's reputation, there was no shortage of arrogant bastards she could have picked from.

When I got back to my office after finishing the afternoon gross, I paged Russ and found out he was in his office and had a few minutes to talk.

Russ, a general surgeon a couple of years older than me, had that slightly plump and rumpled, Norman Rockwell, good ole country doc of yesteryear look, complete with a headful of salt-and-pepper hair and brown eyes under heavy black brows. He was a local boy too, his father and grandfather both having practiced medicine here. His father had been on the medical staff at Perrine Memorial before my time.

I'd always been on friendlier terms with Russ than with any of the other surgeons, but that had never been of any concern whatsoever to his wife, Geri, who was drop-dead gorgeous and had been the only girl for Russ since they were both in first grade. Everybody at Perrine Memorial—er, excuse me, Cascade—knew that Beulah couldn't have picked a more unlikely person for me to have an affair with, and therefore they should have taken her rumormongering with a grain of salt.

Russ greeted me, as always, with a brief hug, and we both dropped into chairs. After the amenities, I got right down to business. "What did Beulah Pritchard have against you?"

"What do you mean?"

"You remember she started a rumor that we were having an affair?"

Russ snorted. "How could I forget? Geri was about to divorce me."

"I know. I talked to her."

"Yeah. You talked her out of it. Did I ever thank you?"

"You did," I said. "Several times. But that rumor made both of us look bad. Why would she want to make you look bad?"

Russ sat down again and lowered his voice. "I don't know for sure, but I have an idea. Did you know that Beulah had a child who died?"

Here we go again. "I'd heard that, yes. When she was married to Marlin Schofield. What about it?"

"My dad did the autopsy."

"There was an autopsy? I didn't know that. What did it show?"

"I don't know. Dad wouldn't talk about it."

"Where's that autopsy report now?" I asked.

"If there is one, it's probably with my dad's stuff in my mom's basement."

"'If there is one'? Are you saying there might not even be a report at all?"

"Times were different then," Russ said. "We didn't have a pathologist here, and Dad didn't want to wait for somebody in Boise to do it, so he did it himself. That report could have been verbal, between Dad and the sheriff."

"Where did he do it?" I asked. "The old hospital didn't have a morgue."

"At Parkside. Rollie's dad was coroner then."

"Would there be any record of it in the sheriff's department?" I persisted.

"Maybe," Russ said, "and maybe not. Why all this interest in that autopsy, Toni?"

"Because nobody seems to know what really happened to Bobby," I said. "Or they don't want to talk about it. Either he wandered off and fell into the coulee, or somebody put him in the coulee. One's a tragic accident. The other's kidnapping and murder. Why all the subterfuge? Toddlers wander off all the time, no matter how careful you are. That suggests to me that the other scenario was the real one. That autopsy could confirm it. Is that why it was hushed up?"

"You don't know that it was hushed up," Russ argued. "And where do you get off suggesting that my dad would be a party to anything like that?"

"It must have been hushed up. Why else does everybody think Bobby just wandered off when Beulah wasn't paying attention?"

Russ stood up, clearly not happy with this conversation. He began to pace. "If anybody covered anything up, it was the sheriff, not my dad. Come to think of it, the sheriff at that time was a Schofield too. So who knows? If the autopsy showed evidence of foul play, he could have hushed it up to protect the family."

"So why wouldn't your dad talk about it?"

"Toni, I don't like where this is going. My dad wouldn't have been a party to a cover-up. But he also didn't talk about patients to his family or anybody else, so why would Bobby's case suddenly become the topic of suppertime conversation in front of us kids? Come on. Get real."

"It left Beulah looking like a bad mother. Maybe that was what she had against you—the sins of the fathers and all that. Could you try to find that autopsy report and let me see it?"

Russ frowned and folded his arms. "You've got quite the nerve, Toni, you know that? First you accuse my dad of covering up the results of an autopsy, and then you expect me to tear apart Mom's basement looking for the report so you can get a look at it?"

"Russ. Please? I promise I'll never say another word against your dad again as long as I live."

Russ relented and let his arms drop. "Okay, Toni," he said. "I'll get Geri to go over to Mom's and look for it."

As I left Russ's office, I saw an attractive, dark-haired woman waiting in the hall. I smiled at her, and when she smiled back, I noticed that her eyes were an unusual shade of cobalt blue. Were they real, or were they contact lenses? "He's all yours," I said to her and walked away down the hall to the elevator. When I reached it, I looked back and saw that the woman had disappeared.

I didn't think anything of it until I was on my way home. I noticed a blue Camry behind me as I left the hospital, and it was still there when I turned off Shoshone onto Montana Street where I lived. As I slowed to turn into my driveway, it went around me and sped on down the street. I didn't get a good look at the driver. It was the license plate that got my attention. It was personalized and said "CANAL2."

Hmm.

Why was someone from the canal company following me home?

Maybe it was just a coincidence. I mean, how stupid is it to stalk someone in a car with personalized plates? Why not borrow some nondescript old clunker nobody'd look at twice—or at least something without a personalized plate?

No coincidence, I decided—not after Beulah's autopsy and Randy's lies. Now, anything concerning the canal company raised red flags for me.

All these thoughts flashed through my head in just the time it took for me to reverse out of the driveway and speed down the street after the Camry. Turnabout is fair play, after all. The Camry turned left at the next intersection. I tried to stay far enough back that I wouldn't be noticed, but that's hard to do in a residential neighborhood with short blocks. At any rate, the Camry finally pulled into a driveway on a street only a few blocks from my house, and as I went by, I noted the address.

In the old days, I would've had to hope that I remembered things long enough to get someplace where I could write them down. But no more. I turned a corner, pulled over, hauled out my smartphone, and recorded the address in the handy-dandy little notebook app. I'd look it up when I got home. Or get Pete to do it.

Hal was fixing dinner when I finally walked into the kitchen. "I thought I heard you pull in a few minutes ago, but I guess it wasn't you."

"It was me," I said, and I explained what had happened.

Hal put his knife down and gave me his full attention. "Someone from the canal company is following you? That's stalking. Have you told Pete?" I'd been stalked before by an old boyfriend, so Hal was a trifle sensitive about the subject.

"Not yet. But what a good idea. I'll do that as soon as I say hi to Mum and Nigel. Want to fix me a drink?"

Pete seemed to find the situation far more interesting than I'd expected him to. After I gave him the license number of the Camry and the address of the house it had gone to, he asked me if I could think of anything else that seemed odd lately. I told him about the dark-haired woman with cobalt eyes lurking outside Russ's office.

"What were you talking to Dr. Jensen about?"

"Bobby Schofield's autopsy," I said.

"Could she have heard what you were saying?"

"I'm sure she could. The door was open. Do you think she was the one who followed me home?"

"I'll tell you in just a minute," he said, and I heard him typing rapidly on a keyboard. "Blue Toyota Camry, license plate CANAL2, is registered to Randall and Carole Schofield. And just so you know, so is CANAL1. That's a black Toyota Tundra pickup, just in case Randy decides to stalk you too."

"Pete, this is creeping me out," I said.

"And so it should," he said. "This tells me that you're onto something, and now they know it. Toni, you and Hal need to watch yourselves. Be very careful what you say and where you say it, and don't go anywhere alone if you can help it. And one more thing."

"What's that?"

"They also know where you live. So if you hear anything or see anything outside your house at night, you call us. Don't go investigating on your own. These people could be dangerous."

Creeped out? I thought as I hung up the phone. No way.

I was now officially scared.

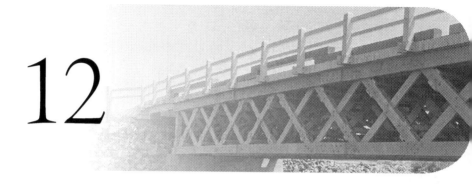

12

Down on me, down on me, looks like everybody in
this whole round world is down on me.
—JANIS JOPLIN

"TONI, YOU'RE SHAKING," HAL SAID as he handed me my drink. "What did Pete say?"

I took a huge swig of scotch and tried remain calm as I told him.

"Antoinette, darling," Mum said. "I do hope you're going to do as Pete said instead of haring off in all directions like you usually do."

"I couldn't have said it better myself, Fiona," Hal said.

"Relax," I said with false bravado. "I have no intention of doing that. I don't want to end up like Beulah."

"I could drive you to work and pick you up," Hal said, "but I can't watch your back at work."

"That's okay. I don't think they'd try anything at work," I said.

"I wouldn't be so sure," Mum said. "Carole was there today, wasn't she?"

"True," I said, "but I have an advantage now that I didn't have before."

"What's that?"

"I know what both of them look like, where they live, and what kinds of cars they drive."

"And they know the same about you," Nigel pointed out. "And here's another thing. Does she know you followed her?"

"I don't know," I confessed. "I tried to stay back, but I suppose she could have seen me. Why?"

"Because," Nigel said, "if she knows her cover's blown, she could become dangerous. *They* could become dangerous. They could also send someone else after you next time, someone you don't know."

"Exactly what did Carole hear you talking to Russ about?" Hal said. "I know you were talking about Bobby's autopsy, but what did Russ tell you about it?"

"He said his dad did it himself because there wasn't a pathologist here then, and he didn't talk about it to anybody but the sheriff, who was a Schofield too. I asked him to try to find the report in his dad's records and let me see it."

"Maybe they have a reason to keep you from seeing that report," Hal said.

"Then there must be something in it that implicates them," I said. "If that's the case, they could come after Russ and Geri too, or burn Russ's mother's house down because the records are in her basement, or they could come after Rollie."

"Rollie? What's he got to do with it?" Hal asked.

"Russ's dad did the autopsy at Rollie's mortuary," I said. "Hey! If Russ and Geri can't find that report, maybe Rollie could tell me what it showed."

"If he remembers after all this time," Nigel said. "P'r'aps you'd better talk to him sooner rather than later, if you think Randy and Carole might do him a mischief."

The doorbell rang.

"Who can that be, I wonder," Mum said.

"Are we expecting anybody?" Hal asked as he went to answer the door.

"Probably Elliott," I said. "I'm being sued."

Mum gasped. Hal stopped short. "What? And you're just telling us now?"

I turned my palms up. "I was going to," I protested. "I just got a little sidetracked by being stalked."

Hal threw up his hands. "*Oy gevalt!* What next?"

Elliott was still in his lawyerly three-piece suit and carrying an attaché case—not alligator, though. It was just plain old brown leather with scuffed corners. Elliott looked a little scuffed around the corners too. He must have had a day like mine.

He also must have heard Hal exploding. He stopped just inside the door, looking around at our faces. "What's going on here?"

Hal explained.

Elliott shook his head. "Does your son-in-law know?"

"He does," I said. "He told me to watch my back."

Elliott sat on the couch, opened his attaché case, and took out a legal pad. It gave me a feeling of déjà vu, the difference being that this lawyer was on my side. "You folks do have a full plate, don't you? Has Toni even had a chance to tell you about this lawsuit?"

"Not really," Hal said.

Elliott fished around in his attaché case and brought out a business card, which he handed to Hal, who looked at it and laughed. "Katz, Klein, Rabinowitz, and Dane? Who's Dane, the office *goy*?"

Elliott chuckled. "Obviously, they don't know your married name is Shapiro," he said to me. He turned to Hal. "Anyway, Toni, her partner, and the hospital are being sued for wrongful death, because the autopsy performed on Beulah while she was still alive caused her death."

"Death by autopsy," Hal said. "In other words."

"Who's the idiot that's suing her?" Mum asked.

"Idiots," Elliott corrected her. "In the plural. Brenda and Mortimer Duke, Beulah Pritchard's sister and brother-in-law."

Nigel chuckled. Mum looked at him. "What's so funny, love?"

"Office *goy*," he said. "Ha-ha. Very good, what?"

"Are you just now getting that?" Elliott asked.

"He's English, dear," said my mother, as if that explained everything. It didn't. "What's that got to do with it?" Elliott demanded.

"English people have a reputation for being slow to get jokes," I explained. "I can't tell you how many times I'd tell Mum a joke and half an hour later she'd start laughing. I'd say, 'Mum, are you just now getting that?' and she'd say, 'I'm English, dear.' Actually, Nigel got it pretty fast, considering."

"Thanks ever so," Nigel said with a little bow.

"Did this guy come to your office?" Hal asked me. "What did you tell him?"

"He actually told me more than I told him," I said. "Once he said they were suing me for wrongful death, I told him I wasn't going to talk to him until I consulted my own legal team."

"Oh, good one," Elliott said. "I don't think anybody's ever called me a legal team before. So, Toni, does this have anything to do with what we discussed before—the puncturing of the heart?"

"It's possible," I said.

Elliott sighed. "Damn it, Toni, talk to me. These people, the Dukes, are claiming that you did an autopsy on Beulah Pritchard while she was still alive and caused her death. Did you or didn't you?"

"No."

"Then why don't you tell me exactly what you did do?"

I took him through everything that happened in the morgue Saturday afternoon.

"When did you actually do the autopsy, then?" Elliott asked.

"Monday afternoon."

"She lived that long?"

"She died Sunday night."

"Do you have any idea why these people think you killed Beulah?"

"I don't know what those people think," I said. "Do they know about the cardiac puncture and the damage to the heart I may or may not have caused? Or do they just think I did the autopsy Saturday instead of Monday?"

"God knows," Elliott said. "You realize that I'm going to have to subpoena all her records, right?"

"No problem," I said. "Mike and I will get you anything you need."

"Do you have an autopsy report yet?"

"No, it won't be complete until I can cut the brain, and that has to fix for another week and a half."

"What's really at stake here?" Hal asked.

Elliott assumed his most pompous demeanor. "There are actually three aspects to this type of situation," he intoned. "First, malpractice."

"Well, duh," I interrupted. "Isn't that what I'm being sued for?"

"Toni, hush," Hal said. "Let him talk."

I subsided. Elliott continued. "The malpractice I'm referring to is premature pronouncement of death."

"That would be Dave," I said.

Hal frowned at me. "Toni ..."

Elliott said, "Dave?"

"Dave Martin. He was the emergency room doc that day."

Elliott made a note. "The second is the duty of the pathologist to make sure that the patient is dead before beginning the autopsy."

"I didn't begin the autopsy at all," I said. "Not that day."

"You said you drew blood from the heart," Elliott said. "Isn't that part of the autopsy? That sounds pretty invasive to me."

"No more so than intracardiac epinephrine during a code," I said. "I used the same size needle. It didn't even leave a mark on the body, or if it did, I couldn't see it with all the hemorrhage from broken ribs in that area, and the broken sternum."

Elliott made another note. "The third thing is that there should be a hospital policy requiring a twenty-four-hour delay between pronouncement of death and the autopsy, simply to prevent that sort of thing from happening. Does the hospital have such a policy?"

"Not that I know of," I said. "I've never heard of a policy like that in any of the hospitals I've worked in. Where would one keep the body during that time?"

"Where do you normally keep bodies?" Hal interjected. "In the cooler, right?"

"Well, that's just it," I argued. "That's fine if you're not dealing with hypothermia. But you can't have dead bodies lying around at room temperature either. You can't leave them tying up an emergency room cubicle, for instance, or a hospital bed."

"Especially in a double room," Hal said. "What would the other patient think?"

"When I was an intern doing my emergency room rotation," I said, "if anybody died while they were still in the ER, they stuck the body in the stairwell on a gurney, until they found out which mortuary to call so someone could come and pick it up. Nobody else ever used that stairwell."

"I wonder why," Hal commented.

Poor, old, tired Elliott didn't see the humor in that. He snapped his case shut and stood up. "I think I've got enough to go on with," he said. "I haven't even been home yet. I need to get out of this freakin' chain mail and have a drink." He strode to the front door, but before he opened it, he turned back to me. "There's one other possibility we haven't discussed. If the Dukes sue and fail, there's one other thing they might try to do."

"What's that?" I asked.

"They could try to charge you with murder."

"Christ on a crutch," I said.

My mother came in right on cue. "Language, dear."

"Actually," Elliott said, "I'm surprised they didn't try that first. Usually people go for the criminal charges before the civil suit, like the OJ Simpson case. There's only one reason I can think of why they'd do it this way."

"What's that?" Hal asked.

"They're more interested in the money than they are in punishing Toni or her partner or the hospital."

"Who are these people, anyway?" Nigel asked.

"I haven't had the pleasure of making their acquaintance," Elliott said, his expression sour, "but I understand that the sister is an actress and her husband is a stockbroker who used to work at Lehman Brothers before the crash."

"So they're from New York," Hal said.

"They were, but they live in Boise now," Elliott said.

"So why didn't they retain some high-powered lawyer from New York?" Hal wanted to know.

"Maybe they can't afford it," Elliott said. "Or maybe they actually did. A lawyer from out of state would have to work with a lawyer licensed in the state. So maybe our old pal Chaim Rabinowitz is just a front for a New York law firm that's a much bigger threat than he is. Or maybe he's licensed in New York as well as Idaho. Anyway, I've scheduled depositions next week for everyone involved, starting with you, Toni, at nine Monday morning, my office."

Then he left.

I turned back to my family. "There's another thing that Elliott didn't mention," I said. "The Idaho State Board of Medicine."

"Your license," Mum said. "Oh dear."

"Naturally, if I were to be convicted of murder, it would be revoked permanently," I said. "But even if I'm not, a malpractice suit will come to their attention, because they do prelitigation screening to determine if a suit has any basis. If they determine that a suit is frivolous, it's unlikely that any lawyer will pursue it."

"But what if they don't?" Mum asked.

"If they don't, the result of that suit will affect my license. If I'm found guilty of malpractice, the board could do anything from a confidential reprimand to revocation."

"You won't be found guilty of anything," Hal said. "None of it happened. The board of medicine will find it frivolous. Fritz won't charge you with murder."

Fritz Baumgartner, the district attorney, knew me pretty well from the Sally Shore affair. Back then, I hadn't even had an alibi, whereas now I had all kinds of witnesses to what I'd done and, more important, had *not* done—with the exception of the role that my cardiac puncture might have played in Beulah's pericardial hemorrhage.

But I was damned if I was going to spend the weekend wondering and worrying if I didn't have to. I picked up the phone and dialed. "Let's just see about that."

"Who are you calling?" Hal asked.

"Fritz," I said.

"Oh, come on," Hal objected. "Can't you let the man have a peaceful weekend?"

"What about my peaceful weekend?" I retorted, and at that moment, Fritz answered. I told him what was going on. "Elliott said these people might want to have me charged with murder," I said.

"On what grounds?" Fritz asked.

I told him about the damage to the heart and the pericardial hemorrhage. "I can't prove that I didn't cause some of that with my cardiac puncture."

"It sounds unlikely," Fritz said. "Besides, the burden of proof is on them. They'd have to prove that you had some kind of premeditation, or at least malice aforethought. Otherwise, it's just accidental, and you're right back to therapeutic misadventure and malpractice. Besides that, aren't they going at it backward? If they wanted to charge you with murder, wouldn't they do that first, and then charge you with malpractice if you were acquitted of the murder charge?"

"That's what Elliott said," I told him.

"And another thing," Fritz said. "What about the paramedics who did CPR on Beulah? If the cardiac damage was caused in any part by what they did, they should be included in the suit as well."

"The paramedics work for the hospital too," I said. "I don't know if they've been named in the suit separately or not."

"Tell you what," Fritz said. "I'll talk to Elliott and get this all straightened out before the deposition. Unless there's something that you haven't told me, I can't see any grounds for a murder charge."

I heaved a sigh of relief, thanked him, and rang off.

"Well?" asked Hal.

I told him what Fritz had said.

"Well, that's a relief," he said. "Now, hadn't we better eat before anything else happens?"

The doorbell rang as we were finishing dinner, and Hal opened the door to admit Pete, sans diaper bag. "Where are the girls?" Hal inquired.

"Home," Pete said succinctly. "Little Toni's got an ear infection. Also, she's teething. You don't want to be around her right now."

I certainly didn't, especially with a cold.

"So, what's up?" asked Hal. "Want a beer?"

Pete accepted and parked himself on the couch. "Just thought I'd give you an update on S & P Pipe Company. I didn't have any luck finding it either. So I got a warrant."

"How did you manage that?" Nigel asked.

"I convinced a judge that a possible fraud involving the canal company might be connected to the death of a canal company employee and his wife who'd had an affair with the current general manager."

"Goodness me," Mum said. "When you put it like that, it sounds terribly illicit."

"It sounds juicy as hell," Hal said. "The stuff soap operas are made of. When's it going to hit the tabloids?"

"Never, I hope," Pete said. "Anyway, I got a warrant that lets me look at the canal company's financials, Randy Schofield's financials, and S & P's financials, assuming I ever find them. I also was able to find out who's paying for PO Box 367. It's not S & P. It's Randy Schofield."

"So maybe he owns S & P," I said.

"Whatever that may be," Pete said. "There's no indication that the company even exists."

"Okay," I said. "What else did you find out?"

"The canal company does get pipe from Pipeco, just as Carole said," Pete continued. "But I went back through their records as far as 2000, and I found entries for S & P every few weeks, all different amounts, anywhere from a few hundred to a couple thousand dollars."

"Was there any documentation of what they purchased from S & P?" I asked.

"There were receipts scanned into the computer, but the items were listed as SKU numbers, so I couldn't tell what they actually were."

"Did you say the payments to S & P have been going on since 2000?" Nigel asked.

"No," Pete said. "They only went back to 2008."

"Wait a minute," I said. "That mailbox was stuffed with mail. Most of it looked like bills. If the canal company only paid S & P every few weeks, there shouldn't have been that many of them in the box at once."

"I thought you said they were all for S & P," Hal said.

"The top one was," I said. "The envelopes all looked alike, but I didn't have time to look at all the addresses. They could have been from other places. I don't really know. If they weren't S & P, what were they?"

"Maybe PO Box 367 is Randy Schofield's personal mailbox," Mum suggested. "Maybe some of those were his own bills."

"There wasn't any record of regular payments to S & P," Pete said. "They weren't at any regular interval or for the same amount. They seemed completely sporadic."

"Even if Randy's personal bills were in that box," I argued, "it wouldn't account for how many envelopes there were. Do you suppose Randy owns more than one company?"

"And uses the same PO box for all of them," Hal said. "That would explain it."

"But if Randy owns all those companies," Mum objected, "what's he doing working for the canal company? One would think he'd be too busy managing them to hold a full-time job elsewhere."

"Unless all those companies were bogus too," Nigel said. "Then there'd be nothing to manage."

"Except the paperwork," I said. "Somebody has to order the stuff, and somebody has to send a bill to the canal company, and Carole would pay it. I wonder if she knows anything."

"She is Randy's wife," Hal said. "And she did follow you home. Why would she do that if she didn't know anything?"

"Obviously you have reason to believe this bloke is embezzling from the canal company," Nigel said. "You should see if you can find evidence of more bogus companies."

Pete groaned. "Do you have any idea what that would entail? I'd have to check out every transaction."

"Not really," Hal said. "Most of them are gonna be legitimate businesses whose names you'll recognize. Just check out the ones you've never heard of."

"Yeah, right," said Pete. "I wonder how long this has been going on. Before 2000, it might not even have been computerized."

"If they've even kept records that far back," I said.

"How long has Randy been general manager?" Hal asked.

"I wonder what it has to do with Beulah and Dwayne's murders," I said. "Maybe Beulah found out about it and talked about it, and

Randy had to kill her to shut her up. Or worse, maybe she tried to blackmail him."

"That doesn't sound so far-fetched to me," Nigel said. "Follow the money, what?"

"No, it actually makes a lot of sense," Pete said. "And Toni?"

"What?"

"Randy knows you saw that envelope, and Carole knows where you live, so watch your back. And stay away from the canal company."

I shivered. Going to the canal company was the last thing I wanted to do.

The threat of being sued or charged with murder was bad enough, but if Randy and Carole thought I knew too much about what they were up to, they could kill me. They could also kill people I cared about, like my family—not to mention Russ Jensen and Rollie Perkins.

After Pete left, I picked up the phone again. "Who are you calling now?" Hal asked. "It's after ten."

"I'm calling Russ," I said, "and after that, I'm going to call Rollie."

"Can't it wait till morning?" Hal asked.

"Only if you're sure Carole and Randy are going to wait till morning," I argued. "Would you, in their position? If anybody finds out that they had anything to do with Bobby's death, their freedom is at stake. There's no statute of limitations on murder."

Hal threw up his hands. "Okay. You've made your point."

I called Russ at home first. The phone went straight to voice mail. His cell phone did too.

Was I already too late?

13

Done to death by slanderous tongues.
—SHAKESPEARE, MUCH ADO ABOUT NOTHING

I CALLED PETE AND TOLD him.

"I'll have someone go by his house and check on him," Pete said, "and his mother's house too. Isn't that where his dad's records are?"

Then I called Rollie at Parkside Mortuary. He and his wife, Wilma, lived in the apartment on the second floor of the funeral home, and I knew that the mortuary phone got switched through to his home when he wasn't at work, so I wasn't surprised when he answered. "Well, now, Doctor," he rumbled, "usually it's me who calls you in the middle of the night. What can I do for you?"

I came right to the point. "Do you remember Dr. Jensen's dad doing an autopsy on a little boy who drowned in the canal?"

"You mean ol' Doc Russell? That had to be thirty years ago or more."

Confused, I repeated, "Doc Russell?"

"That's what everybody called him. And would the little boy in question be Bobby Schofield?"

"So you do remember it! What did he find?"

"Why all this interest in Bobby Schofield?"

"All this interest? Who else wants to know about Bobby Schofield?"

"Some lady called today and asked Wilma about it."

Wilma was also the receptionist at the funeral home.

"Did this lady have a name?" I asked.

"Wilma said she didn't give one. She just asked if we had any records on a Bobby Schofield."

"And do you?" Rollie hesitated, and I went on to explain the situation. "Dr. Russ Jensen, the present Dr. Jensen, told me that his dad did the autopsy right there in your embalming room. He said his dad wouldn't talk about it, and I thought you might remember what he found, because apparently someone doesn't want that information getting out."

"How do you know that?" Rollie asked.

I told him about being stalked by Carole Schofield.

"What's that got to do with me?" he asked.

"What if they think you know what that autopsy showed?"

"You think they might come after me too." It was a statement, not a question.

"Maybe," I said.

"I wasn't actually in the room at the time," he said, "and Dad didn't tell me anything about it."

I remembered Rollie's father, the original proprietor of Parkside Mortuary, who used to stand and watch me do autopsies, smoking a pipe and telling joke after joke. I also remembered the ambulance bringing him in to Perrine Memorial one day as I was leaving work, after he'd collapsed from a massive heart attack. He'd been DOA.

"Why wouldn't he tell you?" I asked. "You were working there at the time, weren't you?"

"I don't know why he didn't tell me." I heard a bell ring in the background and Rollie said, "Sorry, Doctor, gotta go. Got a customer."

"Okay, Rollie," I said. "Just watch your back. I don't want to have to get used to another coroner anytime soon."

No sooner had I hung up than the phone rang. It was Pete.

"There was a fire at Mary Jensen's house," he told me. "It started in the basement. The fire department's there now."

"Is everybody okay?" I asked.

"Yes. Toni, go to bed. Get some sleep. Everything's under control."

In the morning, I called Russ's cell phone and felt a great rush of relief when I heard his voice. "Russ! Where are you? Are you okay? Is your mom okay?"

"She's fine. The fire department put it out before it did any major damage."

"Oh, good. I called to tell you that Carole Schofield was waiting outside your office yesterday afternoon when we were talking about Bobby's autopsy. She had to hear you say the report might be in your mom's basement."

"Why didn't you say something at the time?"

"I didn't know who she was then. I thought she was a patient. I found out who she was after she followed me home last night, and I had Pete run the license plate."

"Good grief," Russ said. "Well, that would explain why the fire started in the basement. Maybe I ought to call the fire department and tell them it was arson."

"They probably look for signs of arson anyway," I said. "But I'll tell Pete. He can take it from there."

"Maybe you ought to call Rollie too," Russ said, "in case the same people come after him."

"I did," I told him. "I called him last night."

No sooner had I hung up than Elliott called.

"Do you have anything you can give me on Beulah's autopsy? Anything at all?"

"I can give you the same provisional report that I gave Rollie and the police," I said, "but all it says about the heart is 'pericardial hemorrhage with cardiac tamponade,' which I'm sure they already know about."

"Well, that doesn't do me any good," Elliott complained. "Got anything else? Pictures?"

Natalie had taken plenty of pictures. They were in our PathPics file where we kept all our pictures and other files having to do with our cases—photomicrographs from the tumor board cases, for example. Or gross pictures of surgicals for when the patient wanted to know what her fibroid uterus looked like, for example. They didn't go in the file with the path reports. Beulah's pictures wouldn't be part of the autopsy report. They were just there in case they were needed in a wrongful death suit—for example.

"Pictures of what?" I asked. "Her heart?"

"I need all of them."

"All of them? You're kidding. We took about fifty of them. The police did too."

"I subpoenaed theirs. I can subpoena yours too. Unless you'd like to send me a set of prints."

"Fifty prints? I can't tie up our printer for that; it'll take forever. Plus, it's not a color printer. How about I e-mail them to you and you print them?"

"Okay. Can you do that today?"

"No problem." I was sure that I could attach that folder to an e-mail in a matter of seconds. "What's your e-mail address?"

He gave it to me, and we disconnected.

So I fired up my computer, opened my e-mail, typed in Elliott's e-mail address, attached the folder of Beulah's autopsy photos, and hit "send."

By then, the pile of slide trays had reached a height that demanded attention, but I had obviously opened quite a can of worms, so I called Pete and told him what I'd found out. Then I went back to work, reading out the slides from the surgicals I'd grossed the day before.

That didn't last long. Arlene interrupted me to say that the coroner was in the emergency room and wanted to talk to me.

"The coroner?" I asked.

"Yes," she said. "Mr. Perkins from Parkside Funeral Home? Isn't he the coroner?"

"Oh. Yes, of course he is," I said. "What's he doing in the emergency room? Did he say?"

"No. He just asked for you."

"Okay. Transfer him."

"He wasn't on the phone," Arlene explained. "It was a nurse who called."

"Huh," I said. "That's weird. I wonder who died."

Arlene shrugged. So I went.

I found Rollie in a cubicle behind a curtain. Dave Martin was with him, suturing a head laceration. "What's going on here?" I asked.

"What does it look like?" Dave retorted. "Toni, what are you doing here?"

"It's okay, Doc," Rollie said from beneath the drape. "I asked her to come."

"Someone attacked him," Dave said. "We've already called the police."

"And here we are," Pete said from behind me. "What happened, Rollie?"

"I don't know," Rollie said. "I guess somebody hit me over the head and knocked me out."

"Who?" I asked. "When?"

"Toni, that's my job," Pete objected.

"I don't know," Rollie said. "Last thing I remember is talking to you last night. I don't remember anything after that."

"Retrograde amnesia," I said. "What about Wilma?"

"Wilma doesn't know anything about it," Pete said. "She was already in bed when you called last night, and she didn't even realize anything was wrong until she woke up this morning and Rollie wasn't there. She called the mortuary and nobody answered. So she went back into the embalming room and found him unconscious on the floor in a pool of blood."

"That makes sense," I said.

"Makes sense?" Pete said. "In what way does this make sense?"

"I called Rollie after I talked to you last night. I told him Carole had been stalking me and that he might be in danger too. That's why it makes sense."

"So you think it was Carole Schofield who attacked Rollie?" Pete asked. "And set fire to Mary Jensen's house?"

"Either her or Randy, or someone they sent," I said. "You should talk to the sheriff and see if he has any record of that autopsy in his files. Rollie told me last night that his dad didn't tell him anything about what the autopsy showed. And then a bell rang, and he said he had a customer and had to go. Oh God, do you think that was who attacked him and he was lying there all night?"

"No way to know," Pete said. "We'll check it out." And he was gone.

I went back to my office, back to the stack of slide trays, which had been merrily reproducing in my absence and obviously having more fun than I was.

But not for long.

Natalie interrupted me to ask if I knew the results of the tests on her blood and Dwayne's. If his viral markers were still negative, we didn't have to worry about hepatitis B or C. But if Dwayne had used intravenous or injectable drugs in his younger days, he could be carrying HIV. And hadn't somebody mentioned anabolic steroids recently? They'd been implicated in liver tumors. Brain tumors also. And weren't anabolic steroids also sometimes given by injection?

I fired up the computer and looked up lab results on Dwayne Pritchard, holding my breath as they came up.

They were all negative except for hepatitis B surface antigen.

Dwayne had hepatitis B antigen but not the antibodies. That was consistent with chronic hepatitis B, which may have been the cause of his cirrhosis and liver cancer, not the alcoholic liver disease that everybody thought he had, or the anabolic steroids he'd used in the past. The Boise gastroenterologist had been wrong about Dwayne's viral hepatitis markers being negative. Perhaps he'd confused Dwayne with another patient. It happens.

Hepatitis B carried a 10 percent risk of chronic liver disease and hepatocellular carcinoma. Hepatitis C, on the other hand, carried a nearly 50 percent risk of those things. There was no vaccine for hepatitis C, but there was a vaccine for hepatitis B, and hospital employees were required to be immunized. Then they were tested at intervals after immunization to make sure they had detectable titers of antibody. If not, they were given a booster shot.

My computer pinged, announcing a new message that informed me that the file I'd tried to e-mail was too big, and reminding me that the maximum I could send was ten megabytes. *Shit. How big are those pictures, anyway?* I opened the file, selected a picture at random, clicked "properties," and found that each of those puppies was 3.5 megabytes, which meant I could only mail two at a time.

The phone jangled, startling me. *Why,* I thought to myself, *did the phone always ring whenever I was in the middle of trying to grapple with a problem?*

"What's taking so freakin' long?" Elliott demanded. "You said you'd e-mail those pictures right over."

"Elliott," I said, "what's the big rush? Why are you in such an all-fired hurry to get those pictures?"

I heard him sigh. I could almost visualize him pushing his fingers through his curly salt-and-pepper hair, making it even bushier than before. "I hate this freakin' case, Toni. That asshole Chaim Rabinowitz is on my case big-time, probably because those damn Dukes are on his case, and apparently he's got a connection to someone in the court system who's pushing for an early trial, and he'll probably get it."

"Wait," I said. "How early is early? Why are they in such a rush?"

"I don't know," Elliott said irritably. "Maybe they don't want to pay for him to drag everything out like he usually does, or maybe they owe money to somebody who doesn't give them a flexible payment plan, if you get my drift."

"What? You mean the mob?"

"I don't know," he said, "but it would explain a lot, wouldn't it? A desperate need for quick money?"

"How smart is it," I asked, "to try to get it by filing a frivolous lawsuit? I mean, lawsuits drag on forever, and this one can't possibly do it for them, can it?"

"You know that, Toni, and I know that, but apparently the Dukes don't. Remember that they're not just suing you. They're also suing your partner and the hospital. They probably figure that with all those freakin' deep pockets something's gotta shake out."

I knew what he meant. Medical malpractice suits generally name everybody who's even remotely connected with the case. They call it "joint and several liability" because everybody shares in it. But if anyone's dropped from the suit or settles out of court, one person could conceivably end up liable for the whole thing, and I really didn't want that person to be Dave Martin or the still-nameless paramedics who were only doing their jobs. But I really didn't want it to be me or Mike either. Cascade Medical Enterprises, on the other hand, probably wouldn't even notice it. It would be the equivalent of swatting a pesky mosquito.

"Those pictures are too big to e-mail," I said, "but I'll download them onto a thumb drive and bring it home with me, okay?"

"How about I send someone over to pick it up?"

Not a good idea, I thought. "Will you know what it is you're looking at without me?"

Elliott clearly hadn't thought of that, and we ended our conversation. Now where was I? Oh, yeah, I was looking up Natalie's medical record.

Natalie was negative for hepatitis B surface antigen, positive for hepatitis B surface antibody, and negative for hepatitis B core antibody. That profile was consistent with having been immunized for hepatitis B. Those who'd actually had hepatitis B, like me in my first year of residency, also were positive for hepatitis B core antibody, which was how you could tell the difference between someone who'd been immunized from someone who'd actually had the disease and shouldn't give blood or be an organ donor.

The other markers were negative also. I called histology and asked Natalie to come to my office so I could give her the good news in person and in private—and also to remind her that she'd have to be retested for HIV at six months and in a year. Dealing with employee health issues like this is all in a day's work for a pathologist.

Lucille had brought me Dwayne's autopsy slides along with the last installment of surgical slides, so after I got those dictated, I pulled the tray containing Dwayne's slides toward me and selected a section of liver. It showed hepatocellular carcinoma—and a really ugly, undifferentiated, rapidly growing form of it too. Another section showed severe chronic hepatitis and cirrhosis. The normal configuration of the human liver had been replaced by crisscrossing and interlacing bands of fibrous tissue, leaving only small islands of functioning hepatic cells, which hadn't been functioning very well, actually. Bile plugs filled the canaliculi, the small spaces between the cells—a condition called cholestasis. No wonder Dwayne was so jaundiced.

This reminded me that I still hadn't downloaded Beulah's picture file onto a thumb drive. I did so and tossed it into my purse before going home.

Now, of course, going home didn't mean merely walking from my office to my car. It meant checking the hallways for tall, sandy-haired men, or attractive, dark-haired women with cobalt eyes, or anyone else who might be waiting to intercept me on their behalf. It meant peering around doors before walking through them, scanning the shadowy underground parking area for moving shapes, checking the backseat of my car before getting into it, and checking the interior of my garage before getting out of the car. Even the brief dash from the garage to the kitchen door included areas where intruders could conceal themselves and leap out at me—or just shoot me and be done with it.

Maybe I should get myself a gun, I thought. Of course, I'd have to get a license to carry one, and take lessons in how to use it safely, and try to get permission to carry it concealed, and even if I managed not to get myself killed while doing all that, I still wouldn't be allowed to have it inside the hospital. I'd have to leave it in my car, where someone could break in and steal it and then lie in wait to shoot me with it when I came out to drive home.

Perhaps it would be more practical to arm myself with a heavy flashlight instead. With that, I could strike first, blinding my adversary before conking him or her over the head. Of course, there was always the risk that I might assault some perfectly innocent person with my flashlight, but at least it was legal to carry it into the hospital.

A note on the kitchen table told me that everyone had gone next door to Jodi and Elliott's house and that the animals had already been fed. Good thing too, because by the way Killer and Geraldine were acting, I might have assumed that they hadn't eaten for days. Just getting from the garage into the kitchen and from the kitchen to the bathroom was a major undertaking, because I had to navigate my way through their obstructing bodies without stepping on them.

But now it occurred to me that maybe they were trying to tell me that someone had been snooping around the house, or had actually been inside the house, or … oh my God … was still inside the house—someone who wouldn't mind killing pets if it suited their purpose to do so. It would send a powerful message that the next to die could be Mum or Nigel or Hal if I didn't back off doing whatever I was doing.

A shiver ran up my spine, and the hairs rose on the back of my neck— just like the hairs had risen on Killer's and Geraldine's backs.

Uh-oh.

Somebody was inside the house.

I had to get out of there—fast.

13

I have been poor and I have been rich. Rich is better.
—SOPHIE TUCKER

I SNAGGED THE FLASHLIGHT FROM the junk drawer in the kitchen and stuck it in my purse. Then I took Killer and Geraldine with me when I went next door, hoping that Spook would have the sense to stay out of sight if there actually was someone in the house.

In the shelter of Elliott's porch, I took out my smartphone and called Pete.

He didn't waste time asking a lot of questions. "Just stay where you are, Toni, and we'll check it out."

The dogs bounded into the Maynards' living room while I hung my coat in the closet and kicked off my shoes. I hugged and kissed Mum and Nigel and sank onto the couch next to Hal. Happy hour was in progress. Elliott and Hal had beers in their hands, Mum and Jodi were drinking white wine, and Nigel had his scotch. Jodi said, "Your usual, Toni?"

I assented. Geraldine sprang into my lap. Hal put his arm around me and kissed me. "What's with the dogs?"

I told him.

He sobered instantly. "Have you called Pete?"

"Yes."

"What did he say?"

127

"To stay put and they'd check it out."

"Good. So have you been looking around corners all day at work too?"

"No, only when I left. But now that you mention it, maybe I'd better start." My heart sank still further as I visualized all the places where I was obliged to go in the hospital during the day: histology, surgery, diagnostic imaging, the cafeteria. Carrying a heavy flashlight for self-defense suddenly sounded a lot less feasible and even a little silly. I pulled the flashlight out of my purse and showed it to Hal. "I stuck this in my purse for self-defense, but I can't carry it all day at work."

"No, you certainly can't. But how about this?" He reached into his shirt pocket and pulled out a slim black tube on which he pressed a nearly-invisible button. A red light showed.

I laughed. "A laser pointer? What am I supposed to do, shine it in their eyes?"

"Certainly. It will temporarily blind them, and you can get away."

I took it and experimentally turned it in my hands. "Cool. That's a whole lot better than a big, honkin' flashlight."

"Keep it. I've got more at work."

Jodi brought me my scotch. I took a sip. "You know about the fire at Russ's mother's house, right?" I said.

Hal nodded.

"Well, somebody attacked Rollie last night too."

"You're kidding."

"No, I'm not," I said, and I told him what had happened.

He sighed. "Well, the police know all about this, right?"

"Yes, they do."

"So there's nothing we can do but watch our backs."

"That's correct."

"So can we talk about something else now?"

I settled myself more cozily into the crook of his arm. "Certainly. So how was your day, sweetie?"

"Okay, I guess," Hal said. "My new lab assistant isn't much help. Makes me appreciate Bambi a whole lot more. Do you suppose I could get her to come back?"

"Only if she could bring Little Toni with her." The thought of a nine-month-old who was just beginning to walk wreaking havoc in a chemistry lab would be enough to drive me screaming into the street. Broken glass, caustic substances …

"Dear me," said Mum with a shudder. "What a horrible thought."

"Bad idea," said Nigel. "Doesn't bear thinking about."

But Hal merely shook his head and said, "*Oy vey.*"

Bambi had been Hal's lab assistant back when she was a nineteen-year-old college student. She was smart as a whip and drop-dead gorgeous—six feet tall with long blonde hair, blue eyes, and a California tan—and Hal had taken a whole lot of ribbing from his colleagues about her looks. I'd even suspected him of having an affair with her.

None of us, including Hal, had known that she was his daughter until her family had showed up for Hanukkah: Hal's ex-wife Shawna and her husband, Marty Bloom, and their two teenage sons, Josh and Jake, who were both short with dark, curly hair like their father's. Shawna, in typical fashion, had taken the opportunity to inform Hal that—oh, guess what—she'd already been pregnant when she'd divorced him and married Marty, and that Hal was Bambi's biological father. And then she'd left it up to Hal to tell Bambi and deal with the fallout.

Then he'd had to tell me.

That had been the most difficult time of our marriage, that difficult time Beulah had been referring to when she started the rumor that Hal and I were going to get a divorce.

"So, Beulah's sister and her husband are suing you for Beulah's wrongful death," Jodi said as she settled into an easy chair with her drink. "I don't get it. You didn't kill Beulah."

"They claim that Beulah was still alive when Toni started the autopsy," Elliott said, "and that it was the freakin' cause of death."

"Death by autopsy," Hal chimed in helpfully.

I wished he'd stop saying that. Doubtless, in twenty years or so, we'd look back on this and laugh, but right now I didn't find it the least bit funny. Even a frivolous lawsuit could do a lot of damage in legal costs, negative publicity, and ruined reputations—*my* ruined reputation, and Mike's. Killing someone by doing an autopsy on them while they were still alive had just the right amount of gruesomeness to make people shiver deliciously and savor the horrified reactions of those they told about it. It might even hit the tabloids. Nobody would ever believe that it really hadn't happened. It was so much more fun to believe that it had and that somebody was trying to cover it up.

"But surely," Mum said, "the record clearly shows that you didn't do any such thing, kitten."

"It does show that I didn't open up the body," I agreed. "It's the damage I may or may not have done to the heart when I drew blood from it that's the problem."

"Well, let's just take a look." Elliott opened up his laptop on the coffee table, inserted the thumb drive I'd given him into a USB port, and downloaded Beulah's pictures. Everyone crowded onto and around the couch to see them, but after the first few shots into the open chest and abdominal cavities, complete with the purple beach ball pericardium, Jodi and Mum withdrew with grimaces of distaste. Hal and Nigel remained, mesmerized, while Elliott opened up one after another until he had seen everything in the file. He went through them so fast that I had no chance to point out the damage I was referring to. He turned to me in frustration. "Where are the ones from Saturday?"

"We didn't take any pictures Saturday," I said, "but the sheriff did."

"Oh, for God's sake," he said in disgust. "Now I've got to get another freakin' subpoena. Why didn't you tell me this was multijurisdictional?"

I shrugged and turned my palms up. "I thought you knew. The canal's in the county, not the city."

"But Beulah died in the hospital, which is in the city," he argued.

"Yes, but when she was pulled out of the canal, the sheriff's department search and rescue was involved, and she was assumed to be dead right up until the time she grabbed my apron strings in the morgue. The sheriff was there at the time, so he took the pictures."

"But that was when you stuck a needle in the heart, right?"

"Yes, but the damage it caused, or may have caused, showed up when I did the actual autopsy on Monday. If you hadn't gone through those pictures so damn fast, I could have showed you."

Elliott ran his fingers through his bushy hair and let out a heartfelt groan. "Shit. I hate this freakin' case."

"You and me both," I said. "Now, can we go back and look at the pictures of the heart and sternum so you can see what this lawsuit is all about?"

The pizza arrived at this juncture, so the discussion was suspended until after we—and the three Maynard children who still lived at home— had eaten and left a wasteland of empty pizza boxes and odd crusts on their dining room table.

Pete and Bernie showed up after dinner. "There wasn't anybody there when we went through your house," Pete said.

"Except the cat," Bernie said. "He came shooting out of a closet, shrieking like a banshee right in front of me. Damn near gave me a heart attack."

Typical, I thought. That was how Spook had gotten his name in the first place.

"Maybe he scared off the intruder too," Pete said. He reached into his pocket and pulled something out. "Does this belong to you?"

In his palm lay an earring inside a baggie. "Can I touch it?" I asked. "Sure."

I picked it up and turned it over. It was very pretty. But it wasn't one of mine.

I handed it back. "Nope. Not mine. Where'd you find it?"

"In the coat closet next to the stairs," said Pete, taking the baggie. "I don't see us getting any usable fingerprints from this, but maybe we can find its mate in Carole's house."

"Jeez," I said with a shiver. "I wonder if they were there when I got home. What if I'd opened the door to hang up my coat?"

"Just as well you didn't," Pete said.

"They would most certainly have done you a mischief," Nigel said.

What a marvelous gift for understatement these Brits have, I thought. What Nigel called a mischief was what nightmares were made of.

After Pete and Bernie left, Elliott and I took the thumb drive into his den to look at the pictures on the larger screen of his PC, while the others watched TV in the living room. "Take me through these one by one," he instructed, "and tell me what each one represents. When I do this in court or in deposition, I need to know what I'm showing, okay?"

I did so, starting with the skin-covered, closed chest with hemorrhage over the broken ribs and sternum, and progressing to the exposed rib cage with the skin peeled back to expose the fractured, caved-in sternum; to the open chest with the breast plate removed to expose the purple beach ball pericardium; to the opened pericardium exposing the heart; to the heart removed from the body, with close-ups of the damage to the left ventricle; and finally, to the breast plate, reversed to show the splintery inner surface of the sternal fracture. Elliott made copious notes.

Then I opened a separate file I'd made on the thumb drive. These were pictures I'd taken while putting in sections of the damaged myocardium for slides to be made. I hadn't actually looked at them myself yet.

"What's this?" Elliott asked.

I told him. "My intention is to actually map the sections I took and to try to correlate them to the fractured part of the sternum. During the autopsy, I painted the inner surface of the sternal fracture with India ink. I put it back in place before I removed the heart, and I pushed down on it as if I was doing CPR, to transfer the ink to the surface of the myocardium. See, in this picture, part of the hemorrhagic area is actually black. When I see the sections I took of this area, I'll be able to see the ink on the slides. Then I'll know which sections correspond to the fracture and which ones don't."

Elliott was impressed and said so. "But you don't actually have those slides yet?"

"I'll have them tomorrow," I said. "I'll tell my histotechs I have to have them tomorrow because of the deposition Monday. I'll be able to take photomicrographs of them, and we can go over them this weekend before the deposition."

At least that was my intention. I hoped that Friday's workload would allow me to get that done so I wouldn't have to do it on the weekend, but one way or another, Elliott and I would be ready for the deposition Monday morning—unless the Schofields, et al, managed to polish me off before then, in which case it would be a moot point, at least for me.

"Oh, no, it wouldn't," Elliott said when I voiced that thought, destroying the only good thing left about being killed. "They can still sue your estate."

Christ on a crutch. I looked at him, horrified. "That's not fair. Hal hasn't done anything wrong."

Hal must have heard me, because he came into the office. "What'd I do?"

"Nothing," I said and explained.

"Neither have you," Elliott added. "Let me explain something to you, Toni. In a malpractice suit, the burden of proof is on the plaintiff. There are three parameters they have to meet. First, they have to prove that you committed an act of negligence, not just a wrong judgment call. Second, they have to show that the act you committed was the immediate cause of harm to the patient. Third, they have to show that the act you committed resulted in serious damage or injuries. If they can't show all three, no law firm will file a suit. And even if a suit is filed, if any one of those parameters isn't proved, the plaintiff will lose."

"Okay. I committed the act of drawing blood from the heart. So if I can prove that that act didn't cause her pericardial hemorrhage, the suit won't even be filed."

"Right," Elliott said. "You catch on fast. But there's more. A malpractice suit can take up to three years and can cost a great deal of money to try. Expert witnesses are expensive. The plaintiff has to come up with a retainer that covers all that."

"So, if these guys are in dire need of money, they can't afford to do this. And if they're in a rush, they're going about it the wrong way."

"That's not all," Elliott said. "In Idaho, noneconomic damages are capped at $400,000, and punitive damages are limited to $250,000—unless you acted recklessly or willfully, or if what you did would be considered a felony under criminal law, which it isn't. Apparently, Rabinowitz and company haven't told their clients that yet, or they wouldn't be bothering to sue."

"Do you plan to do that?"

"One way or another," Elliott said, "they'll know it before we go much farther."

"So, why do we have to go through all these depositions if they're not even going to pursue it?"

"We don't know if they will or not. So the next thing is to make sure they can't meet those three parameters."

"It sounds like Toni doesn't have anything to worry about," Hal said.

"I don't think she does," Elliott said. "This stalking business, on the other hand ..."

"Not to mention the attacks on Rollie and Russ's mother," I said.

But it was Hal who put it into perspective. "You realize what this means."

"Yes," I said. "They're going after us next."

14

Defer not till tomorrow to be wise,
Tomorrow's sun to thee may never rise.
—WILLIAM CONGREVE

I SLEPT BADLY THURSDAY NIGHT. Every little noise sent me running downstairs to peer outside and check that doors and windows were still locked. Of course, whenever I did that, the dogs accompanied me downstairs, and whenever I came back upstairs, either Mum or Nigel peeked out of their bedroom to ask if everything was all right. So nobody got much sleep, and none of us were in particularly good moods Friday morning.

I left my fellow thunderclouds seated around the breakfast table early to allow myself time to check for anyone who might be lurking outside the kitchen door, in the garage, or in my car. I refused Hal's offer to drive me to work, on the basis that anyone stalking me on my way to work could then stalk Hal to the college—not that it wouldn't be a simple matter to just Google Dr. Hal Shapiro and find out where he worked.

On my way to the hospital, I kept an eye out for threatening Toyotas, and in the sprint from my car to the door into Administration, laser pointer gripped firmly in hand, I saw nobody skulking suspiciously about in the underground parking garage. I heaved a sigh of relief when I finally reached my office unscathed and found nobody lurking underneath my desk. But the day was only just beginning.

Word had gotten around with regard to the lawsuit.

Mike came in to ask me about my deposition, because Elliott had scheduled him for one right after mine on Monday. "What can I tell them that y'all can't?" was his take on the situation.

Well, it was a lot easier to put Mike's mind at ease about the upcoming deposition than it was to do the same with Natalie. She'd been scheduled for Monday too, right after Mike, and she was panicked.

Dave Martin charged into my office not fifteen minutes after I finished calming my skittish autopsy assistant and shook his summons in my face. "Toni, what the hell's going on here?"

"What did Charlie tell you?" I asked.

"Some damn idiot is suing the hospital for the wrongful death of Beulah Pritchard."

"Yes. It turns out that Beulah has a sister, and she and her husband are suing us for wrongful death. They claim that the autopsy I did on her while she was still alive killed her."

Dave did an eye roll. "You've got to be kidding."

I waved my summons at him. "Does this look like I'm kidding?" I retorted. "I'm the opening act."

"This is insane! Why are they wasting their time and everyone else's by deposing everybody? Do they think you were lying?"

I shrugged. "Either that, or Elliott wants to cover all the bases by interviewing everybody that had anything to do with Beulah's autopsy. They're not just suing me, you know. They're suing Mike and the hospital too."

Dave sank into a chair. "Oh God, does that mean they'll be asking why Beulah's body got released from the ER so soon?"

"Maybe," I said. "Did you ever find out how that happened?"

"No, we never did. I asked everybody who was on duty that day, and nobody seemed to know anything about it."

"Maybe whoever did it was scared to admit it."

"Whatever," Dave said, "it happened on my watch, and I'm ultimately responsible. What am I gonna say if they ask about it?"

"Wasn't there a note in the chart about the disposition of the body?"

"No, and that's another thing. You don't suppose whoever did it wasn't even anybody who worked in the ER, do you? Like maybe someone was trying to hide something?"

"Jeez, Dave," I said, "you've got a wilder imagination than I do. I hadn't even thought of that possibility."

Dave didn't have a chance to respond, because Jack Allen chose that moment to come charging into my office waving his summons. "Toni, what the hell is this all about?"

I told him, and he started to leave, but I stopped him.

"Not so fast," I cautioned him. "There is one other thing they might bring up, since you're chief of staff. Elliott mentioned that we should have a policy that provides for a waiting period of twenty-four hours between death and the autopsy, just to prevent this sort of thing from happening. Do we have any such thing?"

Jack shook his head. "I'm sure we don't. This hasn't ever come up before."

"Well, don't be surprised if it comes up now," I said. "When are you scheduled?"

"Monday."

"Me too," Dave said.

"Who else are they planning to depose?" Jack asked.

"Probably everybody who had anything to do with Beulah that weekend: me, Mike, Natalie, my stepdaughter, who's an evidence tech, and her husband, who's a detective, his partner, the sheriff, the coroner, the search-and-rescue guys, the paramedics, maybe even the general manager of the canal company, since he operated the excavator that pulled Beulah's car out of the canal." The general manager of the canal company, I remembered with a pang, whose wife had stalked me at work and followed me home, had caused me to fear for my life and the lives of my loved ones, and had cost me a night's sleep—so far.

"Shit," Jack said sourly. "What a royal waste of time. And at $200 an hour too."

I envied him. I wished money was all I had to worry about. I'd have bet nobody was trying to kill *him*.

"Jack, you're hopelessly outdated," I told him. "I know Elliott charges at least $350 an hour, and I bet the guys in Boise charge more than that, and if they're working with a New York law firm, even more."

"New York?" Jack echoed. "What?"

"That's where they're from," I said.

"Damn. I can't do this. I've got patients waiting. I gotta go."

"Me too," Dave said, getting out of his chair.

Me too, I thought, as I eyed the stack of Mike's cases from the day before that I had to review, and the trays of Pap smears to read, plus the morning and afternoon gross.

And before I could do that, I needed to let my histotechs know that I absolutely had to have the slides from Beulah's heart that day. I went into Histology and did that, warning Lucille and Natalie to watch out for possible bone fragments, since, if any were present, they would constitute important evidence that could exonerate their beleaguered boss from possible ruination at the hands of the legal system.

"I hate lawyers," Lucille said. Seeing my look of surprise, she added, "You would too, if you'd been divorced as often as I have."

"Me too," Natalie said. "Except for Elliott. He's okay."

I'd forgotten that Natalie knew Elliott. Back in the day, he'd offered to represent her in case she was accused of murdering her mother: the late, unlamented Dr. Sally Shore. Which she hadn't done.

"You might not think so if you were on the other side," I pointed out.

∞

Lucille brought me Beulah's slides sometime around three, just before she left for the day.

"I did run into a bone fragment," she said, "but I caught it before it popped out of the block. I did step sections with surface decalcification between each one, and I think they turned out pretty good. Let me know what you think."

I told her I would, but I already knew I'd be coming in on Saturday to look at those slides and photograph them.

I went down to the underground parking garage, taking in reverse all the precautions I'd taken that morning, and found that my Subaru had a flat tire. So I called Hal, and he came and got me. "You may as well just leave it there tonight," he said. "We can have someone come get it in the morning."

Bambi and Pete were at the house when we got home. Bambi was just coming downstairs from putting Little Toni down for a nap.

"Don't go up there," she warned me. "She's cranky."

She wasn't the only one. As if to corroborate her mother's statement, Little Toni let out a scream that threatened to rupture my eardrums. I winced. "Are you sure she's all right?" I asked.

I had difficulty hearing Bambi's answer as my granddaughter continued to wail. "She's fine," Bambi said. "She's been fed, she's been burped, and she's been changed. She's just pissed off. She'll get over it."

"Yeah, but will we?" Hal said with a smile that indicated he didn't really mean it.

"You should have heard Antoinette carry on whenever I made her take a nap that she didn't want to take," my mother remarked.

"Was she that bad?" asked Nigel.

"Worse," said Mum. "We lived in a very small flat when she was that age. One couldn't get away."

We'd still lived in England then. We hadn't emigrated to the United States until I was three years old.

"Should I apologize?" I asked her.

"Don't be silly, kitten."

"Did you get everything done?" Hal asked me.

"I got the grossing done," I told him, "but I'm going to have to work tomorrow to photograph Beulah's slides for Elliott."

"Well," Pete said with an air of great satisfaction, "I had a nice chat with the Commander today."

"Good," Hal said. "What did you find out?"

"He said that Bobby didn't wander off and fall into the coulee. Beulah had put him down for a nap, and when she went to check on him, he was gone. Next day, they found him in the coulee."

As he said this, I became aware that Little Toni had stopped screaming. For now.

"So he was kidnapped?" I said. "Who did it?"

"They never found out. Whoever did it didn't leave any evidence. But Marlin blamed Beulah anyway."

Hal said, "That seems unfair."

"Did he know that he wasn't Bobby's father?" Mum asked. "Perhaps that was why he divorced Beulah. They do say that the loss of a child either brings couples closer or tears them apart. If he knew Beulah had cheated on him, Bobby's death would certainly tear them apart."

"Ray told me that Marlin insisted at the time that Bobby was his son," Pete said.

"It would be interesting to see what he has to say about it now," I commented. "Is he still living?"

"I should think it would be very painful for him to talk about it," Mum said. "Besides, he must be quite old by now."

"Not so old," Pete said. "He retired about four years ago. That would make him about seventy now. If it's pertinent to the case, Bernie or I could go talk to him—or maybe Ray could. They're more of an age, and I think Ray knows him."

"Is that when Randy became general manager?" I asked. "When his father retired?"

"Yes," Pete said. "He was dispatcher before that."

Things suddenly fell into place. "So that was when Dwayne Pritchard became dispatcher."

"That's right," Pete said.

"Damn," I said. "I was wondering if Dwayne blackmailed Randy into giving him that job. Or maybe Beulah did."

"Why wouldn't Randy give him that job anyway?" Hal asked.

"Ray said that Dwayne was injured badly in a work-related accident about four years ago and they wanted to give him early retirement," Pete said, "but then they gave him the dispatcher job."

"Possibly because Dwayne knew about Randy embezzling from the canal company and blackmailed him into giving him that job," I persisted.

"Four years ago," Hal observed, "would be 2008."

"Exactly," I said. "The same year Marlin Schofield retired, and Randy, who was dispatcher, became general manager."

"Very neat," said Nigel. "Almost too neat, eh what?"

"What kind of accident was it?" Hal asked.

"Ray said he thought it was a dragline that tipped over," Pete said.

"What's a dragline?" I asked.

"It's what they used to use to clean out the canals before they used excavators," Pete said, "but they haven't used draglines since the nineties. In 2008 it would have to have been an excavator that tipped over on Dwayne. But that's not what happened. I went back into the police files to see if there was a report on that accident."

"Randy told me that excavators are counterweighted so that they can't tip over," I said.

"When?" Hal demanded, "Don't tell me you—"

"Went to the canal company after Pete asked me not to?" I finished for him. "Relax. It was at Beulah's autopsy. You know, the one that didn't happen."

"Wouldn't an accident on a canal be in the sheriff's jurisdiction?" Hal asked.

"Well, as it turns out, that accident happened inside city limits," Pete said, "which is why we had a record of it, and it wasn't an excavator, it was a pickup. The brakes failed. Dwayne went off the road into a ditch and flipped over. Nobody else was hurt."

"Didn't you say it was a work-related accident?" I asked.

"It was a canal company pickup," Pete said. "Dwayne was out on a job that took several days to complete. So he left the excavator out there with the trailer and was driving the pickup back to the canal company when he crashed."

"You seem to know an awful lot about it," observed Hal.

"I went out there and interviewed people," Pete said.

"Did you find out anything about whether Randy is embezzling from them?" I asked.

"I tried. Everybody denied knowing anything about it. Of course, I couldn't just come right out and ask people if they knew Randy was embezzling, but I did ask if it would be possible for someone to do that, and they all said there was no way. I had Carole show me how things got ordered. If someone needs something, they go to the dispatcher, and he fills out a purchase order. With the PO number, the employee goes to the vendor and gets what he needs, then signs the receipt and brings it to the dispatcher, who attaches it to the PO and puts it in the PO book. When the bill comes in, Carole checks to see if it's in the PO book, and if it is, she pays it."

"So, when Randy was dispatcher, he could create a PO for merchandise from one of his shell companies, make up a fake receipt, sign it, and put it in the PO book without ever leaving the comfort of his own office," I said. "Then he could send in a fake bill, and Carole would pay it."

"Right," Pete said. "Then the check would go to the address on the bill, which would be Randy's post office box."

"That's all well and good," Nigel put in, "but when Randy became general manager and Dwayne became dispatcher, how did he manage it then?"

"He's got a point there," I said. "Randy would have to go to Dwayne to get a PO number. Dwayne might wonder why the manager needs a PO number. That's not his job."

"Unless he's in on it," Pete said.

We all looked at each other. Nigel was the first to speak. "He'd be daft to let anybody else in on it. That person might let it slip to somebody else. Somebody could tell the authorities. More to the point, somebody could blackmail him."

"If he told Dwayne, Dwayne could have told Beulah," I said.

"Even if he didn't tell Dwayne, Dwayne might figure it out on his own," Mum said.

"And then tell Beulah," Hal said.

"Then Beulah could go around dropping little hints about it," I said, "because that's what she did best."

"But Dwayne could blackmail Randy," Pete said. "Weren't you just saying, Toni, that you thought Dwayne had blackmailed Randy into giving him the dispatcher job? Maybe it was because he already knew Randy was embezzling."

"But what about Carole?" Bambi asked. "She pays the bills. Wouldn't she have to know what Randy is doing? If that's what he's doing, I mean."

"Not necessarily," Pete said. "She could pay the bills and not suspect a thing, as long as all the paperwork jibes."

"Here's another thought," I said. "Randy and Carole are married. Surely Carole knows what everybody's salary is, because she cut the paychecks, doesn't she? And puts money into the pension funds?"

"What are you getting at, Toni?" Pete asked.

"She'd know what Randy's salary is supposed to be. How would he explain all the extra money he's getting? Don't they file a joint tax return? She'd have to know."

"If Randy's an embezzler," Nigel said, "what makes you think that he's honest enough to declare that extra income in the first place? He could be keeping it completely separate from the family pot and stashing it away in a Swiss bank account or something."

"Problem is," Pete said, "we can't find any evidence of an account for him to put that money into. Their joint account shows no deposits other than their paychecks. Ray and I looked for other accounts, like brokerage accounts, even offshore accounts, but came up empty. Where's that money going?"

"Into an account under somebody else's name," I suggested.

"Not Carole's," Pete said. "We checked for that."

"Wouldn't it have to be someone who had no obvious connection to either Randy or Carole?" Mum asked.

"That makes sense," Hal said. "Especially if Carole doesn't know anything about it."

"Okay, I grant that it's possible that Randy could hide the whole scheme from his wife," Pete said, "but what about Dwayne? If Dwayne questions what he's doing, wouldn't Randy have to let him in on it to shut him up?"

"Either that or fire him," Mum said.

"And what reason would he give for that?" asked Pete. "Dwayne could file a wrongful dismissal suit. That would be the last thing Randy would want. Everything would have to come out into the open. No, I can't see that firing Dwayne would help. Randy would have to kill him."

"Even more so if Dwayne already knew about it," Nigel said. "If Randy fired him, what's to stop Dwayne from letting the proverbial cat out of the bag?"

"If Dwayne was already in on it, he'd be just as guilty as Randy," Pete said. "It would be in his best interests to keep quiet about it."

"Did anybody check to see if that truck had been tampered with?" I asked.

"No," Pete said. "There was no mention of that in the report."

"Why would anybody tamper with a canal company pickup?" Hal asked.

"Maybe somebody had a reason for putting Dwayne out of commission," I said. "If that person knew Dwayne would be the next person to drive that pickup."

"But why put Dwayne out of commission in the first place?" Pete asked.

"Maybe," I said, "Marlin was planning to give Dwayne the dispatcher job before the accident. Maybe he was going to promote his son to assistant manager back then, and Randy needed to keep the dispatcher job so that he could keep embezzling."

"So you think," Nigel said, "that Randy tampered with that truck to keep Dwayne from getting his job."

"That makes sense," Pete said, "but there's no way of proving it now after all this time."

"Did anybody repair the truck," I asked, "or was it a total loss?"

"I think it was a total loss," Pete said, "but I wouldn't swear to it. I'd have to check."

"I know something else Dwayne could do," I said. "He could ask Carole why Randy would need PO numbers. Then she'd get suspicious and start asking questions."

"So Dwayne could tell Carole his suspicions …" Hal said.

"Why would he do that?" Mum asked.

"Pillow talk," I said. "They were having an affair."

All eyes swiveled to me. "What?" I asked. "Didn't I mention that?"

"When did you find that out?" Hal asked. "And from whom?"

"Lucille told me. Her boyfriend Kenny bowled with Dwayne in the canal company league."

"You mean Kenny works for the canal company too?"

"He's a ditch rider," I said and explained what Lucille had told me.

"Oy vey," said Hal. "We have canal company employees coming out of the woodwork, already."

"Seriously," I said. "So Dwayne could tell Carole his suspicions, and she could check the paperwork."

"And tell Dwayne," Hal said.

"And she could tell Randy."

"And Dwayne could tell Beulah."

"And Beulah could tell everybody," I said.

"So now we have three people who know. Randy would have to kill them all," Hal said.

"Well, Beulah and Dwayne are dead," Pete said, "but Carole's not."

"Yet," my mother said. "if there's any truth to this at all, she's in absolutely horrible danger. Pete, isn't there anything you can do to protect her?"

"Hang on," I said. "Aren't you forgetting something? Carole may or may not know about the embezzling, but she knows something about Bobby's death that she doesn't want us to know. She's the one who stalked me, remember?"

As if on cue, a noise from outside startled us, and Pete went out to investigate. We heard a shout and a crash, and Pete came back in, cursing. "Whoever it was got away," he said ruefully. "But I can tell you it wasn't Carole. Whoever it was, was male."

At this point, Little Toni woke up and announced her readiness to rejoin the party, and Bambi went upstairs to get her. Pete said, "Do you want me to stay here tonight?"

"I don't think that's necessary," Hal said, "although we appreciate the offer. You'd all have to stay. I'm not sending Bambi and Little Toni home without you. They could be in danger too."

"How do you figure?" Pete asked. "They don't know who we are."

"They do now," I pointed out. "Whoever it was just now saw you. They know you're related to me. They could threaten you and your family to get me to back off."

"They could try," Pete said stoutly, "but it won't work."

As I prepared for another sleep-deprived night, I wished I could be as sure of that as he was.

But I wished in vain, because I was awakened sometime in the wee hours of the morning by Killer's and Geraldine's frantic barking and the smell of smoke.

15

I SHOOK MY SOUNDLY-SLEEPING HUSBAND—and none too gently either. "Hal! Hal! Wake up!"

Hal opened one eye and peered at the clock radio. "This better be good. Do you realize that it's three-fucking-thirty in the morning?"

"The house is on fire! Is that good enough for you?" I demanded.

At that, Hal woke all the way up and leaped out of bed. "Call 911!" he commanded. I did so while he rooted around in the closet and hauled out the chain ladder we kept there for just such an emergency. By the time I'd informed the dispatcher of the emergency, Mum and Nigel were up and knocking at our bedroom door in their bathrobes and slippers. Killer and Geraldine raced up and down the stairs, barking.

"We might not need that thing," I told Hal. "The dogs have been downstairs, so it doesn't look like the stairs are cut off yet."

"Are you sure enough to go down and see for yourself?" he challenged me.

But by that time, the fire department had arrived. Not for the first time, I reflected on how lucky we were to live so close to downtown Twin. A few years earlier, a firebug had targeted several houses belonging to friends and had nearly succeeded in burning ours down as well. But this

147

time the damage was limited to some bushes around the front porch, and the firemen made short work of putting those out. Hal and Nigel went around the property with one of the firemen, checking for any other areas of incipient conflagration, but they didn't find any.

No doubt, the present firebug had intended to cut off escape through the front door but hadn't done anything to cut off the exit to the garage or the French doors into the backyard. "Maybe he was just trying to scare you," the fireman joked.

I wasn't amused. "Well, he succeeded," I growled.

Pete showed up right after that and went round again with the firemen, but outside of posting armed guards around the house, something the Twin Falls Police Department was singularly ill-equipped to do, there didn't seem to be anything else to do about the situation other than catch the culprit.

While all this was going on, I'd brewed a pot of coffee, Mum had heated up the teakettle for herself and Nigel, and the sky was beginning to lighten in the east. Pete joined us for some coffee before going home.

"Are you working today?" I asked.

"No, I'm off. But Ray's there. Why don't you drop in? I'm sure he'd love to see you."

"It has been a while," I agreed. "Maybe after I get done with work I'll do that."

"Work? You're on call?"

"Yes, and I need to get ready for a deposition on Monday." I told him about the lawsuit, and as I did so, his expression changed from mild incredulity to outright disbelief.

"That's the dumbest thing I ever heard," he said. "I was there when you did that autopsy. I never saw anyone deader."

"I know, but you weren't there Saturday after they pulled her out of the canal. She wasn't dead then, and that's when I'm supposed to have killed her with an autopsy."

"Which, of course, you didn't."

"I didn't do an autopsy then, but I was getting ready to, and I drew blood from the heart, like I always do. That's where things get a little murky." I told him about the situation. "And that's why I have to work today."

Pete drained his coffee cup. "Well, I wish you luck with that. I'm gonna go back to bed when I get home."

With a nine-month-old in the house? *Good luck with that,* I thought, but I didn't say it. "Give Little Toni a kiss from her Bubbe and Zayde."

"Grammy and Grampy too," added my mother.

∞

Since my Subaru still languished in the underground parking garage with a flat tire, Hal drove me to the hospital. He left me with a kiss and a reminder to call the tire place, which I did as soon as I got to my office. The hospital corridors were practically devoid of human life at that early hour on a Saturday morning, which made it easier for me to spot and avoid possible stalkers. Nonetheless, I let the door to the department close and lock behind me. Anyone wishing to get in would have to have a key.

Unless they were lying in wait inside one of the other offices.

I did a brief reconnaissance to relieve my mind before settling down to work. Nobody was there.

Beulah's slides lay on my desk, right where Lucille had left them. I fired up the computer and opened the picture file of the sections I'd taken from the damaged area of Beulah's heart. I'd drawn a sketch of the area, outlined the damage, divided the area into a grid according to the sections I'd taken, and numbered them. Another picture showed the actual pieces of tissue, lying on the grid in plastic cassettes labeled with numbers corresponding to the squares on the drawing in addition to the case accession number.

Now I prepared another display with the actual slides lying on the grid according to their numbers and photographed that. Using that, I could make notes on the actual grid if I found anything in the slides. I could also use the camera mounted on my microscope to photograph my findings and number the photomicrographs accordingly. Just getting that all set up took nearly an hour before I actually even looked at a slide.

I spent less time than that actually looking at the slides, because most

149

of them showed, as I suspected, just a lot of hemorrhage and early scar tissue. Lucille had marked all the sections containing bone fragments with a little green *x* on the label, as well as notations of "decal" (for decalcification) and "recut," with additional numbers denoting the level at which they were cut. This provided a three-dimensional picture of the tissue in which each fragment had been lodged and the direction in which the fragment had been pointing. I stacked them in descending order on their corresponding grid square.

There wasn't just one bone fragment. There were several, and they all pointed downward from the epicardium, where the black ink was clearly visible, to the endocardium, the inside of the left ventricle, which I'd marked with green ink, also clearly visible.

No one bone fragment pierced the myocardium; but taking them in concert, level by level, their path was unmistakable.

Sections of the pericardium, where blood had leaked, also contained bone fragments.

Whatever damage my cardiac needle might have done was insignificant in comparison to that done by the fractured sternum. No other sections from the damaged area showed anywhere near the degree of damage that the bone fragments had caused.

A picture is worth a thousand words. A thousand pictures are worth a million words. I photographed each section, each level, downloaded the photos onto the thumb drive, and called Elliott, who came and picked me up so that we could spend the next two hours arranging them to be shown at the deposition.

"Of course, you realize," Elliott said, "that this particular aspect of the case may not even come up at the deposition."

To my surprise, I felt a stab of disappointment. "So all this may be for nothing? After all this work?"

"Don't worry," Elliott said grimly, "with any luck, the Dukes will be paying for it."

At that point, I got a call from the tire place saying that their man was at the hospital and needed to know where I'd parked my car. I told them it was in the underground parking garage—and then realized that I'd need to go swipe my badge to let him into it. There were damn few places one could go in this fancy new hospital without swiping a badge. Cascade was all about security. I practically needed to have my retinas scanned to get into my own computer, and then it locked me out every ten or fifteen minutes so that I spent more time unlocking and logging back into it than I did actually using it.

All of this made me wonder why they'd designed an open-air underground garage where anyone could just walk in and vandalize, break into, or steal somebody's car.

So Elliott took me back to the hospital, where I swiped my badge for the tire guy to drive his truck in. He made short work of removing my tire and putting the spare on. Then I had to follow him back to the shop so they could repair or replace my tire with another all-weather radial to match the other tires.

But once he got my tire out into the light where he could see it clearly, he looked up at me with a frown. "This tire isn't just punctured," he said. "It's been slashed."

16

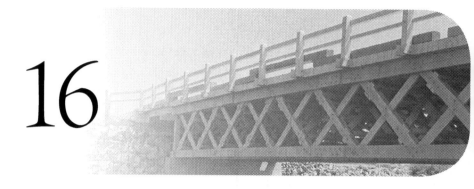

Everything happens to everybody sooner or later if there is time enough.
—GEORGE BERNARD SHAW

THE COMMANDER SHIFTED THE ever-present toothpick from one side of his mouth to the other and shook my hand. He was a few inches taller than I was and somewhat stocky, and he still wore his iron-gray hair in the same crew cut he'd probably had in high school. He was in his sixties now and getting close to retirement. His gray eyes smiled behind wire-rimmed spectacles. "Well, Doc, are you ever a sight for sore eyes! I swear, you get prettier every time I see you."

"And you become a better liar every time I see you," I responded with affection.

The Commander and I went all the way back to the Sally Shore affair. He'd been the one who thought up the scam we'd run to flush out the real killer.

Once the tire guy had finished with my car, I'd gone straight to the police station. Besides having a chat with my old buddy, the Commander, I needed to report my slashed tire, which was still at the tire place. I'd told them it was evidence and that the police would want to look at it.

"You don't say," was the Commander's reaction. He hitched forward in his chair and leaned his elbows on the desk. "I heard about all the other stuff, but I hadn't heard about that."

152

"I know. I'm telling you now. Last night when I left work, my tire was flat. Today the guy from the tire place came and changed it, and he told me it had been slashed. It's still there if you want to look at it."

"Where was your car parked?"

"In the physicians' underground parking garage."

"I thought that was secure parking," the Commander said. He gestured at my badge, which I'd forgotten I was still wearing. "Don't you have to swipe that thing to get in?"

"You do if you're driving a car," I explained, "but anybody can just walk in."

"Not very secure at all, in other words," he said. "I'll send someone out to look at that tire. Come, sit," he invited, and I followed him back to his desk.

"You've lost some weight since I saw you last," I observed.

"I've been on medical leave, dealing with this here prostrate cancer."

Prostrate. To my ears, it was like fingernails on a blackboard. But the Commander belonged to that generation of folks who had less than a nodding acquaintance with medical terminology and said things like "prostrate" and "larnyx" and "nucular."

"Prostate cancer?" I echoed, shocked. "I didn't know. Tell me about it."

He leaned back in his chair and took the toothpick out of his mouth. "Well, I didn't have to have surgery, so that's a good thing," he began. "They did radiation instead. Plumb wore me out. Once a week for two months, and now I'm supposed to be cancer free. They'll be checking my blood from time to time to see if it comes back or not."

"My stepfather has prostate cancer too," I told him. "He and Mum are in the process of deciding between that and having those little radioactive seeds put in."

He shook his head. "I wasn't about to have them put no seeds in me. What if they left one in by mistake?"

I laughed. "I'm sure those seeds are inside a tube or something so that none get left behind."

"Is that so?" He put the toothpick back in his mouth. "Well, that's why I didn't go that route. So you've got a stepfather now? When did that happen?"

"A couple of years ago," I said. "He's a retired Scotland Yard detective. He met Mum on the Queen Mary, and it was love at first sight."

"Well, congratulations. So what else can I do for you?"

"I was just wondering what you know about Marlin Schofield."

"Why do you want to know about him?"

"I've heard that he had a son, and that his wife died in childbirth. I also heard that he married again when his son was grown, and he had another son who drowned in a coulee when he was eighteen months old. I got the impression that there was more to that than met the eye."

"Well, that's something we never quite figured out. Marlin, he blamed her. He said she wasn't paying attention and just let the boy wander off. But she swore she never took her eyes off him while he was outside. She said he wasn't outside. He was in the house. She'd put him down for a nap, and when she went in to check on him, he was gone. He said she made the whole thing up. We never found any evidence that someone kidnapped the boy. He just disappeared, and his body was found the next day in the coulee. Marlin divorced her after that."

"I also heard," I said, "that the boy was the result of an affair that the wife had with the son."

"I heard that rumor too, but Marlin denied it. Said of course the boy was his. O' course, maybe he didn't want to admit that his wife had cheated on him. She was a pretty young thing, and much younger than him, and that son of his was a spoiled brat—obnoxious, ignorant, and ugly, in that order."

That pretty much jibed with my impression of Randy Schofield. But Beulah? A pretty young thing? "You know who his wife was, of course."

"I do?"

"She's Beulah Pritchard."

"Well, I'll be damned. I remember ol' Marlin calling her 'Bee.' I thought her name was Beatrice, not Beulah. Are you sure?"

"Positive. I also know that Randy Schofield is now general manager of the canal company, and that Beulah's husband, Dwayne, was the dispatcher."

The Commander leaned forward and shifted the toothpick to the other side of his mouth. "It can't be a coincidence that so many people involved in this case are associated with the canal company. Besides, I don't believe in coincidences."

"I don't either," I told him. "I also don't think it's a coincidence that Randy Schofield may be embezzling from the canal company."

"Yes, Pete told me about that. I've got his report right here. He and Kincaid got a warrant to search Randy's office and his home. That package he was supposed to pick up was from an online stationery store, and the letterhead was for some local hardware outfit, but we can't find any mention of it anywhere. It's like it doesn't exist."

"You mean S & P Pipe Company?"

"That's the one," the Commander said. "But maybe that's not the only one. Maybe he's set up a bunch of shell corporations and has been running canal company money through them and right into his own bank account. Trouble is, we can't find it. His bank account doesn't show any unusual activity. No big deposits or withdrawals. Just the usual—utility payments, groceries, house payment, and so on."

"Maybe he's got another account."

"We couldn't find one."

"Maybe it's offshore. Remember Jay Braithwaite Burke?"

The Commander snorted. "Who could forget him?"

"You found his offshore account. You could find Randy's too, if he's got one."

"Mmm. Another possibility is that he's got an account under another name."

"Carole's?"

The Commander shrugged. "Possibly. But maybe he's got a whole slew of 'em under the same names as his shell corporations. Damn. That means another warrant."

"You didn't find any bank statements in his house or his office?"

"Not for any account besides his and Carole's joint checking account."

"Could he have a brokerage account somewhere?"

"Didn't find one."

"Does S & P Pipe Company have a bank account?"

"Didn't find one. Don't worry, Doc, when we find out who all those shell companies are, we'll look."

I wasn't ready to quit. I had another idea. "Do you suppose Beulah and Dwayne knew about it?"

"Do you mean you think they were blackmailing Randy?"

"I don't know, but if Beulah told anybody about it, it could have gotten him caught."

"Would she do that?"

"She liked to drop hints that she knew more than she was saying. Oblique references. If somebody had a guilty conscience, she could make him very uncomfortable. Somebody might kill her just to shut her up."

"What about Dwayne?"

"I don't know about Dwayne," I said. "I didn't know him. I've heard one person call him a jerk. But Carole was having an affair with him."

"You don't say," the Commander said. "You know, now that I think about it, there was something else that happened to Dwayne too. An accident or something."

"Pete told us," I said. "He drove a canal company truck into a ditch and flipped over when his brakes went out."

The Commander took the toothpick out of his mouth, looked at it, made a face, flipped it into his wastebasket, and took another one out of his shirt pocket and stuck it in his mouth. "They airlifted him to Boise for back surgery, and he was out to the Elks for months after that." He was referring to Elks Rehabilitation in Boise. "He was stove up for quite a while. They didn't think he'd ever walk again. The canal company paid all his expenses and offered him early retirement. They said he'd never be able to run a dragline again. But he didn't want to quit, so they gave him the dispatcher job."

"What made them change their minds?"

The Commander shrugged and turned up his palms. "Maybe the old dispatcher quit, or maybe the job just happened to be vacant for some reason."

"Or maybe Dwayne blackmailed them into it. Maybe he knew something they didn't want made public."

"Oh, hey, now, wait a minute ..."

"Or maybe Beulah did the blackmailing on her husband's behalf. Maybe that's why they're both dead."

The Commander sat back. "Do you suppose that these two things—the possible embezzlement and the autopsy report nobody wants us to know about—are connected?"

"It would be a hell of a coincidence if they weren't," I said. "And you don't believe in coincidences."

"No, I don't," the Commander said. "Looks to me like somebody at the canal company wants to keep those things quiet—and doesn't mind killing to do it."

∞

The doorbell rang Saturday night after we'd all gone to bed. Hal went downstairs to answer it, accompanied by two barking dogs. No sooner had he left the bedroom than the phone started ringing. I answered it. The caller spoke in a whisper.

"Back off. Back off now. Or next time it won't be just your tire that gets slashed."

17

Man is the only animal that blushes. Or needs to.
—MARK TWAIN

THE IMPLICATION WAS UNMISTAKABLE. MY hand went involuntarily to my throat.

"Who are you?" I demanded. "Identify yourself."

But the caller had hung up, leaving me to rail at empty air.

Hal returned, looking grim, with an envelope in his hand. "Who was on the phone?" he demanded.

"I don't know," I said. "Whoever it was talked in a whisper." I repeated what the voice had said.

Hal's expression grew even grimmer. He handed me the envelope. "Nobody was there when I answered the door, but this was taped to it."

I opened the envelope. Inside was a note that said, "Back off. Back off now. Or next time it won't be just your bushes that burn."

I looked up at Hal. "These are warnings."

"No shit, Sherlock," he said and reached for the envelope.

I shook my head. "I don't think we should handle this any more than we have to. It might have fingerprints on it."

Hal said, "I'll call Pete."

I went downstairs to the kitchen, found a baggie, and put the note and the envelope in it.

By the time Pete arrived, all of us were up, with Mum and Nigel warm and snug in their bathrobes and slippers. "Antoinette, dear, whatever is going on at this ungodly hour?" Mum asked.

"Yes, please tell us," Pete said. "I'd like to hear this too."

Oh dear. I didn't want to tell him in front of Mum. It would scare her to death. I looked helplessly at Hal and then at Nigel, who said gently, "It's no use keeping it from her, you know."

So I told them. Mum gasped and put her fingers to her mouth but said nothing. Nigel put his arm around her, and she turned her face into his shoulder.

Pete studied the note without removing it from the baggie. "In my opinion, these are just warnings," he said. "They're telling you not to pursue your investigation of either Randy's embezzlement or the autopsy of Bobby Schofield or both, and I think it has to be both. It's too much of a coincidence not to be."

"That's what the Commander said," I told him. "Do you suppose Russ and Rollie have gotten warnings too?"

"I'll check with them tomorrow," Pete said. "And don't worry. You can back off and let us take it from here."

"What if they blame us anyway?" I asked. "How do we let them know that we backed off, just as they asked?"

"I guess we'll cross that bridge when we come to it," Pete said.

"Are you going to be able to tell anything from that note?" Hal asked.

"You mean like fingerprints? Sure, if the dirtbag was stupid enough to handle it with his bare hands."

"What about the printer?" I asked. "Is it possible to identify the printer that was used?"

"It's possible," Pete said. "Some folks at Purdue found that they can analyze the banding artifacts printers leave on the paper."

"Oh," I said. "Sort of like the marks guns leave on bullets. Printer ballistics."

"All we'd have to do is run paper through the printers or copiers in question and have them compare them to this note."

"So if this was printed at the canal company, or on Randy and Carole's home printer, they could match it."

"Conceivably," Pete said.

"That'd be one in the eye for the note-writer," Nigel commented. "He probably thought that if he didn't use a typewriter he'd be home free."

"Hardly anybody uses typewriters anymore," I said. "And everybody knows typewriters can be identified."

"It'd be pretty stupid," Hal agreed. "But then, aren't criminals in general stupid?"

"Only the ones who get caught," Nigel said.

I presented myself at Elliott's office at nine on the dot Monday morning. Betsy, the receptionist, told me that everybody was in the conference room. "Everybody" consisted of Elliott, Clark Dane, and Fritz Baumgartner. I had known beforehand that Fritz would be there, because he'd called me Sunday night and told me. A court reporter sat at the end of the table, already typing—although nobody was talking.

Fritz could be a pretty scary person. He looked like a caricature of a German SS officer from an old World War II movie: bald head, rolls of fat on his neck, gimlet eyes behind wire-rimmed round spectacles, and a lipless mouth. One expected him to say something threatening like "ve haf vays of making people talk" in a fake German accent. But when he smiled, his face lit up, his eyes twinkled, and he was instantly transformed into a kindly grandpa. He wasn't smiling now, but when I caught his eye he winked.

Elliott stood up. "Welcome. I know most of us know each other, but let me introduce everyone so that we all know who we are, and we can get it on the record. This is Dr. Antoinette Day, pathologist at Cascade Perrine Regional Medical Center, one of the defendants, whom I represent as hospital counsel. To my left is Clark Dane of Katz, Klein, Rabinowitz, and Dane of Boise, for the plaintiffs. Across from me is Fritz Baumgartner, Twin Falls County district attorney. Fritz is here because of the possibility that the plaintiffs might want to bring a charge of murder against the defendant."

The court reporter dutifully typed it all into her laptop.

Clark Dane shoved his chair back and stood up too. "Now, just a minute, counselor. Nobody said anything about murder."

Elliott put out a hand, palm down, as if to pat the younger man on the head and say "there, there." "I know that, sir. It just had occurred to me that the plaintiffs, being of a mind to bring this utterly ridiculous suit against Dr. Day in the first place, might possibly resort to bringing a murder charge against her if all else failed."

Clark Dane raised both hands, opened his mouth to speak, and apparently found himself at a loss for words. He hadn't seen that one coming, I guessed. I was willing to bet that he hadn't known who Fritz was either. He'd probably thought Fritz was just one of Elliott's partners, and wily old Elliott had just let him keep thinking that. He slapped his thighs, expelled a breath, and sat down heavily.

Elliott sat down too, having gotten the upper hand without even breaking a sweat. I looked at Fritz. He winked again. I felt better. These guys weren't going to let anything bad happen to me. They had my back.

Elliott took me through all the same questions he'd asked me before at my house. I answered them the same as I had then. I thought we'd covered it pretty exhaustively, but when we were done, Clark Dane started in on me, asking pretty much the same questions that Elliott had, and I objected.

"We've covered this," I pointed out.

"Just answer the questions," Elliott advised me. "He's trying to trip you up in case you're lying."

"That's not it at all," Clark Dane objected. "I'm just trying to get everything clear in my head in case we actually go to trial."

In case we actually went to trial? Did this mean that opposing counsel didn't think this would actually go to trial? My spirits rose a notch. It gave me courage.

"It's a waste of time," I declared, "because I'm not lying. But go ahead, if you must. Ask your questions."

A sheen of sweat began to appear on Dane's patrician forehead. Was I getting to him? Or was he just embarrassed to be involved in such a ridiculous lawsuit? One could only hope.

"Tell me what you did when you had the deceased on your autopsy table," he began.

"Which time?" I asked.

"What do you mean, which time?"

"I had her there twice," I told him. "The first time was on the day they pulled her out of the canal, Saturday, and then again after she died, on Monday."

Dane looked confused, and I began to get a glimmer of understanding of why he'd taken the case. Could it be that he hadn't yet grasped the fact that I'd had two different opportunities to autopsy Beulah?

Apparently it could. "Wait a minute," he said. "You're saying you had her on your autopsy table on two different occasions?"

Praise the Lord, he's actually beginning to get it. "Yes, yes," I said. "Two different times, two days apart."

"So what did you do the first time?"

I told him.

"You said you drew blood from the heart. How did you do that if you didn't open the body?"

I described the procedure.

"Doesn't that damage the heart?"

"It shouldn't. It's a very tiny needle, only twenty-five gauge. The puncture site clots off almost immediately."

"Was the heart beating when you punctured it?"

"No."

"How could you tell without opening the body?"

"The needle didn't move. It would have, if the heart had been beating."

Clark Dane leafed through a stack of papers in front of him and pulled one free, waving it in the air like a flag. "This is a procedure note describing something called 'pericardiocentesis.' What is this procedure?"

"It's the process of removing fluid from inside the pericardial sac, the sac around the heart."

"What happens if they don't remove the fluid?"

"If enough fluid builds up inside the pericardium, it can cause pressure on the heart and interfere with it beating efficiently, a condition called cardiac tamponade."

"Yes, it mentions that here. What conditions, Doctor, can cause fluid to accumulate in the pericardium?"

"Infection, malignancy, congestive failure, uremia, or some autoimmune diseases such as lupus."

"What about a hole in the heart?"

I winced and tried not to let it show. Elliott had been right when he said they'd descend like freakin' vultures. Mr. Dane appeared to be practically salivating at the prospect of devouring the carrion that my reputation was about to become if I couldn't get him off this subject. I looked at Elliott. He nodded. "Answer the question, Toni."

"In that case, the fluid would be blood," I said.

"As it was in this case, isn't that right, Doctor?"

"Yes."

"What caused that?"

"There was some damage to the heart."

"Caused by your needle?"

"No."

"How do you know that?"

I turned to Elliott. "Shall we show him?"

"I think that's a dandy idea," Elliott said and opened up his laptop. "I've got this rigged to project on that screen over there on the far wall. That way the pictures will be much larger than life and everything will show up clearly."

I looked at Clark Dane. He wasn't looking so hungry anymore. In fact, he looked a little nervous.

Elliott projected picture after picture, with me narrating what each one showed, and by the time we got to the purple beach ball pericardium, Clark Dane had begun to sweat profusely and had turned much the same color that Randy Schofield had when confronted with Beulah's battered, naked body on my autopsy table. I hoped he wouldn't hurl on Elliott's gorgeous carved antique mahogany conference table.

"Are you all right, Mr. Dane?" Elliott asked. "Do you need to take a break?"

"I'll be okay," Clark Dane said weakly. "Are we almost done?"

"Oh, no," I said. "We're only getting started."

Clark Dane sighed. "Go ahead. I'm fine."

"Bathroom's on the left if you need it," I said helpfully, and Clark Dane gave me a baleful look.

Elliott flashed the next picture, and the next, until we came to the naked heart with the hamburger-like area over the left ventricle in close-up. At that point, Clark Dane lost the battle and dashed, hand-over-mouth, from the room. We heard the bathroom door slam and water running. The groaning pipes in the century-old Bank & Trust building covered up any other sounds, for which I was grateful.

"Hope he doesn't do that in court," Fritz said, startling me. He'd been so quiet, I'd forgotten he was there. "You two put on quite a show. Did you know he had a weak stomach?"

"No, that was just luck," I said.

Elliott sighed and leaned back in his chair. "This is gonna take for-freakin'-ever," he complained. "How about some coffee?"

Fritz and I assented, and Elliott had Betsy bring some in. Clark Dane returned from the bathroom, looking pale. "How much more?" he asked in a strained voice. "I'm not sure how much more I can take."

"Relax," I said. "There are only two more, and the rest are slides and photomicrographs."

We got through the remainder of the slides without incident, by which time Mr. Dane seemed inclined to absolve my dinky little cardiac needle from any wrongdoing, especially as viewed in the context of the relatively major damage done by the fractured sternum.

"Just in time too," Elliott said. He pressed a button on the phone. "Betsy, is Dr. Leonard here yet?"

"No, not yet," Betsy's disembodied voice said.

"He can't leave until I get back," I explained. "He's covering me."

"Well, then, get out of here!"

I got.

"Who was it that said to keep your friends close but your enemies closer?"

With a sigh, Hal put his book down on the bedcovers. "That is generally attributed to Sun Tzu. Why?"

"I was just thinking about Carole."

"Toni, don't even go there."

"There's got to be a way."

Hal turned his palms up. "Like what? Follow her around? How do you suggest we do that? We'd have to keep her under surveillance day and night. We can't do that. We have jobs. We have lives. We need our sleep." With that, Hal reached out and turned off his bedside light.

"Maybe you're right," I said sullenly and returned to my book.

"Love you, honey," Hal said sleepily and turned over on his side, facing away from me and my bedside light.

"Love you too," I responded.

I continued to read until long after Hal had begun to snore, but my mind wasn't on my book. It was going round and round on ways to get to Carole. I could take her to lunch or something, just us girls, and get her to talk about her marriage or maybe about Beulah—or Dwayne, or even Marlin. Something might shake out.

I didn't know if she knew that I knew she was stalking me. I might be putting myself in even more danger than I was in already.

On the other hand, I could just call her. She couldn't hurt me over the phone, and lunch would be in a public place. Surely she couldn't hurt me there.

Could she?

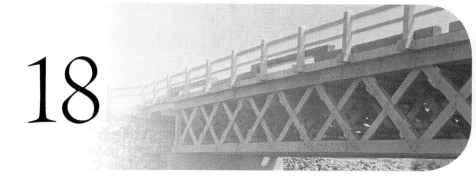

18

You are not permitted to kill a woman who has wronged you,
but nothing forbids you to reflect that she is growing older every minute.
You are avenged 1440 times a day.
—AMBROSE BIERCE

I WENT IN TO WORK early on Tuesday in hopes of finishing up those two autopsies—with the exception of the brains, which would have to fix in formalin for another week—but I really wasn't expecting any more information from them than I already had. I wasn't expecting anything earthshaking from the slides I had either.

One of the things that always amazed me about autopsies was not the things that people died of, but the things they lived with. There was no shortage of things people could have that were not the cause of death.

By that time, it was nine o'clock, and I figured that the Twin Falls Canal Company was open for business and that Carole was at work. So I called the canal company and invited her to lunch—one o'clock at the Cove, that dark, smoky place where nobody would recognize us and we could talk undisturbed once the lunch rush was over. And they had the best cheeseburgers in town. She accepted, and I figured I should have a good many of the surgicals signed out by then.

When I got to the Cove, Carole was already there. She waved at me from the booth in the back—a good thing, because after coming in from the sunny day outside, I could hardly see anything in the dim interior. She already had a beer in front of her. "Want one?" she asked.

"Better not, more's the pity," I told her. "I have to go back to work after this."

"Me too," she said, "but my job's not life and death like yours. Do they ever call you in after hours?"

"Not very often," I said. "But I know if I had, say, a couple of drinks after work, that'd be the time they'd call. So I don't. The last thing I need is a DUI, or for somebody to smell it on my breath at work and report me to the state board of medicine."

"Could you lose your license over something like that?"

"Possibly. At the very least, I'd have to get into a diversion program and submit to random drug testing and go to AA meetings, and if I failed to do that just once and got caught, it'd be all over. So I just don't do it."

"I get that," Carole said and changed the subject. "What did you want to talk about?"

"I was just curious," I said. "I thought maybe you could clear up some points of history dealing with the canal company. How long have you worked there?"

"Why do you want to know that?"

"Well, I'm kind of involved, being that I fell into the canal trying to rescue Beulah, and your husband had to get the car out using an excavator, and I did autopsies on both Beulah and Dwayne, and I've heard some stories about Marlin Schofield and his son who drowned, and about Dwayne's accident, and I wondered if you'd been there long enough to know about all of that."

The waitress appeared, and I ordered a cheeseburger and a Coke. Carole ordered fried shrimp and planks, big slabs of fried potatoes. I'd never understood why those were so popular; my own taste ran to skinny, crispy shoestring potatoes, which meant that most people's French fries were too thick and mealy for my taste.

Carole took a sip of her beer. "I started working there right out of high school," she said, "in 1981."

"So you knew Marlin Schofield," I said.

"Marlin was the general manager until he retired," Carole said. "He's a sweet man, and I hope you're not going to do or say anything to destroy his reputation. He doesn't deserve it. He's been through enough."

"You're the second person I've heard say that," I said. "I have no intention of doing that. I'm just trying to fit pieces together. It might help me understand what I found in the autopsies better."

"Why, what did you find?" Carole leaned forward, eyes avid.

"The patterns of injury don't make sense, given the evidence," I explained, hoping that obfuscation would suffice to satisfy her curiosity without leading to more questions. I wanted to be the one asking the questions, not answering them. "Was Marlin still married to Beulah when you started working there?"

"No, they were divorced by then."

"So, I'm guessing that Bobby had drowned prior to that?"

"Oh, the poor man was devastated," Carole said. "Everybody was tiptoeing around, trying not to say the wrong thing. I swear, you could have cut the tension with a knife."

"Did you know how it happened? I've heard more than one version."

She thought for a minute, twisting a lock of dark hair around her finger. I noticed an unusual ring on her hand and thought about asking her where she'd gotten it, but I refrained because I didn't want to interrupt her train of thought.

"Marlin didn't want to talk about it, but from what he said, I got the idea that Beulah wasn't paying attention and Bobby just wandered off. But Beulah swore that Bobby was in his crib taking a nap and had been taken from his crib."

"Did Randy live with them?"

"Yes. He was still in high school when Marlin married Beulah. Then he went to college but still lived at home. So he could have still been living there at the time Bobby died."

"I heard a rumor that Marlin might not have been Bobby's father. Do you know anything about that?"

"There was talk around the office that Randy might have been the boy's father, not Marlin. None of us wanted to just come right out and ask either one of them. You know how it is."

I allowed as how I did. "What was Randy's job at that time?"

"He was a dragline operator," Carole said.

"Did you ever see Beulah after the divorce?"

"Oh, yes. One time she came in to talk to Randy, and you could hear them shouting all over the office, even from behind closed doors. She went stomping out of there, spitting nails. Randy told me about it afterward. Apparently Beulah thought Randy should marry her, since he was responsible for breaking up her marriage, but he refused. Then she threatened him."

"How?" I asked, although I had an idea that I knew.

"She told him if he didn't marry her, she'd tell everybody that he had killed Bobby."

"Oh my God!"

"He told her to publish and be damned."

"Good for him," I said. "Of course, there's no truth to that, right?"

"Of course not," Carole said indignantly. "By then, Randy and I were engaged, and there's no way I'd ever marry a man who could kill anyone. I'd know, and I wouldn't do it."

Our food arrived. I thought the waitress would never stop fiddling with things on the table and let us get back to our conversation, but of course she did.

I took the top bun off my cheeseburger and inserted the slices of tomato and onion and lettuce leaf. "Did you ever see Beulah again?"

"She came in to see Marlin one time."

"What about?"

"Well, I didn't know at the time, but then she started coming in around lunchtime to just shoot the breeze, you know, so we started eating lunch together, and she complained that the alimony she was getting from Marlin wasn't enough, because she'd started nursing school at the college and had expenses. But he wouldn't budge. I figured that was it."

"Maybe he didn't have it to give," I suggested.

"Well, that's what I said," Carole agreed. "Randy and I were married by then, and I was appalled at how little he was getting paid. So I told her that if Marlin couldn't even pay his own son a decent wage, why should Beulah expect more alimony? That pretty much ended that conversation."

"Did you stay friends after that?"

"Oh, yes. Of course, once she graduated and got a job at the hospital, she couldn't come to lunch anymore, but we still got together once in a while. Then Randy became dispatcher, and Marlin hired this other guy, Dwayne, to replace him. I introduced him to Beulah, and eventually they got married."

"Someone I talked to at work said that Beulah met Dwayne in a bar," I remarked.

"That's true. We were here at the Cove when I introduced them."

While we'd been talking, I'd gradually become aware that I needed to go to the bathroom. Now the feeling had reached the stage where something needed to be done about it. "Can you excuse me for a minute?" I asked. "I'll be right back."

I did my business as quickly as I could, because it had occurred to me that Carole might take advantage of my absence to take off. But to my relief, she was still sitting right where I'd left her. "Everything okay?" she inquired, as I slid back into my seat.

"Uh-huh. So, what year did Randy become dispatcher?"

"I think it was 1983, but I wouldn't swear to it."

Wow. That meant the embezzlement could have been going on almost thirty years. Randy could conceivably have quite a big nest egg stashed away in his Swiss bank account by now.

I changed the subject. "Do you remember Dwayne's accident?"

Carole snorted. "How could I forget it? It was pretty awful. The poor man broke his back, did you know? For a long time, they said he'd never walk again."

"But he did."

"Yes, he did. It took months and months of rehab, but one day he came walking in here just as good as new and asked for his job back."

"Did anyone check the truck he was driving to see if it had been tampered with?"

Carole looked startled. "I don't know. I never heard anything about that. Who would do such a thing?"

I shrugged. "If you don't know, then I certainly don't. So, did Dwayne get his old job back?"

"No," Carole said, "Marlin wouldn't give him his old job back. He said Dwayne hadn't been cleared by his doctor for that kind of work, and besides, he'd already replaced him."

"Didn't Dwayne know he hadn't been cleared before he came waltzing in asking for his job back?"

"I don't know," Carole said. She licked salt off her fingertips. "They went round and round on it, until Marlin offered him the dispatcher job."

"He offered Dwayne Randy's job?"

"Well, he also offered to make Randy assistant manager, because he was going to be sixty-five in a few months and wanted to retire."

"Cool. That meant more pay, didn't it?"

"I'm sure it did, but Randy didn't want it. He liked being dispatcher. I told him he was crazy to turn down an offer like that, and finally he gave in."

"So Randy's been general manager since …?"

"Two thousand ten," Carole said. "When Marlin retired."

"So, is he making enough money to satisfy you now?"

The question took Carole off guard. She made a show of dabbing her lips with her napkin and then dug in her purse, coming up with a lipstick with which she touched up her lips. "We do okay," she finally said.

"I was just noticing your ring. What's the stone?"

She held out her hand and admired the ring. "It's a tanzanite," she said, "set in white gold with diamonds."

"Such a beautiful color," I commented. "Matches your eyes."

She smiled self-consciously, showing dimples. "That's what Randy said when he gave it to me."

"What was the occasion?"

"Our thirtieth anniversary."

"Wow," I said admiringly. "He must really love you."

"He does," she said complacently. "He gave me these for our

twenty-fifth," she went on, pushing her dark hair aside to show me tanzanite drops surrounded by diamonds in her ears.

"Those are gorgeous," I said, meaning it. "Matching set?"

"There's this little shop downtown," she said. "This guy makes all his own jewelry. You should give me a call sometime, and we'll go shopping. I was noticing your necklace. That's unusual too."

"It's a star of David," I said. "Sapphire and diamonds in white gold. My husband gave it to me on our first anniversary."

"Your husband is Jewish?"

"Yes."

"How did that happen?"

"We met in college," I said, "in California." How neatly she had turned the conversation around so that it was now about me. But maybe that was a good thing. If I was forthcoming about my marriage, she might be more forthcoming about hers.

I wasn't so sure about the shopping, though. I couldn't afford to deck myself out in expensive jewelry. It was interesting that she could. She and Randy were obviously doing more than just okay.

"How long have you been married?" she asked.

"Twenty-one years," I said. "We've got a ways to go to catch up with you guys. Do you have kids?"

She shook her head. "Several miscarriages. We quit trying after the last one. I guess it just wasn't meant to be."

"Me too," I said. "I never even got pregnant in the first place."

She reached out and put a hand over mine. Our eyes met in an exchange of sympathy. I guessed that meant we'd bonded.

I wondered what Hal would say when I called Carole and asked her to go shopping with me.

✺

It was nearly three o'clock when I got back to the hospital. "Your parents are in your office," Arlene told me.

I dashed into my office. "I'm so sorry to keep you waiting," I exclaimed. "How long have you been here?"

"Not too long," my mother said. "Nigel's appointment was at one-thirty."

"So how did it go?"

"I'm scheduled for tomorrow at seven-thirty," Nigel said. "Then I have to stay overnight, and I'll be discharged Thursday morning, barring catastrophe."

"Really?" I asked. "Why does it take so long?" I knew in principle how HDR worked, but I'd never before had occasion to know the details of the procedure. I'd had the hazy idea that it was a same-day surgery procedure, but apparently it wasn't.

"Dr. Nichols said that while Nigel is under anesthesia, he'll insert some hollow plastic needles into the prostate," Mum said. "Then, during the next twenty-four hours, they'll hook Nigel up to the brachytherapy machine three different times and put the radioactive seeds in through the needles and then take them out again. Then, after twenty-four hours, they'll pull the needles out."

"And Bob's your uncle," Nigel added complacently.

"How long do the seeds stay in each time?" I asked.

"They calculate that by the size of the tumor, I think," Mum said.

Nigel glanced at his watch. "We'd better get going, love," he said. "I'm supposed to get some blood tests and an EKG and a chest X-ray. Might as well get it all done while we're here, eh what?"

After a bit more chitchat, they left, and I fired up my computer and Googled "HDR brachytherapy." I found a site that described the procedure in detail, and it was pretty much as Mum and Nigel had said. Armed with that information, I felt confident that I could field any questions my family could come up with regarding Nigel's surgery.

Too bad I couldn't do the same with all the other chaos going on in my life.

However, I could get the rest of these surgicals signed out if there were no other interruptions.

That turned out to be more of a chore than it should have been.

I began to feel dizzy and light-headed. It became difficult to focus on what I saw under the microscope. If I didn't know better, I'd have thought

I was drunk. Was it because of my cold? Maybe this was the next stage of that fatal, incurable, exotic infection that I'd contracted while in the canal, which only started out looking like a cold and then turned into an encephalitis or something.

Or maybe it was something I'd eaten—or drunk.

Eaten or drunk where? What had I eaten or drunk today?

A toasted English muffin with marmalade for breakfast, with coffee, at home.

That wouldn't be it.

But lunch? A cheeseburger and a Coke at the Cove?

I'd eaten at the Cove lots of times and had never had anything like this happen. What had been different about this time?

Carole.

Had Carole slipped me a mickey? How could she do that?

Easy, you idiot. She did it when you went to the bathroom.

So much for being safe in a public place.

So, what had she given me? Was it just another warning? Or was it going to kill me?

Either way, I couldn't continue to sit here and sign out surgicals. I needed medical attention, and the sooner the better, while I could still ambulate.

I told Mike I wasn't feeling well and wouldn't be able to finish the surgicals, and then I went down to the emergency room.

◇

"Are you out of your friggin' mind?"

Hal was somewhat unimpressed and definitely not amused by my lunch date with Carole. "I told you to stay away from the canal company," he railed. "Pete told you to stay away from the canal company. And what do you do? You totally ignore both of us and go charging off to the canal company, stirring up trouble. Are you fuckin' nuts?"

"I didn't go to the canal company," I protested. "I met her at the Cove."

"You went to the Cove for lunch? You never go to the Cove for lunch."

"I do when I don't want to be seen or heard, and I didn't."

"The last time you went to the Cove with somebody, she turned out to be the murderer!"

"True," I said. "But she didn't kill me at the Cove. And all Carole did was put vodka in my Coke."

"'All she did'?" Hal mimicked. "She could have killed you doing that. What if you'd had a car accident while driving drunk? At the very least, you'd get a DUI and then the board of medicine would get involved and you could lose your license. You career could be over."

"I probably gave her the idea," I said. "She had a beer and offered to order one for me, and I told her all the reasons why I couldn't have one. And now I'm on record as having been over the legal limit at work, so all that could happen anyway."

"Not if Dave doesn't report you," Hal said, "and you have extenuating circumstances. Dave knows that, and he got the police involved. You're the victim here."

I certainly felt like a victim. I'd spent a very unpleasant afternoon in the ER, post-syrup of ipecac, while the lab performed a urine tox screen and a blood alcohol on me. Now we were having this conversation in the car on the way home.

Pete had arrived after it was all over but the shouting. He announced his intention to arrest Carole for attempted murder, and apparently he succeeded, because the Commander called shortly after we got home and asked us to come down to the station.

Mum and Nigel insisted on coming with us. The Commander took me into the interrogation room and asked Hal and my parents to wait in the waiting room. "We've got the Schofield woman in the holding cell," he told me. "Now we need to get a statement from you, Doc. Tell me what happened at lunch."

"Nothing happened at lunch," I said. "I had to get up and go to the bathroom once, but I felt fine until I got back to work."

"You didn't notice that your food tasted funny? Or your drink?"

"No."

"Can you tell me how long it was before you started feeling drunk?"

"I'd guess about a half hour to forty-five minutes. My stepfather had an appointment with his oncologist, and he and Mum stopped by after it was over. I didn't start feeling funny until after they left."

"What did you do then?"

"I went to the emergency room."

"Then what happened?"

I described my treatment. "My blood alcohol was over the legal limit, and my tox screen was negative."

"So it was alcohol that she put in your drink."

"Apparently. I'm guessing vodka, because it doesn't taste like anything."

"Why did you go to lunch with her in the first place? Isn't she the person who's been stalking you?"

"I just wanted to talk to her," I said, not wanting to get into the philosophy of Sun Tzu right at that moment. "I wanted to know more about the history of the canal company with regard to Marlin and Beulah, and what happened to Bobby, and who his father was."

"Did she tell you?"

"Yes, she did, but I'm not sure she really knows the truth. She was mostly just repeating rumors."

"Did you talk about anything else?"

"Yes," I said. "Jewelry."

The Commander seemed taken aback. "Jewelry?"

"Yes. She was wearing a very unusual ring, and I admired it, and she told me about the shop where she got it and suggested that we go shopping together sometime."

"So she didn't seem hostile to you in any way?"

"Not at all."

"So you had no reason to suspect that she'd put anything in your drink when you went to the bathroom?"

"I suppose I should have," I said. "After all, she did stalk me, and somebody did set fire to our bushes and to Russ Jensen's mother's house—and attack Rollie and leave threatening notes and make threatening phone calls. And speaking of that, did anyone leave notes or make threatening calls to either Russ or Rollie?"

"I believe so," he said, "but I don't know the details. Pete talked to both of them yesterday."

"What's going to happen to Carole now?"

"She'll be arraigned tomorrow, and bail will be set. If somebody bails her out, she'll be released on her own recognizance, seein' as it's a first offense, until her trial."

"What's she being charged with?"

"I guess that's up to the lawyers. It's probably something related to the laws against date rape, except that there's no rape involved. She might have to spend some time in jail, or she might get off with a fine."

"Do I have to be there?"

"No. You'll have to be at the trial, though."

"Are you done with me now?"

"Yes, for now, but I'd sure like to meet that stepfather of yours."

"Of course. I'll introduce you."

He came with me out to the waiting room and sat down on the couch next to my mother. "It's good to see you again, Mrs. Day," he said.

"Likewise, I'm sure," said Mum with a coy little smile. "But it's Mrs. Gray now. This is my husband, Nigel."

The Commander reached across Mum to shake Nigel's hand. "Ray Harris," he said. "Commander, Twin Falls Police. The doc tells me you're retired from New Scotland Yard."

Nigel smiled. "You obviously know whereof you speak."

"Was there an Old Scotland Yard?" I asked.

"No," Nigel said. "It's actually the Metropolitan Police Service of London. Its original location on Whitehall Place had its public entrance off a street called Great Scotland Yard, so after a while people just called the police station Scotland Yard, rather like your Wall Street in New York City being synonymous with the financial district. But headquarters moved in 1890, and it's been called New Scotland Yard ever since."

"I guess 122 years is considered new in England," Hal said. "Here, that would be considered really old."

"What was your rank, if you don't mind me asking?" the Commander asked my stepfather.

"Chief Superintendent," Nigel said. "Probably equivalent to yours here in Twin Falls."

The Commander looked at his watch. "Wish I could stay and chat, but there's too much going on right now."

"Come round to the house when you're off duty," Nigel suggested, and then he turned to me. "If it's all right with you, dear girl."

"Sure," I said. "Come and have a drink."

"Thanks. I believe I will."

As we were leaving the station, I saw an officer bringing Carole, in handcuffs, to the interrogation room that I'd just left. Unfortunately, she saw me too.

"You bitch!" she screamed. "How could you do this to me?"

"Excuse me," I said to my family, and I walked over to her. "Who did what to whom?" I demanded. "You spiked my drink. What did you expect?"

"It was just a joke!" she wailed.

"Make it funnier next time," I suggested.

At that moment, a lawyer I didn't recognize dashed into the station, rushed over to Carole, and told her not to say anything more without his permission.

She paid no attention to him. "I'll get you for this if it's the last thing I do!"

The lawyer and the police officer rushed her into the interrogation room and shut the door.

Slowly, I walked back to my family. Hal put his arms around me. "She can't do anything to you. She's in jail."

"Until Randy bails her out tomorrow," I said.

"After that performance, it's not likely she'll be able to make bail," Nigel commented. "They'll set it way too high for Randy to pay."

"What's Randy going to do in the meantime?" Mum worried.

We all stood and looked at each other. I voiced the thought that had to be going through all our minds.

"Come after me," I said.

19

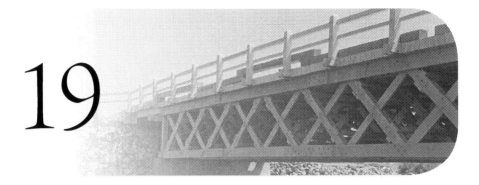

You don't need a weatherman to tell which way the wind blows.
—Bob Dylan

TRUE TO HIS WORD, the Commander came by a couple of hours later. After drinks were poured and everyone was settled, he said, "Well, I went and visited my old friend Marlin Schofield last night. No offense, Doc, but I was afraid you'd go and question him and piss him off, and I thought, as a police officer and an old friend, that I might be able to get more out of him—especially in regard to who Bobby's father was and who killed him. Know what I mean?"

I nodded. He wasn't the first person to suggest that I pissed people off by grilling them about matters that appeared to be none of my business, at least as far as they were concerned. Hal mentioned it frequently, and so did Pete. I resolved to take it easy on whomever I talked to next.

"The old boy's kind of fragile these days," the Commander went on. "He's got some kind of cancer, not sure what—pancreatic, maybe. Anyway, he doesn't have much time left. So after we got all the niceties out of the way, I kind of started reminiscing about the old days, about school and our kids and our wives and what everybody's doing these days—you know what I mean—hoping he'd drop something I didn't already know about."

"And did he?"

"Toni," Hal said, "Shut up, and let the man talk."

"Sorry, Commander."

The Commander continued, unperturbed. "Luckily the old boy was in a reminiscing mood. It didn't take much to get him going. Did you know that I was his best man when he married Janae, his first wife?"

"Really?" I interrupted. "Wasn't he LDS?"

"He was," the Commander said, "but they were married by a justice of the peace on account of Janae was already pregnant. Can't get married in the temple, ya know, unless the girl is a virgin, and they do check."

"You're kidding," I said. "What, they have somebody stick a finger up her—"

"*Antoinette!*" my mother exclaimed.

"Well?" I shot back. "Do they?"

Apparently I'd put the Commander on the defensive. His face had turned bright red. "I don't know how they do it, but they do," he said. "Maybe they take her to a doctor for that. Anyway, that's how come they weren't married in the temple."

"Toni," Hal said, "quit interrupting."

The Commander continued. "Then Janae died in childbirth when Randy was born. That kid was trouble from day one. Marlin turned him over to a nanny and pretty much ignored him while he went cattin' around, trying to drown his sorrows in loose women. Lots of women tried to make an honest man of him, but ol' Marlin wasn't havin' any truck with that. Not until he met Bee."

"That's what he called Beulah," I interjected helpfully for everyone else's benefit.

"Met her at a square dance," the Commander went on. "The boy had just graduated from high school, and she wasn't much older than he was. Maybe even younger. Marlin said she was like a breath of fresh air, and just like that, he was ready to settle down. He was hopin' to have a bunch more kids, and when Bee got pregnant, he was over the moon about it. That son of his, though, was right pissy about the whole thing. Jealous, maybe. Marlin put him to work runnin' draglines on the Low Line Canal, just to get him out of the house. He said he was afraid the boy might try to harm the baby, and he hired a nanny to help

Bee take care of him. Not the same nanny who raised Randy; she was already retired."

"You mean to say," Mum said, "that your friend's older son threatened to harm his little brother?"

"Half-brother," I corrected.

"Ol' Marlin said Randy was 'hostile' to the baby," the Commander said. "That's the word he used. Hostile."

"So what really happened to Bobby?" Nigel asked. "I've heard that he wandered off when Beulah wasn't paying attention, and I've heard that he was taken from his crib during a nap. Which was it?"

"Marlin didn't really know," the Commander said. "He was at work. He said Beulah swore that Bobby was taking a nap. Randy claimed that Beulah had him outside and that he just wandered off because Beulah wasn't paying attention. He said that Beulah probably had a visitor and was distracted."

"Was Randy at home at the time?" Nigel asked. "Did he see the visitor? Did he know who it was?"

The Commander shook his head. "Randy wasn't home either. He was at the canal company, same as Marlin."

"I suppose Marlin knew that if Randy was at work he couldn't have been home kidnapping Bobby," I said.

"Didn't you say that Randy was a dragline operator?" Nigel persisted. "What was Marlin doing at the time?"

The Commander held up a finger. "I know where you're going, Superintendent. If Marlin was in his office and Randy was out on the canal running a dragline, who's to know if he takes off in the middle of the afternoon to go kidnap Bobby and throw him in the coulee and then go back to the dragline and pretend he'd been there all afternoon?"

"Precisely," Nigel said. "And please call me Nigel. I haven't been Chief Superintendent for some time now."

"Where was the nanny while all this was going on?" I asked.

"It was her afternoon off," the Commander said.

"So," I said, "who do we have for witnesses? I suppose that other canal company employees could vouch for Marlin's whereabouts but not for Randy's or Beulah's, right? Except for her visitor. Who was that, by the way?"

"I don't know," the Commander said. "Marlin didn't know. He said Randy told him that Beulah probably had a visitor and that was why she wasn't watching Bobby. Randy suggested that Beulah had a boyfriend, but Marlin didn't believe it. He just put it down to Randy's natural cussedness."

"The guy's a piece of work, isn't he?" Hal commented.

No shit, I thought. Randy hadn't changed much, in my opinion.

"No shit," said the Commander, and then he caught Mum's eye and said, "Sorry, Mrs. Gray. But like I said, the boy was trouble from the get-go. We got to know him real well down at the station during his high school years. A spoiled brat, if you ask me."

"Spoiled brat, my ass," said Hal. "Juvenile delinquent sounds more like it."

"Did he say anything about Bobby's true parentage?" I asked.

"I asked him about that, but he wouldn't talk about it. He said, and I quote, 'Ray, I'm not going there. The boy was mine, and that's all I'm gonna say about it.'"

"Does Marlin still blame Beulah for Bobby's death?" I asked.

"Yep. He still claims that's why he divorced her. My take on it is that he suspected Beulah of cheating on him—with Bobby wandering off while she was otherwise occupied, if you get my drift."

"But didn't you say that Marlin didn't believe Beulah had a boyfriend?" Mum inquired.

"Yes, ma'am, I did. That's what he said, but it's my feeling that he was lying. What man wants to admit that he can't satisfy his young wife?"

"I get that," Hal said. "He was covering up for that, and he was also protecting Randy."

"That's it!" I exclaimed. "If Randy really was Bobby's father, maybe he and Beulah were still having their affair. Maybe Randy took off from work to have an 'afternoon delight' with Beulah, and that was when Bobby wandered off."

"Or maybe somebody snuck in and kidnapped Bobby while Randy and Beulah were otherwise occupied," Hal suggested.

"Like who?" I demanded. "Who else was there that had access to Bobby?" Then it hit me. "The nanny!"

"She had the afternoon off, kitten," Mum reminded me.

"I know," I said. "But she could have come back unbeknownst to Beulah, especially if Beulah was having a romantic interlude."

"How would she know that Beulah would be distracted just at that time?" Hal asked. "Surely Beulah wouldn't confide in her that she was going to have an assignation with Randy and at what time, would she?"

"It's not impossible," I argued. "Women do talk about such things with each other. Beulah and the nanny were probably about the same age. They could have been confidantes. That would have to be it—unless Randy told her."

"Why would Randy tell the nanny?" asked Hal. "Are you suggesting that Randy and the nanny were in cahoots to get rid of Bobby?"

"It's possible, isn't it?" I persisted. "What happened to the nanny, anyhow?"

The Commander didn't know, and I'd run out of questions.

But Hal had one. "Did you hear Carole Schofield threatening Toni this afternoon?"

"I sure did." The Commander picked a fresh toothpick out of his shirt pocket and put it in his mouth. "Good thing she's in jail."

"But Randy's not," Hal said. "What if he comes after Toni?"

The Commander looked uncomfortable. "We've talked about this before. You know we don't have the manpower to have an officer stake out your house all night, and who knows when he might decide to do that, anyhow? We can't have someone here day and night for an indefinite period of time. All we can do is have someone drive by from time to time."

"That won't do any good," Hal said.

"He really can't guarantee your safety, you know," Nigel said. "So it's a good job you've got dogs, eh what?"

⁂

We'd spent an uneventful night, but none of us slept particularly well, except for the dogs upon whom our safety apparently depended. At six o'clock, Hal drove me and Mum and Nigel to the hospital so that Nigel could check in for his surgery.

At work, I sat screening the same Pap smear over and over, checking and rechecking to make sure I hadn't written a diagnosis on the wrong patient's requisition. Then I thought of how nervous Mum must be up there in the waiting room. I wondered whether I should go up there to be with her, but I couldn't because I was on call. The minute I left, my phone would ring with the news that I had a frozen section.

The minute that thought entered my consciousness, my phone did ring. I reached out and punched the speaker button, expecting it to be Histology. "Yes?"

A tremulous voice said, "I'm sorry, do I have the wrong number? I was looking for Dr. Toni Day."

I picked up the receiver hastily. "This is Dr. Day," I said, feeling guilty about being so abrupt for no reason. *How the hell had the call gotten past Arlene?* I wondered, and I glanced out the door to see if Arlene was at her desk. She wasn't. I glanced at my watch and saw that it was five minutes to eight. Arlene started work at eight. "What can I do for you?" I asked the caller.

"My name is Norma Lou Gibson," she said. "Beulah Pritchard was my daughter. I wondered if you could possibly spare some time to talk to me."

Shit. I hated this. Talking about autopsies with bereaved loved ones was my least favorite thing to do. Oh, sure, the promotional films that the College of American Pathologists put out show a medical examiner reassuring the next of kin that their loved one hadn't suffered, that his/her untimely death had not in any way been their fault, et cetera.

Hogwash. Nothing that I'd ever been able to tell the bereaved had ever reassured them. To the contrary, it usually upset them more, for reasons totally unforeseen on my part. More often than not, the family would consult a lawyer and try to get a second autopsy done because I'd failed to check out something that nobody had mentioned to the attending physician and wasn't in the medical record. Of course, those cases usually went nowhere, but they were upsetting for everyone involved.

And those were people whose relatives weren't already planning to sue me.

I've never understood just what a second autopsy consists of, anyway. The internal organs have already been dissected and sliced up and have had samples taken, and then they've been put back into the body cavity inside a plastic bag before it's sewn up. Anything of interest was in formalin in our lab and most likely had been embedded in a paraffin block. Nobody had ever exhumed a body on my account, but they had requested my slides for review. Nothing had ever come of that either.

But Mrs. Gibson was waiting. "Of course," I said in the most soothing voice I could muster. "Do you want to come to my office, or shall I come to you?"

"You'd do that?" she asked. "I didn't think doctors made house calls anymore."

"I can if you can wait until I'm off work, about five o'clock. I can't leave sooner because I'm on call."

"That would be lovely," Mrs. Gibson said. "I'm disabled, and it's hard for me to get out."

And so it was arranged that I would visit her as soon after five as I could get there. I immediately called Hal at work to let him know I'd be late, and I got his voice mail. I left a message there and another one at home on our answering machine. The rest would be up to him.

I looked up with a start to see Mum in my doorway. "Nigel's in recovery," she said. "He seems fine. They'll be moving him to a room after a while. May I wait here with you, kitten?"

"Of course, Mum. Do they know where to find you?"

"I asked them to call me here." With that, she collapsed into my visitors' chair and stretched her feet out in front of her.

"I need to keep working," I told her.

"That's all right, kitten," she said faintly, and the next time I looked over at her, she was sound asleep. I suspected she'd not gotten much sleep the night before, worrying about Nigel. I wondered how she'd do tonight. To my knowledge, it was the first time they'd been separated since they were married, and maybe longer. They'd lived together without benefit of clergy for at least a year before they were married.

I finished the Pap smears and signed them out. Then I started in on Mike's slides from the day before. The phone rang, startling both Mum and me. I punched the speaker button. This time I was more polite and said "hello" instead of "what?"

"Dr. Day, is your mother there with you?" I recognized the voice as one of the nurses that worked in PACU, or Post-Anesthesia Care Unit, as they call the recovery room nowadays.

"Yes, she is, and we're on speaker phone," I told her.

"Mr. Gray is being moved to room 2335 on the surgical floor," she said.

"Okay. We'll meet you there. Thanks." I punched the button again and turned to look at Mum. She was wide awake. "I'll take you there. Are you ready?"

She was. I poked my head into Mike's office to let him know where I was going, and we took the elevator up to the surgical floor. Nigel was already there, being transferred from the gurney to the bed, and we waited outside while nurses got him settled. When they finally let us into the room, Nigel was sitting up in bed with pillows behind him, looking alert and in no particular distress. He had an IV in his left hand. Everything else was discreetly hidden under the covers.

My mother went over and kissed him. "How do you feel, love?"

"All right, I guess," he said. "I keep waiting for those bloody needles to start hurting, but they haven't yet."

"They won't," the nurse assured us. "He's got an epidural. It'll stay in until he goes home tomorrow."

"Is there anything we can get you?" I asked him.

"Breakfast," he said. "I'm bloody starving."

"Coming right up," the nurse said. She then turned on the TV and handed the remote to Nigel, showed him where the call button was, and then bustled out of the room.

"Have you seen the doctor yet?" he asked us. "Because I haven't."

"He's got six of these on the surgery schedule," I told him. "You were the first one. He's going to be pretty busy, getting all those done and doing three treatments on each one."

"Hmph," he said.

"He's a bit grumpy," my mother said apologetically to me.

"It's the anesthesia," I said. "It hasn't completely worn off yet. I've heard that some patients say perfectly awful things. It'll get better after a while."

"I certainly hope so," Mum said. "But if it doesn't, I know where he sleeps."

"Are you threatening me, woman?" Nigel demanded.

Mum raised an eyebrow. "I wouldn't dream of it."

I checked my watch. "I gotta go back to work. Are you two okay without me?"

"Of course, kitten. Now, what are you going to do about your car?"

I frowned, puzzled. "What about my car?"

"Hasn't it been down in the doctors' car park all night?"

I still didn't get it. "Yes, why?"

"Is that a secure parking garage?" she asked.

Oh. Suddenly I got it. "Not really. It's open air. Anybody can walk in. You think maybe someone tampered with my car?"

"Yes, dear. Or put a bomb in it, perhaps."

Oh my God. A bomb hadn't even occurred to me. Suddenly I couldn't seem to get enough air into my lungs. "I'll get it checked out before I come home," I told her.

When I got back to my office I called the police station. Pete said he'd send someone right over.

I debated calling Hal too but decided against it. No use in getting him all upset too. Besides, I didn't want him to know I was planning to visit Beulah's mother. I already knew it was a stupid thing to do, but I just didn't know how to say no to the poor lady.

The morning wore on while I resisted the urge to go out to the parking garage and see what, if anything, was going on.

Mike came back from lunch and told me he'd had to park in the outside doctors' parking because the police had the underground garage roped off with caution tape that said "bomb squad" on it.

Whereupon I got that "not enough air in my lungs" feeling again. "Huh," I said, feigning ignorance. "Wonder what that's all about."

But I knew.

They'd found something.

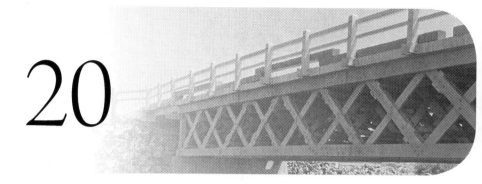

20

Hatred comes from the heart; contempt from the head;
and neither feeling is quite within our control.
—Arthur Schopenhauer

PETE CALLED ME ABOUT AN hour later to tell me they'd found a small explosive attached to my car that had been set to go off two minutes after I started it. "Just long enough for you to get off the hospital campus," he said. "We'll be sending it off to Boise so they can do their thing, but I feel pretty sure about who did it."

So did I.

But for now, I was safe to drive.

❧

Norma Lou Gibson lived in a small bungalow in a neighborhood of small bungalows and big trees. All the houses dated back to the forties and fifties and were built of brick, with carports rather than garages. Her carport contained an ancient Chevy Bel Air with tail fins, which I guessed was a '57. I wondered who was maintaining it. A classic car like that deserved better than an open carport, in my opinion, but that was not why I was there.

I rang the doorbell, and a young girl came to the door. She was about my height, had curly blonde hair and freckles, and wore a nursing student uniform with a hospital badge. "Yes?" she greeted me.

"I'm Dr. Toni Day," I said. "I've come to see Mrs. Gibson."

"Let her in, Crystal, dear," said a voice from behind her. "I asked her to come. You go fix that tea now."

"Okay, Grandma," the girl said and opened the door wide.

I stepped into the tiny living room, which was crammed with knickknacks. Mrs. Gibson sat in a recliner chair with a walker next to her. Her white hair was thinning, but her round, pink cheeks and faded blue eyes resembled Beulah's. She put her knitting down on the table on the other side of her chair by a lamp. I saw that her fingers were swollen and gnarled with arthritis. I went over to her, and she started to get out of her chair. It was one of those electric recliners that lifted its occupant to a standing position. All she had to do was push a button. I hurried over to her, hands outstretched. "Oh, please don't get up on my account," I begged. "I'm Dr. Toni Day. I got here as soon as I could."

Mrs. Gibson sat back down as her chair slowly returned her to her original position. "Thank you so much for coming," she said. "Tell me about my Beulah. What happened to her?"

I felt at a loss as to where to start. "What have you been told so far?"

"They said she drowned in the canal," Mrs. Gibson said in her tremulous voice, "but then they kept her in the hospital for two days. My daughter Brenda claims that someone killed her by doing the autopsy too soon. I don't understand."

Oh jeez. How much should I tell her? A lawyer—that is to say, Elliott—would have told me not to come here in the first place. But now I was here and on the spot. I had to say something. "It is pretty confusing," I agreed. "Beulah didn't drown in the canal. Her car went into the canal, but Beulah didn't drown. Her head was out of the water. But she was in that cold water long enough to be hypothermic. She appeared to be dead. I was about to start her autopsy when she showed signs of life."

Mrs. Gibson leaned forward, her faded blue eyes drilling into mine. "You mean you were the one who did the autopsy and killed my Beulah?"

"No, no, not at all," I protested. "Beulah grabbed my apron strings. She took a breath. I called the emergency room doctor and he admitted her to ICU. She was still alive. But she only lived for two days. I did the autopsy the day after she died, on the following Monday."

"Well, now I'm really confused," she complained. "Where does that child get off suing the hospital for something that didn't happen?"

Assuming it was Brenda she referred to, I shrugged, palms up. "I have no idea. You know her better than I do. What do you think?"

At this point, Crystal came back in with the tea tray. She set it down on the coffee table. Then she set up a TV tray in front of her grandmother and set the tea tray on it. "Do you want me to pour, Grandma?"

"No, dear. We can handle it. Don't you have homework?"

Crystal nodded. "I sure do. Got an exam coming up. Just holler if you need anything." And with that she was gone.

Mrs. Gibson beckoned me closer and handed me a cup of tea. "I don't want Crystal to hear me say this, but her mother is a piece of work. I'm afraid we spoiled her when she was a child. She was so pretty and so talented. We would have done anything for her that she wanted—piano lessons, dancing lessons, singing lessons. Poor Beulah got pushed into the background. She was the brainy one, always reading and studying. She wanted to be a doctor. Did you know that?"

I took a sip of tea. It was weak. "I heard that. What happened?"

Mrs. Gibson poured herself a cup of tea and took a sip. "She was accused of stealing some examination questions. They found them in her locker. She always insisted that she didn't do it, but they gave her an F in the course, and she had to repeat the semester."

I put my cup down on the coffee table. "I bet she was devastated not to graduate with her class," I said. "Did you believe she did it?"

"I didn't know what to believe at the time. Beulah said she was innocent, but Brenda said she was lying. I didn't know who to believe."

"Did you ever think that maybe Brenda was the one who was lying?"

"Not then. I'm not so sure now."

"What did Beulah do after she graduated?"

"Nothing at first. She lived here with her father and me for a year and worked at odd jobs—waitressing, mostly. She didn't have much of a social life. Then one Saturday night a friend asked her to go to a square dance, and she met a man. Suddenly she was happy, going out every night with this man, and every time we suggested that she bring him home, she made up some excuse. Of course, when we finally met him, the reason was obvious. He was three times her age! But he was a good man. He had a good job. He wanted to marry Beulah, and we went along with it. She gave him a son, and he doted on that child. He even hired a nanny to help Beulah take care of him. That's why I can't understand what happened to that child."

"You mean Bobby," I said.

"Yes. How could he wander off and fall into a coulee with two women taking care of him?"

"I heard that someone kidnapped him," I said.

"How, with two women in the house?"

"I also heard it was the nanny's day off."

"Young lady, you will never convince me that my Beulah neglected that child to the point where either of those things could happen. She was a good mother—unlike her sister."

"What happened to Brenda?" I asked. "Someone told me she went to Hollywood to become an actress."

"Oh, she did," Mrs. Gibson said. "She got a few bit parts. But it wasn't until she went to New York that she really became successful."

"Was she on Broadway?" I asked.

"Oh, no, she never made it that far. She was a showgirl, you know, doing burlesque and things like that. One night a man saw her from the audience and swept her off her feet. They were married two weeks later, which really isn't long enough for an engagement, but he's a very wealthy man, and he's been very good to her."

Translation: she was a stripper.

"Is Crystal her daughter?"

"Yes. But Bert and I raised her. Brenda and Morty were much too busy."

Too busy doing what? "What does Morty do?"

"He's in business."

"What kind of business?"

191

"In the stock market, dear. He worked for Lehman Brothers until the crash. They lost everything."

"What does he do now?"

Mrs. Gibson was prevented from answering that question by the arrival of two more people who breezed in the front door, bringing a blast of cold air with them and arguing at the tops of their voices. They took up far too much space and too much oxygen in that tiny house. The woman in the full-length ranch mink coat was tall, blonde, and gorgeous, but her beauty was spoiled by her sullen expression. The lines around her eyes and mouth suggested that she'd spent a lot of time with that expression on her face. She had to be Brenda. Therefore, the portly man with the slicked-back black hair, red face, rimless spectacles over beady dark eyes, and the diamond pinky ring had to be Morty. I diagnosed high blood pressure. This was clearly not a marriage made in heaven.

Shit. Here I sat, like a deer in the headlights, unable to move without calling attention to myself. I wished I had Harry Potter's cloak of invisibility. These weren't nice people. They were loud, cheap, and aggressive. They'd eat me alive. Did I dare just excuse myself and slip out before they found out who I was? They were still in each other's faces, ignoring Mrs. Gibson and me, so it was worth a try. I stood up and gestured to my hostess that I was going to just tiptoe out, when Brenda turned away from Morty and saw me. "Who the hell are you?" she screeched, from which I deduced that the lovely singing voice she'd once had was no longer.

"I was just leaving," I said and headed for the door, but it was nothing doing. Brenda reached out and grabbed my arm, jerking me back. "Oh, no, you don't. Come back here and identify yourself."

"Brenda!" Mrs. Gibson's voice was uncharacteristically strident. I guessed it had to be if it was going to be heard over Brenda's. "That is no way to treat a guest in our home!"

Brenda let go of me but continued to glare at me. "I know who you are. You're that bitch doctor who killed my sister!"

I shook my head. "No, I didn't."

She put her hands on my shoulders and pushed me. Hard. I fell back into my chair. "The hell you didn't!"

Mrs. Gibson pushed the button on her chair and propelled herself to a standing position. "Brenda Renee, that will be quite enough! I won't have you assaulting someone I invited here."

Brenda switched her glare to her mother. "You invited her here? Whatever for?"

Morty, who up till now had been positively sphinxlike in his silence, suddenly came to life. "Bren, your mother's right. You need to apologize to the lady."

Brenda turned on him. "Apologize? The hell I will!"

Morty seemed to grow taller as he stepped closer to his wife and stared down into her face. "You will apologize. You won't like the consequences if you don't." His voice was low and threatening.

Brenda wilted visibly as she turned to me, face suddenly drained of color. "I'm very sorry, Dr. Day. I had no right to act that way. I hope you'll forgive me."

I felt like taking a leaf out of her book and yelling "The hell I will!," but Mum had brought me up better than that. So I merely nodded, excused myself, slipped past them, and left the house. Once outside, my knees began to shake so much that I nearly didn't make it to my car. My hands shook too, making it difficult to get the key into the ignition and also to back up without hitting the black Escalade parked behind me, which was almost but not quite blocking my exit. No way was I going back into that house and asking Brenda and Morty to move their car. I oozed out of the driveway and drove home with white knuckles and gritted teeth.

I walked into the kitchen, looking forward to comfort and succor from my family, only to hear Elliott's voice. "She did what? Is she out of her freakin' mind?"

He didn't sound happy. I heard Hal's voice say, "I don't know any more than you do. You heard the same message I did." He didn't sound happy either.

Christ on a crutch. More screaming people. Just what I need.

I walked into the living room, dropped my purse on the coffee table with a thump, and faced Elliott with my feet apart and my hands on my hips. "Just what is your problem, Elliott?"

"Tell me you didn't go talk to Beulah's family."

I sank into my recliner. "Beulah's mother called me. She wanted to talk about how Beulah died. She's heard all kinds of rumors and wanted to know the truth. I had no idea that Beulah's sister and her husband would show up."

Elliott dropped onto the couch and put his head in his hands, making his bushy hair even bushier. "Did you talk to them too?"

"Not any more than I could help," I said.

"What did you say?"

I told him what had happened.

"Holy shit," Hal said. "Are you okay?"

"That's assault," Elliott said. "Want to press charges?"

"She didn't really hurt me," I said. "What do you think? Do you think it would help with my defense?"

"Definitely. It would show her up for the nutcase that she is. Not to mention that it would mitigate the fact that you fornicated skyward by going to see them in the first damn place!"

"Well, then, let's do it."

"Done," Elliott said. "I'll get going on it first thing in the morning." And he left, slamming the door behind him.

"He seems pissed," I observed.

Hal cranked his recliner all the way back. "Toni, you are one of the most infuriating people I know. Of course he's pissed!"

"But you love me anyway," I said.

"What was Beulah's mother doing while all this was going on?" Mum asked. "Surely she didn't condone that sort of behavior."

"She didn't," I said. "She told Brenda she wasn't going to have anyone she'd invited to the house treated that way. But Brenda didn't back down until Morty told her to apologize."

"Who's Morty?" Hal asked.

"Brenda's husband," I replied and described him. "Looks like a mobster. He had to threaten Brenda to get her to apologize. She's scared of him."

"Scared of him?" repeated Hal.

"She looked scared to me," I said. "The blood drained right out of her face. I'll bet he hits her."

"They sound like thoroughly unsavory people," Mum observed. "Not our sort at all."

"How's Nigel doing?" I asked her. "I didn't have time to check on him before I left work."

"He's not enjoying having to stay in bed all day," she said. "He'd had two treatments by the time Hal picked me up at five. I expect he'll get the third one either tonight or in the morning before they let him go home."

"What time did they say he could go home?"

"They didn't," Mum said. "I expect it depends on how many cases Dr. Nichols has in the morning."

"He might not have any," I said. "He doesn't do them every day. Usually it's just one day a week."

"Well, then, it might be early," Mum said. "We can always hope."

⚬⚬

Thursday morning, I took Mum to work with me, expecting to have to take her and Nigel home whenever he was discharged. She appeared at the door to my office shortly after nine o'clock. "Nigel's ready to go home, kitten."

So I took them home, stopping at Walmart to pick up Nigel's prescribed pain pills. Mum and I got him into the house and settled him on the couch. I got him some water so he could take a pain pill. Mum said, "I'll put the kettle on for some tea. Can you stay for tea, kitten?"

"No, sorry. I've got to get back to work. Are you two going to be okay here alone?"

"I'm sure we will be, kitten."

Nigel said, "No worries," which were the first words out of him since we'd left the hospital. "Sorry to be such a grouch."

"How do you feel?" I asked him.

"Bloody uncomfortable," he admitted. "I wish that sodding pill would hurry up and work."

Mum came back into the living room. "Nigel, really, your language," she admonished.

I burst out laughing.

It was the last laughing I was to do that day.

Elliott called shortly after I got back to work. "We need to talk," he said. "Can you come to my office?"

"I just got back from taking Nigel home from the hospital," I told him. "Work is piling up here. Can you possibly come here?"

"I guess so," he said. "Maybe it's just as well. That way I can talk to your partner too."

He arrived about half an hour later with his scruffy briefcase. In a way, Elliott's well-used brown leather briefcase was as much of a statement as Clark Dane's shiny, black alligator one. It said "good ole country lawyer," while Clark Dane's said "slick, expensive, big-city attorney." However, I knew that Elliott's fees were considerable, and I was grateful that Cascade was paying them and not me.

I went next door and got Mike. "Hey," he said, shaking Elliott's hand. "What's up with y'all?"

"Here's the thing," Elliott said as he opened his briefcase and hauled out a handful of papers. "Brenda Duke is determined to pursue this lawsuit, even though the state board of medicine has ruled that it is without merit. Chaim Rabinowitz told me he advised her to drop it, but she refused. So he's dropping her."

"You could have told me this on the phone," I said. "What's really going on here?"

"That's really what's going on," he said, "but you wanted to press assault charges against Brenda Duke. There are things you need to sign. Have you told the police yet? You need to do that before I can do anything."

"Assault?" Mike echoed. "She assaulted you, Toni? How did that happen? I thought you weren't supposed to have contact outside of court with people who are suing you."

"I didn't intend to," I said. "Beulah's mother wanted to talk to me about how Beulah died, so I went to her house after work yesterday, and Brenda and Morty showed up while I was there."

"What are they like?" Mike asked.

I described them. Mike made a face. "Sounds like a mobster and his gun moll."

"That's pretty much the impression I got," I said and told him what had happened.

"There's another angle," Elliott said. "I know he was supposed to have worked at Lehman Brothers and lost everything in the crash and that's why he needs money, but I'm willing to bet there's more to it than that. The crash was four years ago. That's when he should have needed money. Why now?"

"Maybe he borrowed it from the mob, and they want it back," Mike suggested.

"What I'm saying is that those two need to be investigated," Elliott said. "We can go about it two ways. Either I can put a PI on it, which will cost money that you might end up paying if we don't find anything pertinent to the lawsuit, or the police can put a detective on it."

"That means Pete or Bernie or the Commander," I said. "They're busy going through canal company records to trace Randy's possible embezzlement. But don't the police have to have a crime to investigate? You can't just hire them like you would a PI."

"You can hire a PI to find a crime and then have the police investigate it," Mike suggested.

"But if there's a crime in their past, it wouldn't be in Twin Falls," I argued. "They lived in New York City."

"They live in Boise now," Elliott said. "Okay, there's a lot to think about here, but right now you need to call the police and get those assault charges filed."

"Oh, right," I said and dialed.

Bernie Kincaid answered. After identifying myself and dealing with the amenities, I said, "I want to press charges against Brenda Duke for assault."

Bernie wanted details. I gave them to him. He said he'd take care of it, and we disconnected. "Now," I said, "the police have a crime to investigate."

"Peachy," Elliott said. "Now, let's get these freakin' papers signed, and then we can move on."

He laid the papers out on my desk and indicated where I should sign, and I did so. I hoped that would be an end to the day's festivities so I could get some work done, but it was not to be.

It was really nobody's fault but mine. I knew I wouldn't be satisfied until I did a little snooping on my own. I fired up my computer, got online, and Googled Mortimer Duke. There were fifty-two million entries. I looked at the first forty or so, most of them either Mortimers or Dukes but not both. There were only three Mortimer Dukes, all of whom had lived in the eighteenth or nineteenth centuries and were long dead. There was no record of a present-day Mortimer Duke who had worked at Lehman Brothers. There was no record of a present-day Mortimer Duke, period.

Next, I Googled Brenda Duke and found thirty-seven million entries. It was pretty much the same story. There was no mention of a present-day Brenda Duke, let alone one that was in showbiz. Of course, if she really was in showbiz, she would most likely use a stage name.

So I Googled Brenda Renee Gibson instead. That brought up a mishmash of Brendas, Renees, and Gibsons—but not a single Brenda Renee Gibson. On a hunch, I deleted Brenda and searched for a Renee Gibson. There was an entry titled "Images for Renee Gibson," which I clicked on, and there she was. Renee Gibson-Dubois, actress. Bit parts in several off-Broadway shows. Pictures of her in glitzy costumes and chorus lines, in poses that stopped just short of pornography. A single picture of a pretty teenager with long blonde hair and a sweet smile contrasted harshly with later pictures of an older Brenda who had grown hard and cynical with experience. I e-mailed the link to both Elliott and Pete.

So Brenda existed, but her husband didn't. Where had the name *Dubois* come from? I Googled Mortimer Dubois. Out of the first forty of nearly three million entries of Mortimers and Duboises, there was only a single Mortimer Dubois, and he had died in 1985.

So, who was Brenda married to—the Invisible Man?

There were two choices. Either he was in organized crime or he was a spy. And he sure didn't look like a spy to me.

Of course, a spy that looked like a spy wouldn't get much spying done, because he'd get caught. Better to look like a mobster and fool everybody.

Okay, enough, I told myself. The stack of slide trays had been steadily growing to a claustrophobia-inducing height. So I closed out Google and got back to work.

I'd managed to get through about twenty cases when Pete called. "You didn't tell me you'd been assaulted. Why not?"

"It just happened yesterday," I protested. "I wouldn't have said anything about it except that Elliott thought it would be a good way to show what a nutcase Brenda Duke is. You know, at the wrongful death trial."

"The wrongful death trial that isn't gonna happen," he returned. "What were you doing at her mother's house in the first place?"

"Her mother called me," I explained. "She wanted to know the truth about Beulah's death. I didn't see any harm in telling her, and she's disabled, so instead of having her come to my office, I went to her house."

"So what's this link you sent me? Who's Renee Gibson-Dubois?"

"Brenda," I said. "Apparently that's her stage name."

"Huh. How'd she come up with that, I wonder?"

"Renee is her middle name," I explained. "Gibson is her maiden name. I don't know where Dubois came from."

"What's her husband's name?"

"Duke. Mortimer Duke. She calls him Morty. Of course, yesterday she was calling him every name in the book."

"What were they fighting about?"

"I couldn't tell. But she was pretty riled up before she even knew I was there or who I was."

"What exactly did she do to you?"

I described yet again what had happened. I was beginning to regret having told Elliott to go ahead and file charges. This was shaping up to be a real pain in the ass—not that this whole wrongful death business wasn't already causing major discomfort in that location.

"How much do you know about these people?" he inquired.

"How fortuitous that you should ask that question," I replied, and I told him about my Google search. "I can't find any evidence that Morty Duke even exists."

"That's okay," Pete said. "We have access to other databases. Police sites. We can contact the New York City police and see if he has a rap sheet. Maybe the FBI too, if he's into organized crime. We'll find out who he is."

I changed the subject. "Have you found out anything about Randy Schofield and his shell companies?"

"Bernie's working on that. I'll have him call you."

∞

Nigel was feeling much better when I got home and was much more inclined to talk.

"I had a rather interesting chap for a roommate," he said. "Fellow works for the canal company too. Nice chap."

"What did you talk about?" I asked.

"We started out talking about you, actually. Fellow said he knew you. Said he was living with one of your techs."

Kenny. Of course. "I do know him," I said. "He's a ditch rider for the canal company. But Lucille never said anything about him having prostate cancer."

"He must," Nigel said. "He had the same procedure I did. So we got to talking about the canal company, and I found out something very interesting." He paused and looked expectant. I looked at Mum, whose green eyes twinkled.

"Well?" I demanded. "Are you going to make me guess?"

"I found out who the nanny was," he said, "and you're not going to believe it."

"Don't tease her, dear," Mum said to her husband.

"Randy's wife," Nigel said. "Carole."

200

21

The law hath not been dead,
though it hath slept.
—Shakespeare, *Measure for Measure*

WOW! WHO'D 'A' THUNK IT?

Nigel was happy to enlarge on the subject. Kenny bowled on the canal company league—not only with Dwayne but also with Randy and Marlin. He'd heard about all the goings-on in the Schofield family straight from the horse's mouth. The only thing he didn't know was what had really happened to Bobby, because everybody had told him that Bobby had wandered off and drowned in the coulee.

"So Randy married the nanny," Hal mused.

"Why didn't Carole mention that at lunch?" Mum asked.

"Maybe it had something to do with Bobby's death," I said. "Maybe the reason she didn't want me to know what was in that autopsy report was because Bobby didn't drown."

"You mean, because maybe she had something to do with it, don't you?" Hal said.

"Well, we were speculating that Randy and the nanny were in cahoots, weren't we?" I said. "What do you think about that now?"

"Judging from how she acted toward you at the police station Tuesday," Nigel said, "I've no doubt she's capable of murder."

"Well, I've got no doubt that Randy is too," I said, "if he's the one who put the bomb under my car."

"Bomb? What bomb?" demanded Hal.

"Whatever are you talking about, kitten?" Mum asked.

"You were right, Mum," I said. "You were the one who suggested that I should get my car checked out after being in the underground parking all night, and you were right. There was a bomb. You saved my life."

Mum burst into tears. Nigel pulled her close and put his arm around her.

Hal turned to me. "Why didn't you tell me?"

"Because Elliott was here yelling at me," I said, "wanting me to press charges against Brenda Duke. We did that today, by the way."

Elliott must have heard me, because the doorbell rang, and there he was.

"What happened with Carole?" I asked. "Did she get out on bail?"

"She did," Elliott said with a sour expression. "God only knows why, especially after the way she threatened you. Ray told me all about it."

The doorbell rang again, and Hal got up to answer it.

"Guess we're not going shopping for jewelry," I said.

Pete came in just in time to hear that. All eyes turned to me. "What?" I said. "She invited me to go shopping with her. Didn't I mention that?"

Apparently not.

"Are we talking about Carole?" Pete asked. "She's out on bail, by the way. I suppose Elliott told you."

"He did," Hal said. "How the hell did that happen?"

"It wasn't supposed to," Pete said. "The judge set bail at a hundred grand. Nobody expected Randy to be able to pay that. But he did."

"Don't you only have to pay ten percent?" I asked.

"How many people do you know who can pony up ten grand on a moment's notice?" Pete demanded. "Besides doctors and lawyers, that is."

Not this doctor. "Or movie stars and mobsters," I added, thinking of Beulah's sister.

"Did it come out of his bank account?" Elliott asked.

"He paid cash," Pete said. "The bank has no record of him withdrawing that much in cash."

"I should think you could use this as evidence that Randy has money for which he cannot account," Nigel said.

"I know another thing you could use," I said. "Carole's jewelry."

"Carole's jewelry?" Pete echoed. "How?"

"She was wearing earrings and a ring that must have cost at least five thousand dollars apiece," I told him. "Tanzanites and diamonds in white gold."

Pete hauled out a notebook and made a note in it. "Where'd she get it?"

"She said there was a little shop downtown where the guy makes all his own jewelry," I said, "but I have no idea where it is. Too bad. If she hadn't spiked my Coke, she could have taken me there."

"What was the occasion?" Mum asked.

"Occasion?" Pete looked bewildered.

"The occasion for Randy to give Carole jewelry," Mum explained. "One doesn't usually give one's wife expensive jewelry unless there's a special occasion."

"She got the earrings for her twenty-fifth anniversary," I said, "and the ring for her thirtieth."

"One could postulate that he gave her something for every anniversary," Nigel said, "to say nothing of birthdays and Christmas. If you could find that shop, you could look at the receipts and see just how much he was spending there."

"I think I know that shop," Pete said. "We've responded to several robberies or attempted robberies over the years. It's down on Main Street South, on the second floor over a law office and a computer store. There's a narrow staircase that you'd never notice if you weren't looking for it. It's owned by a little old Jewish guy who escaped from Nazi Germany." He made another note. "Shouldn't be too hard to get a warrant for that."

"Of course, it's possible that Randy gets his cash by selling Carole's jewelry," Nigel continued. "You'd actually have to prove that wasn't the case."

Pete looked up from his notebook. "You mean I'd have to go to Carole's house and account for every piece he bought."

"Precisely," Nigel said, "and document it."

"That means another warrant," Pete said and made another note.

"This is too bad." I sighed. "Carole was positively radiant when she was talking about her jewelry. She looked so in love with her husband that I can't picture her having an affair with Dwayne Pritchard."

"For God's sake, Toni," Hal said. "She's got to hide that from Randy, doesn't she? If she can fool him, she can fool you without even breaking a sweat."

"That would be the least of her crimes," Nigel observed. "At least it's legal. Stalking, setting fires, and slashing tires aren't."

"We don't know that Carole did all those things," I objected. "She followed me home one night. She spiked my drink. Randy could have done all the other stuff. Maybe she only did those things because Randy asked her to."

"You keep defending her," Hal said. "But the only thing we know she couldn't have done is put the bomb under your car, because she was in jail that night."

"And speaking of that," Pete said, "we got a report from the Boise bomb squad. They said there wasn't much firepower to that bomb. If it had gone off, it probably wouldn't have done more than disable your car."

"If I was out in the middle of traffic when that happened, it could still have gotten me killed," I retorted.

"That puts it on about the same level as spiking your drink," Nigel said. "All it did was make you drunk. But depending on where you were and what you were doing at the time, it could have gotten you killed too."

"What that tells me," Pete said, "is that they aren't trying to kill you. They're trying to send a message."

"Or maybe they are trying to kill me and are doing a really bad job of it," I said. "And how long is it going to take for them to get really pissed off that I keep not dying and step up their efforts?"

"It doesn't really matter which one is behind all this," Hal said, "because neither of them is in jail tonight. They're both out there, plotting God knows what."

Pete sighed. "And there's not one thing we can do about it."

Thank God for our canine early warning system, I thought—especially since Pete and Elliott had no sooner left than Killer and Geraldine started making a ruckus and scratching at the French doors into the backyard.

22

But there's nothing half so sweet in life
As love's young dream.
—THOMAS MOORE

HAL GOT UP AND HEADED for the garage. "I'll take care of this."

So will I, I thought, and I let the dogs out. Still barking and growling, they raced toward the blue spruces, where a frantic rustling suggested that someone was making a hasty exit over the back fence. Hal came out the side door of the garage with the CO_2 pistol—which I'd forgotten he had—in one hand and a flashlight in the other and started firing in the general direction of the commotion.

"Are you nuts?" I demanded in a stage whisper that probably could be heard in the next county. "You could hurt somebody."

"That's the point," he said, not bothering to lower his voice. "Well, well. What have we here?"

I looked where he was pointing the flashlight. "Why, I do believe it's a footprint. Hang on a minute." I picked up a large clay flowerpot that sat outside the garage door and had not yet been planted for the summer and put it upside down over the print. "Maybe that'll keep the dogs off it until Pete or somebody can make a cast of it."

"Well, aren't you the little Sherlock Holmes," Hal said, shining the flashlight on the fence. "Bastard broke the corner off this board."

"He did better than that," I said, peering at something orange in the crack. "Have you got some tweezers or forceps?"

"Tweezers or forceps? Isn't that more your department?"

"Have it your way," I said. "I'll go get my tweezers. Stay here and guard this."

I took the opportunity to call Pete while I was in the house, and then I had to explain what was going on to Mum and Nigel, who then had to go out and see for themselves, while the dogs ran around sniffing and growling. When I got back outside, I not only had tweezers but also a baggie. Hal took the tweezers, extricated the orange fragment from the fence, and put it into the baggie that I held open for him. By then, Pete had arrived.

He looked at the fragment under a magnifying glass. "This looks like it's off one of those blaze-orange vests that hunters wear. We'll have to see if Randy has one—and if it has a hole that matches this."

After Pete left, a lively discussion ensued. Would the intruder come back to finish what he had started? Or had he already succeeded? We finally decided that Killer and Geraldine wouldn't have waited to sound the alarm and hadn't given him a chance to complete his mission—and if he came back to finish it, they'd alert us again. After that, we all slept surprisingly well.

On Friday morning, none of us showed any signs of sleep deprivation. I went to work in a much better mood than I had the day before, and it turned out to be a very productive day.

Enough time had passed that I could now cut Beulah's and Dwayne's brains and complete their autopsies. Once I got those reports done, I could get any number of people off my back.

The brains didn't provide any additional information. I didn't even put any sections in. I just took pictures after I'd sliced them, which showed the extent of the damage that had killed both of them much better than any microscopic section would have done.

Charlie brought me his yearbooks—all four of them.

I spread them out in chronological order, ignoring all the work I had to do, and started with Charlie's senior year. Back then, Charlie had been a cute, pudgy little guy with curly, dark hair, round cheeks, and an impish grin. If he'd worn glasses back then, he'd taken them off for the picture.

Beulah's picture showed shoulder-length, curly, blonde hair held back from her face with a pair of barrettes. A sprinkling of freckles decorated her pug nose and cheeks that were as round as Charlie's. *Wow*, I thought, *Crystal looks just like Beulah did back then.*

Brenda's hair—much longer and blonder than Beulah's, and not so much curly as wavy—had been pulled to one side to flow over one shoulder and drape seductively over one eye. Her face was delicate, her skin clear, her lips pouty, and her eyes framed by impossibly long, dark lashes. They didn't look anything like sisters, let alone twins.

I gazed at her in awe. Or was it envy? Charlie hadn't exaggerated. She really had been a knockout back then.

I continued to leaf through the group pictures and pictures of special events. Brenda seemed to show up everywhere. She'd been homecoming queen. I didn't recognize the boy who'd been homecoming king, and his name wasn't familiar either. Brenda had played the lead in the drama club's production of *The Sound of Music*. She'd been a cheerleader. She'd been senior class president. She was featured in numerous pictures of random groups, all of which looked like everybody in them was having fun. She was the girl everybody wishes they could be.

Beulah showed up only in pictures of Scholarship Society and National Honor Society, which must have been taken before the end of the first semester, considering what had happened then.

I ran through the pictures of everyone in Charlie's class. I recognized a lot of people I knew, but nobody else connected to this case.

Then I looked through the yearbooks from Charlie's freshman, sophomore, and junior years and hit pay dirt: Dwayne "Boomer" Pritchard, who had been a senior when Charlie was a sophomore. He'd been the quarterback on the football team. He'd been a handsome devil back then, unlike the cadaverous individual I'd autopsied. I wondered if he'd still looked like that when Beulah married him.

I moved on to Charlie's freshman year. When Charlie was a freshman, the homecoming king and queen had been Randy Schofield and Carole Anne Witt. Randy had been really cute back then. He'd looked like Ron Howard when he played Richie Cunningham on *Happy Days*. Carole Anne Witt had black hair piled up on her head, and she looked like … Carole Schofield.

Well, well.

So Randy was actually older than Beulah, not younger. Or had he been really smart and skipped a couple of grades? Nah. How could he do that and be constantly in trouble with the cops as the Commander had told me?

Had Randy and Carole been an item way back in high school? Was that how Carole had gotten her job as Bobby's nanny?

I leafed through the pictures of seniors and suddenly recognized one of them. The name under the picture was Martin Dubois. It was Morty.

Oh, my God. That was where the name Dubois had come from. Brenda hadn't married a man from New York after all. She'd married a hometown boy from right here in Twin. And her own mother didn't know that. Or maybe she did and was ashamed of it for some reason. Had Martin Dubois been a bad boy in high school, somebody no mother would want her daughter mixed up with?

I couldn't wait to tell Pete, so I called the station—and got Bernie Kincaid. "Hey," I greeted him. "How's it going?"

"Just peachy," he grumbled. "I'm sitting here going through the canal company books from 2000 all the way back to 1983."

"How's that going?" I asked. "Does that mean you've already gone through everything from 2000 on?"

"Pete did," he said. "So far we've found fourteen shell companies, with which Randy's managed to embezzle $6.5 million."

"Well, isn't that enough to arrest him?"

"Not really," Bernie said. "I misspoke when I said Randy'd embezzled $6.5 million. What I should have said is that *someone* has embezzled that much. We don't have a money trail that leads us to Randy. We have no proof that Randy's the embezzler."

Excuse me? "What do you mean, you have no proof? Didn't Pete find payments from the canal company to S & P in the canal company's financial records?"

"He did. But there's no money trail that leads to Randy."

"Wait a minute," I said. "You know that there was an envelope addressed to S & P in Randy's PO box. What address did the other shell companies use? Isn't that enough of a connection?"

"It may have to be if we don't find anything else," Bernie said.

I changed the subject and told him what I'd found in Charlie's yearbooks. "Now I know where Brenda got the name Dubois."

"Toni, what are you talking about?"

"Her stage name is Renee Gibson-Dubois, with a hyphen."

"How the hell do you know that?" Bernie demanded.

"I Googled her. But I couldn't find Morty. It's like he didn't exist. But now I can Google Martin Dubois."

I heard Bernie sigh. "Toni, could you please let us do the investigating for once?"

"If I had," I countered, "would you know what you know now? I mean, all these people are interconnected from high school on. Seems to me they all need to be investigated."

"For once I agree with you. Now could you get off my phone so I can get on with it?"

"Okay. Bye." I disconnected, fired up my computer, and Googled Martin Dubois.

Out of approximately fifteen million entries, I found one Martin Dubois, born January 4, 1963, in Twin Falls, Idaho, to Forrest Dubois and Marlinda NaDeane Sorenson Dubois. He graduated from Twin Falls High School in 1981, attended Idaho State University in Pocatello, and apparently did not graduate. He married Brenda Renee Gibson on June 24, 1987. One child, Crystal Dawn Dubois, was born January 30, 1988. He resided in Manhattan.

There was no information beyond 1988. Martin Dubois seemed to have disappeared from the face of the earth.

Why? Was that when he had become Mortimer Duke?

Had he changed his name legally, or was it an alias? What would he need an alias for?

If it was an alias, was it the only one, or did he have others?

Had Brenda legally changed her name as well? Or was she still legally Brenda Renee Dubois? What was Crystal's legal name?

Well, that was easy. I'd just Google them too.

I hadn't been able to find Brenda as Brenda Duke, only as Renee Gibson-Dubois. But I found Brenda Renee Dubois, née Gibson, married to Martin Dubois in New York City on June 24, 1987, with one child, et cetera. That was it as far as Brenda was concerned.

But Crystal was another story entirely. She was on Facebook, Twitter, and a number of other social media sites. She even had a blog, on which she posted frequently.

Everything that happened in Crystal's life—from high school, from nursing school, from her clinical rotations at the hospital—was described in great detail. Everything she did, either alone or with friends, was out there. Everyone she dated, everyone she did anything with, every book she read, every thought. She shared everything she bought at the mall or online.

She posted innumerable pictures of friends, taken at places, such as the campus, the mall, or a favorite hangout. There were also pictures of family: her grandparents, her aunt Beulah, and her uncle Dwayne. But there were no pictures at all of her parents—none.

It was difficult to imagine that someone who turned herself inside out online would have any secrets, but having no pictures of her parents suggested that she was hiding something. So I went to her blog.

I'd grown up in a time when people had talked to each other. They'd bragged about their children and grandchildren and what they did on their vacations. They'd showed each other pictures. But they hadn't broadcast all that to the world.

Now they do. Everybody has a Facebook page on which they post every picture they take with their cell phones. They post videos of their babies and their pets, pictures of whatever they're eating in a restaurant. Every little thing gets tweeted. Nothing is private anymore. Kids are going to grow up with their toilet training immortalized online for the whole world to see.

Crystal was no exception. I found her blog to be typical of a teenage girl: joyous about getting a good grade on a test; romantic about a certain handsome boy; jealous of a certain girl who also wanted said boy; her twenty-first birthday, when she went out with friends and had her first hangover—even to the number of times she threw up, which she really could have spared us. But no, it all had to come out, so to speak.

Several posts dealt with her secret desire to be a doctor and her decision to go into nursing school because of a lack of money. She hadn't mentioned it to anybody in her family, because they would just laugh, but of course on her blog the whole world would know—or at least anybody interested in some teenager's blog, which would be mostly other teenagers. I doubted that her grandmother or her parents or her aunt Beulah had ever read it.

Two posts in particular interested me.

July 7

My friend Karleen invited me to her family's Fourth of July celebration. Her parents had everybody up to their cabin in the Stanley Basin, just north of Stanley on the Salmon River. There must have been twenty people there—aunts and uncles, cousins, nieces and nephews. We all went rafting in the afternoon, and then they had a huge picnic with fried chicken, corn on the cob, all kinds of salads, watermelon— you name it, they had it. They had fireworks when it got dark. The little kids all ran around with sparklers.

I love Karleen's mom and dad. They treated me just like one of their own kids. They have five. The youngest one is six. They all seem to love each other so much, and even when they argue or chew out one of the kids, it's done with love. Why can't my family be like that?

Don't get me wrong; I love my grandma and Aunt Beulah. I miss my grandpa. He died last year. I don't like

Uncle Dwayne much; he's a jerk. He's mean to Aunt Beulah, and I don't like it.

But my parents live in New York. I hardly ever see them. They only call once in a while. They say they're coming to visit, and then something comes up with Dad's business or Mom's acting career. She gets a part in a play or a movie and all bets are off. Then when they do come visit, they argue all the time and don't pay any attention to me, or Grandma either. Why bother?

When Dad lost his job at Lehman Brothers, I thought things might change. I thought maybe they might come back here to live. But then Dad got a new job. He won't tell us what it is or who he works for. Nobody will talk about it. What's the big secret? Does he work for the Mafia or what?

Even now that they live in Boise, they don't pay any attention to me.

What's wrong with me?

Why can't I have a loving family like everybody else?

Oh, my God. If that wasn't a *cri de coeur,* I don't know what is. Crystal's anguish poured right off the screen at me and brought tears to my eyes.

What's wrong with me?, she'd asked, and the implicit question was: why is it that my own parents don't love me and my grandparents and aunt and uncle just put up with me, because if they don't, who will? If Crystal hadn't developed a Texas-sized inferiority complex by now, she was stronger than the average child. No wonder she hadn't confided her desire to go to medical school.

The other blog was a little more recent.

March 18

My Aunt Beulah died today.

They brought her in to the ER by ambulance this afternoon. They said she'd driven off the road into the canal. They were doing CPR on her, but they stopped as soon as

Dr. Martin showed up. He told me to take her vitals every fifteen minutes and release her body to the morgue as soon as her temp was 95. I didn't tell him she was my aunt. I cried the whole time I was in there with her.

Why did it have to happen today? This was the last day of my ER rotation. I know this is a small town, and sooner or later you end up having to deal with someone you know, even a loved one. But Aunt Beulah! Oh, God!

She looked awful. All blue and swollen up. She had a black eye and a big welt on her cheek. I bet Uncle Dwayne did that. Maybe she was running away. I hate him.

I don't understand any of this!

I'm going to miss her so much.

Poor kid.

So it was Beulah's own niece who had released the body. Or had she? She hadn't actually said so. Maybe somebody needed to ask her that point-blank.

And then there was this:

March 19

Uncle Dwayne's dead too.

What's going on here?

That was the last blog.

Why? Wouldn't someone who enjoyed spilling her guts into cyberspace be even more likely to keep blogging after suffering a loss like that? Why'd she stop?

Maybe Crystal had decided that she'd said too much already. Or had her parents shut her up? Maybe they didn't want her talking about the lawsuit. Or maybe her mention of the Mafia got her father's attention. If he was really mixed up in something illegal, he sure as hell wouldn't want his daughter blogging about it.

Was Crystal in danger too?

Russ Jensen came into my office to ask my opinion of a colon he'd resected for cancer. He had a folder in his hands. "Is it as bad as it looks?" he asked. "It looks like a stage four colon cancer."

"No," I said. "It's not anywhere near stage four. The cancer obstructed a diverticulum, and it got infected and caused an abscess. It's the abscess that made the mass look so big. What's in the folder?"

He tossed it on my desk. "That's Bobby Schofield's chart from my dad's office," he said. "There's no autopsy report as such, but there's a note at the end of the chart you might find interesting."

I looked up at him, perplexed. "But—"

"Dad kept his records in a fireproof file cabinet," he said, "so the fire didn't get to them."

"Sweet." I opened the folder. The notes on the last page were handwritten in typical doctor fashion—that is to say, unreadable. I squinted at them. It didn't help.

"Russ, help me out here," I requested. "Can you read your dad's handwriting?"

"Sort of," he said, taking the chart from me. "I think it says, 'Patient's body brought to my office by Sheriff Clint Schofield. Found in coulee. No pulse or respirations. Pupils fixed and dilated. Bruises on throat. Will request autopsy.'"

"That sounds as if Bobby was strangled," I said.

"The next note says, 'Autopsy consent denied by parents. Will contact coroner.'"

"Who was coroner back then?" I asked. "Surely it wasn't Rollie. Was it?"

"No, it was his dad," Russ said. "Rollie was working there at the time, though. He might remember."

"What's the next note say?"

Russ peered closely. "I think it says, 'Body released to Parkside Funeral Home.'"

"That's it?"

"No, there's another note. 'Autopsy performed by sheriff's request at mortuary. Hyoid bone not broken, but no water in lungs.'"

Shazam!

"Aha!" I said. "That means Bobby was already dead when he went into the coulee. He was murdered. No wonder everybody is so reluctant to talk about it. I wonder who else knows."

"Well, Rollie's dad is dead, so that's not a problem," Russ said.

"If Rollie remembers anything about this, he'd better not let on," I said. "He could be in danger too. So could you, for that matter."

"Don't worry about me," Russ said, rising to leave. "I know how to keep a secret. I'll just think about HIPAA and federal prison."

And now I knew about it too, I thought. So if I hadn't been in danger already, I certainly was now.

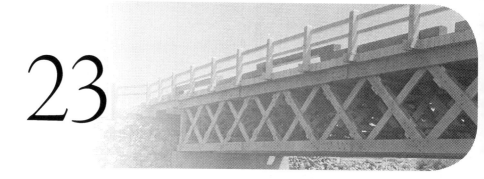

23

There was a little girl
Who had a little curl
Right in the middle of her forehead;
When she was good
She was very very good,
And when she was bad she was horrid.
—Henry Wadsworth Longfellow

I LOOKED UP AT RUSS. "You need to take this to the police."

"I will," he said, "right after my last surgery." He started to pick up the report, but I stopped him.

"Let me make a copy first."

"Why?"

"Just in case," I said.

"In case what?"

"In case somebody gets to you before you can go to the police," I said. "Or in case you have a car accident on the way to the police station. In case—"

"Okay, Toni. You made your point."

❦

Bernie would tear me a new one if I bothered him at the station again. But he needed to know about that autopsy report.

Also, Crystal might be in danger—but from her parents? Surely not. What kind of parents would kill their own child?

Well, that was just it, wasn't it? I had no idea what kind of parents they were, but having met them, I knew they weren't nice people. They certainly didn't seem to care much about their daughter, did they?

So I called.

Bernie didn't disappoint me. "Toni, what do you want now?"

I told him.

Silence ensued, during which I visualized him gritting his teeth and pulling out his hair while his frustration wrestled for supremacy with his professionalism. Then he cleared his throat. I tensed.

"Okay, Toni. I'll check it out."

∞

Elliott called to tell me that the Dukes had filed for civil damages.

"So, what exactly does that mean?" I asked. "Are they still suing the hospital as well as Mike and me, or is it just me?" I may as well know the worst right off the bat, I figured.

"They're still suing the hospital," Elliott said. "It has the deepest pockets, after all."

"What's the difference between this and the malpractice suit?"

"The only thing of significance is that the state board of medicine has nothing to do with it. They don't even have to change lawyers. We're still dealing with Katz, Klein, Rabinowitz, and Dane, but now we have to deal with Katz and Klein instead of Rabinowitz and Dane."

"Do we have to do all those depositions again?"

"We shouldn't," Elliott said. "They have all the information they need."

Oh, goody, I thought as I hung up the phone. I knew it was just a matter of time before Dave Martin and Jack Allen would descend upon me in a rage, because Elliott would also be informing them that they were still at the mercy of Beulah's crazy relatives—and our crazy legal system, which allowed crazy people to waste our time and the hospital's money when none of us had done anything wrong.

Well, maybe Dave had. There was still the matter of Beulah's body being prematurely released to the morgue.

Briefly, I considered paying Charlie a visit, but I still had a few more surgicals to sign out first. That took about half an hour. Then I went to Charlie's office. But he was busy.

Jack Allen and Dave Martin were already there.

Undecided, I stood there for a moment outside Charlie's glass wall, debating. Were they there for the same reason I was, or was it something that was none of my business? Or were they there to discuss firing me because I was a liability to the hospital? Maybe I should just go back to my office and call Charlie. By that time, the decision was made for me.

Charlie raised his arm and beckoned me in.

Jack pushed a chair toward me as I walked in. "So, Toni. Heard the latest?"

I sat down. "Do you mean about the Dukes suing us for civil damages?"

"In the amount of $60 million," Charlie said.

"Sixty million!" Until that moment, nobody had mentioned an amount. "Why so much?"

Charlie snorted. "Don't you mean, 'why so little'? Usually civil suits against hospitals are a lot higher than that."

I must have looked as shocked as I felt, because Dave reached over and patted my hand. "Toni, you've led a sheltered life. Civil suits against hospitals are usually in the hundreds of millions."

"Of course, they usually end up settling for less," Charlie said, "so they start out much higher than what they really want so they have bargaining room."

"Not only that," Jack said, "but these people are really in a hurry. They're pushing to settle out of court."

"If they settle out of court, they'll have to settle for a lot less than they asked for," Dave said.

"Maybe they don't care," I said.

This time it was Jack's turn to snort. "Not care? Then why sue?"

Dave frowned. "Toni, do you know anything about these people?"

"Well, I know that Brenda Duke is an actress whose stage name is Renee Gibson-Dubois, and that her husband Morty used to work for Lehman Brothers, and that his name is really Martin Dubois, and that he graduated from Twin Falls High School and went to ISU but didn't graduate from there."

"Jesus," Jack began, but I wasn't through.

"I also know that they have a daughter, Crystal Dawn Dubois, who was raised here in Twin by her grandparents and her aunt Beulah."

"She's a nursing student," Dave said, "who was responsible for releasing Beulah's body to the morgue before it was warm."

"But in her defense, she didn't know that," I said, anxious not to get Crystal into trouble. "She wasn't using a clinical low-temp thermometer, because the ER didn't have one."

"They don't have one?" Charlie asked. "Why not?"

"We never needed one before," Dave said.

"I can't believe that," Charlie said. "Surely we've had hypothermia cases before. Does that mean they were all misdiagnosed because we didn't have the right kind of thermometer?"

Jack and Dave looked at each other. Then they both turned and looked at me.

"What?" I asked.

"That doesn't leave this office," Dave said.

"What Dave means," Jack added, "is that we don't want you doing one of your chart reviews for quality assurance on the subject of hypothermia."

Them's fightin' words, by gum. "I wasn't going to," I protested. "But now I might."

"Gentlemen," Charlie interjected. "Ladies. Never mind the thermometer. Let's get back to the subject at hand. Doc, how do you know all this about the Dukes, or Duboises—or whatever the hell they are?"

"Google," I said, "and your yearbooks."

Charlie looked blank. "My yearbooks? You mean I went to school with this guy?"

"You did," I told him, "but you were a freshman and he was a senior. You probably didn't know him."

"Martin Dubois," Charlie said slowly. "Marty Dubois. Kind of a big, beefy guy with greasy black hair and a red face?"

"Yes," I said.

"He was the guy everybody went to for drugs on campus," Charlie said. "Not me, of course."

"How did you know about him?" Jack asked.

"Everybody knew about him," Charlie said defensively. "Except the cops, apparently."

Except the cops? I'd have to check on that. The Commander would probably know without even looking at the records.

That would explain Mrs. Gibson's not wanting to tell people who Brenda's husband really was—if she even knew who he was. She might not, if Brenda hadn't told her.

I stood up. "Do you guys need me anymore?"

"We know where to find you if we do," Charlie said.

Dave walked back to my office with me.

"Crystal was just finishing her ER rotation," he told me. "The day Beulah came into the ER was her last day, and she was off duty at three-thirty. She released Beulah's body and forgot to document it."

"So, how did you find out?"

"Marilyn Sanderson was the one who figured it out. Remember her?"

I did remember Marilyn. Formerly an ER nurse, she had been teaching in the nursing program at the college since 2008. I nodded.

"She was reviewing charts. She reviewed Beulah's. She called Crystal and asked her to come back and finish her nurses' notes. But Crystal said that she hadn't released the body. She took a bathroom break, and when she came back, the body was gone."

"You said it yourself," I reminded him. "Maybe someone who doesn't even work in the ER released that body. If that was the case, that person wouldn't write a note in the chart. But that person would have to sign a transfer form."

"A what?"

"When transport comes to pick up a body, don't you have to sign some kind of form? A release, or something?"

"Oh. You mean …"

"Exactly. Transport would have a record of who signed that form."

Arlene had everything typed by the time I got back. I signed the cases out and then called the station again.

Pete answered. "Bernie? He's not here. Can I help?"

I knew where Bernie was. He was here at the hospital, talking to Crystal. She'd finished her ER rotation, but now she'd be on some other rotation. "Call him," I urged. "Tell him to check into the possibility that someone released Beulah's body who wasn't even an employee. Tell him to ask people working that day—"

But Pete interrupted me. "Oh, he's back. Hey, Bernie! Toni wants to talk to you."

Too late.

Bernie's was the next voice I heard. "What now, Toni?"

"Did you talk to Crystal?"

"Yes. She said she didn't release the body. She said she took a bathroom break and when she got back the body was gone. It was the end of her shift, so she signed out and went home."

"So who released the body?"

"I asked Crystal if she had any idea who it might have been, and she told me that whoever it was would have to sign—"

"You talked to Transport?"

"Yes, Toni, I talked to Transport. I have a copy of the form. But I can't read the signature."

"Did you—"

"So I took it back to the ER," he went on, ignoring my interruption, "and nobody recognized it. So I asked if anyone there had worked that day, and one person had. She remembered that there was a new nurse who came on for the second shift that she'd never seen before. She remembered because this nurse had really unusual eyes. A deep cobalt blue."

Carole.

It was no use trying to decipher the signature. Carole wouldn't have signed her real name, and she would have made her signature illegible on purpose.

Carole had been responsible for the premature transfer of Beulah's body to the morgue cooler.

Why? Because she hadn't wanted Beulah to warm up and possibly regain consciousness.

And why would that be? Because she hadn't wanted Beulah to talk.

Ergo, Carole had murdered Dwayne.

"It was Carole," I said. "She's the murderer."

24

Golden lads and girls all must
As chimney-sweepers, come to dust.
—SHAKESPEARE, CYMBELINE

PETE, BAMBI, AND LITTLE TONI came to dinner Friday night, as they usually did.

It seemed that Pete had had as productive a day as I'd had. Once we all got settled with our drinks, he produced an iPad from the depths of the diaper bag. He switched it on. "Check this out."

We all gathered around to see picture after picture of the most gorgeous display of jewelry I'd ever seen outside of a jewelry store—more gorgeous than that, even. "What is this?" I asked.

"That," Pete said, "is Carole Schofield's jewelry collection. And before you ask, Toni, we did find the mate to that earring we found in your coat closet."

"My stars and garters," Mum breathed. "I've never seen anything like that."

"What would be the value of a collection like that?" Nigel asked.

"Well, that would be the rest of the story," Pete said. "We got warrants to photograph Carole's jewelry, and also to look at the jeweler's financials. Luckily, the man is a meticulous bookkeeper, and he had receipts for every piece Randy had bought. There were even photographs attached. That's how we know that we were right about Randy selling Carole's jewelry to raise money."

"There were receipts for items that weren't in Carole's collection," Mum guessed.

"Got it in one. It was the jeweler I told you about, by the way. His name is Leopold Witt."

Witt? Where had I heard that name before?

It didn't take me long to remember, seeing as I'd just seen it earlier that day. "Is he related to Carole Schofield?" I asked.

"He's her great-uncle," Pete said, surprised. "What made you ask that, Toni?"

"It's her maiden name," I said.

"How'd you know that?" Hal asked.

"Charlie brought me his yearbooks from high school," I said, and I told them what I'd found.

"Martin Dubois?" Pete said. "That name sounds familiar."

"You mean he's got a rap sheet?" Nigel asked.

"I think so, but not recently. I've heard Ray mention it, like it was years ago."

"Since he was in the same class as Randy, maybe they got into trouble together," I suggested. "Charlie told me that he was the big drug guy on campus when he was in high school."

"I'll ask Ray about it tomorrow," Pete said. "Did you find anything about Mortimer Duke online?"

"No," I said. "It's like Martin Dubois disappeared from the face of the earth in 1988."

"Well, we'll find him," Pete said.

"Not to change the subject or anything," Nigel said, "but what was the value of Carole's jewelry?"

"Six hundred seventy-five thousand dollars," Pete said. "That's the total value according to Leo Witt's records. Matching the receipts to what she has in her possession now, she still has six hundred thirty thousand dollars' worth."

"So what happened to the other forty-five thousand?" I asked. "If it didn't go into his bank account, where did it go?"

"We got a warrant to look into Leo's financials, and we paid a visit to his establishment. Your friend Leo does have a local bank account, in which we found no unusual activity—that is to say, we found nothing that matched deposits of checks from any of Randy Schofield's shell companies. Everything matched his books."

"What about brokerage or offshore accounts?"

"Well, that's where we hit pay dirt," Pete said. "Our friend Leo had a Swiss account with $15 million in it, give or take a few hundred. He opened it in 2007."

"Fifteen million!" I exclaimed.

"But he closed it in 2011."

"Where'd the money go?" I asked.

"We don't know," Pete said. "It seems to be another dead end."

"Back to Lehman Brothers, maybe?" Hal asked.

"But Lehman Brothers went bankrupt in 2008," I objected. "Do they even exist anymore?"

"You're right, Toni," Pete said. "They declared bankruptcy on September 15, 2008, to be exact, and the North American investment-banking and trading divisions were acquired by Barclay's on October 13."

"So any accounts remaining in Lehman Brothers after that would now be Barclay's," I said. "Assuming Barclay's hasn't also gone belly up by now."

"Nope. Barclay's is alive and well."

"Does Leo have a Barclay's account?" I asked.

"Nope. Leo doesn't have a Barclay's account, either in banking or trading."

Struck by a sudden revelation, I slapped my forehead. "Of course he doesn't. Who was it that worked at Lehman Brothers in the first place?"

"Morty Duke," Pete said.

"So, maybe it was Morty with the Lehman Brothers account. Maybe that account carried over to Barclays."

"Well, that's what we thought," he said, "so we checked. Mortimer Duke does have a brokerage account. But there's not much money in it. Only a few thousand dollars. Where'd the rest of it go?"

"Would it be possible," I wondered aloud, "to make a timeline showing how much money was in Leo's Swiss account and his Lehman Brothers account and his Barclay's account and the times that large amounts of money were transferred from one to the other?"

"Follow the money, in other words," Pete said. "Well, let's see. We know that Leo opened his Swiss account in 2007 with $15 million, and he closed it in 2011 with about the same amount. We also know that Lehman Brothers went belly up in 2008. Leo would have been smart to get Randy's money out of the stock market before the crash, which would account for the timing of his opening the Swiss bank account. So we may be wasting our time looking in Barclay's for an account carried over from Lehman Brothers. Leo could have put that money anywhere."

"Bernie told me today that Randy has embezzled six and a half million from the canal company, and if you subtract the jewelry from that, it would still leave nearly six million. But fifteen million? Where did all that come from?"

"Randy's been embezzling for nearly thirty years," Pete said. "Maybe it increased that much in that time. Interest rates, especially back in the eighties, were a lot higher than they are today. And maybe some of that money is actually Leo's."

"So," I said, "Randy was laundering the money he embezzled by putting it into Leo's brokerage account with Lehman Brothers, and Morty was managing the fund. Leo moved the money to the Swiss account in 2007, so when Lehman Brothers went under four years ago, the money wasn't there anymore. But then he closed the Swiss account in 2011. Where'd the money go then?"

"I rather think," Nigel said, "that it's now in a Barclay's account belonging to Mortimer and Brenda Duke."

"I thought Swiss bank accounts were numbered," Hal said. "How'd they manage to find Leo's?"

"Oh, no, Hal, dear," Mum said. "One has to present identification to open one. Ever since 9/11, even Swiss banks have to be careful. Moreover, in 2010 the US and Swiss governments signed an agreement to allow banks to share information with the US authorities in regard to tax fraud and tax evasion."

226

"So that explains why Bernie was able to find out about Leo's Swiss account," I said. "He was also able to find out about Morty's brokerage account at Lehman Brothers and at Barclays."

"Is that where all Randy's ill-gotten gains are located?" Nigel asked.

"Not exactly," Pete said. "Leo keeps an extraordinary amount of cash in his safe. He could easily buy back the jewelry, give Randy cash, and leave no paper trail. He could also cash Randy's checks for him and deposit them directly into his brokerage account, wherever it may be."

"But don't Randy's checks have to come back to the bank where they were issued?" I asked.

"All he'd have to do is endorse them over to Leo," Hal said.

"I know, but then wouldn't Leo have to sign them over to his brokerage account? Wouldn't they come back with both signatures on them?"

"No, dear," Mum said. "Checks under $10,000 don't have to be endorsed any more if they're being deposited directly."

"As far as I could see, none of the payments to Randy's shell companies were anywhere near that much," Pete said.

"Here's another thing," I said. "How could Morty more than double the size of that account and then know when to get it out of Lehman Brothers just in time for the crash?"

"Can you say 'insider trading'?" Hal asked.

"This is getting really complicated," Pete said.

"Let me complicate it some more," I said. "Elliott told me today that the Dukes have dropped the malpractice suit and are now filing a civil suit against the hospital for sixty million."

"Sixty million!" Hal exclaimed. "Why so much?"

"Charlie said that was an unusually small amount," I said.

"Charlie's right," Mum said. "Civil suits usually run into the hundreds of millions. Sixty million is a relative pittance."

"How did you know that?" I asked in surprise.

"You forget that I was an executive secretary," Mum said. "My company went through several civil suits during my forty years there."

"Charlie also said that the Dukes are in a big hurry and are pushing to settle out of court," I said.

"Well, then, they'll be settling for much less than what they're asking for," Mum said. "Why are they in such a hurry?"

"Especially if they lost everything in the crash, as they say," Nigel said. "Why are they suing you now instead of four years ago?"

"Something changed," Hal said. "Something came up. We need to find out what."

"Maybe not," I said. "They didn't have anything to sue about until Beulah died. Maybe they've been desperate for money all along, and this was their first chance to get some."

"Maybe they borrowed money to live on after he left Lehman Brothers," Pete said, "and the loan came due."

"Four years' worth?" Nigel asked. "How much would that amount to? And they'd have to have been making payments on it. Unless ..."

"Unless they borrowed it from someone other than a bank," Nigel said. "Here's another thing. Did he leave Lehman Brothers voluntarily, or was he fired?"

"Crystal said in her blog that he lost his job," I suggested. "If he'd been doing insider trading, he could have been caught and fired, or he could have left to avoid being caught."

"Securities fraud," Pete said. "Maybe the SEC caught up with him after four years. Or was about to."

"I understand they do levy some very punitive fines," Mum said.

"Fines?" I asked. "What about jail sentences?"

"The SEC doesn't deal in jail sentences," Mum said. "Not unless the Department of Justice gets involved."

"A fine would explain why the Dukes are in such a hurry for money," Hal said.

It certainly would, I thought, and that brought up another subject.

"That reminds me," I said. "Russ brought me a copy of Bobby Schofield's chart today."

"I thought they had a fire," Hal said.

"It was in a fireproof file cabinet," I said.

"What about the autopsy report?" Hal asked. "Was it there too?"

"There wasn't a report, as such," I said. "Russ warned me that there might not be. He said it could have been verbal, between his dad and the sheriff. But there was a note in the chart that Bobby had bruising on his neck, which was why he requested the autopsy from the parents."

"Did they consent?" Mum asked.

"No. So he turned it over to the coroner, who was Rollie's dad."

"So Russ's dad did the autopsy right there at the mortuary, and his conclusion was that Bobby hadn't drowned. He'd been strangled."

"Broken hyoid and no water in the lungs?" Hal asked.

"The hyoid wasn't broken, but there was no water in the lungs."

"I thought strangling always broke the hyoid," Hal said.

"Usually it does, but Bobby was only eighteen months old," I said. "The hyoid is still mostly cartilage. It bends but doesn't break."

"My stars and garters," Mum said. "Whoever would do such a thing?"

"I've been thinking about that," I said, "and I wondered what motive there could be for murdering a child, and the only one I can come up with is money."

"Money?" Mum asked. "How ..."

"It might be worthwhile to look at Marlin's financials," I suggested. "If Marlin has a lot of money, it would have been divided between Randy and Bobby when Marlin died."

"You're right there, Toni," Pete said. "I thought of that and got a warrant. Marlin's grandfather was one of the founders of the canal company, one of the original investors, and over the last hundred-plus years that investment has returned big-time. Marlin's worth several million dollars in stocks and real estate. The real estate he bought back when he was young has been sold or developed, and he's still raking it in, hand over fist. He lost relatively little in the crash of 2008."

"So Randy's the only person with a motive to kill Bobby," I said. "And Carole was the nanny, who was conveniently off the day that Bobby disappeared, and she'd have access to the boy's bedroom."

"Are you saying that Carole murdered Bobby?" Pete asked.

"I'm saying a good deal more than that," I declared. "I think Carole murdered Dwayne and tried to murder Beulah." I told them what I'd learned from Bernie about the strange nurse with cobalt eyes.

"I think," Pete said, "we've got enough to arrest Randy for embezzlement and Carole for suspicion of murder." He stood up. "I've got to go back to the station and get that going."

"Oh, honey," Bambi said. "Can't that wait till after dinner?"

He kissed her. "We'll go get 'em, and I'll be back before you know it," he said. "In time for dessert."

She sighed melodramatically. "That's what I get for marrying a cop," she said.

∾

Pete didn't come back. Bambi took Little Toni home after dinner. We didn't hear from Pete until he called after we'd gone to bed.

"Randy's gone," he said. "He's not at home, and he's not at the canal company either."

"What about Carole?" I asked.

"She's gone too," Pete said. "We've got a couple of officers checking with other canal company employees to see if they know anything."

"What's going on?" Hal asked.

"Pete says Randy and Carole have disappeared," I told him.

"'The guilty fleeth where no man pursueth,'" Nigel quoted. I hadn't seen him come up behind us. He held out his hand. "Let me talk to him," he said.

I gave him the phone. "They're both gone?" he demanded. "Have you checked with the airport? Did you put out an APB or a BOLO, or whatever it is?"

I was sure they had, but I said nothing. Nigel said, "Okay, do keep us posted, won't you?," and he hung up. "They're gone," he said. "Flown the coop. On the lam. In the wind."

"Yes," I said, "I know."

"So now what?" Hal asked.

"We go to sleep," I said, "and the dogs will let us know if anything happens."

∾

The phone rang at three in the morning. I answered it, praying that it would be a blood bank problem or something else that I could handle on the phone, but it was no such luck. It was a frozen section, so I had to haul my sleepy ass out of bed and go to the hospital.

"Be careful, sweetie," Hal said. "Remember, they're still out there somewhere."

As if I needed to be reminded. "Tell you what. When I leave the hospital, I'll call on my cell and leave the line open until I get home."

The frozen section consisted of a colon resection—unprepped, of course, since this was emergency surgery, and chock-full of you-know-what. The patient was an elderly man with symptoms suggesting acute appendicitis, but when the surgeon got into the abdomen, he found a mass in the colon, which he was sure was a colon cancer that had grown into the pericolic fat. But it wasn't. It was diverticulitis with a ruptured diverticular abscess.

When I left, I called Hal's cell phone from my cell, told him I was on my way home, left the line open, and stuck the phone in my bra. I thought I was being careful, looking around the underground parking garage and checking out the interior of my car before getting in. I could have sworn there was nobody around, but I was wrong.

I bleeped my car open with my remote and started to open the door. An arm snaked around my neck and immobilized my head in a firm headlock. My heart jumped into my throat.

Randy. Shit.

25

Beware the Jabberwock, my son!
The jaws that bite, the claws that catch!
Beware the Jubjub bird, and shun
The frumious Bandersnatch!
—Lewis Carroll

I FELT SOMETHING HARD AND cold against my temple. "Randy? Is that you?" I said.

The arm jerked my head back. "Shut up," he growled.

"Randy? Oh my God, is that a *gun?* Are you planning to shoot me?"

"If you don't shut up, I might."

I felt someone snatch the keys out of my hand. My hands were jerked behind me and secured with what sounded like a cable tie being ratcheted tight. I quickly flexed my wrists so that there was space between them and hoped nobody would notice.

They didn't. They shoved me into the backseat of my own car and pushed me face down on the floor. "Carole, have a heart," I said. "This is really uncomfortable."

"Shut up," she barked. She got into the backseat with me and continued to hold the gun against my head. Randy got into the driver's seat, started the engine, and drove us out of the parking garage.

Right, I thought, *you need a badge to drive in but not to walk in—and not to drive out either.* I tried to keep track of the turns and figure out where we were going. It was exceedingly uncomfortable, and the dust in the carpet made me want to sneeze. I raised my head once, but the barrel of the gun pushed it down again.

I sneezed, and sneezed again—and again, and again. It became difficult for me to catch my breath. I began to wheeze. Again I raised my head. When the gun barrel pushed it down again, I turned my head so that it glanced off. "Let me up," I said. "I can't breathe down here."

"Shut up," Carole said.

I continued to sneeze. My nose was plugged up and running. "Can I have a Kleenex?" I asked.

I heard Carole snap the clasp on her purse with the hand that wasn't holding the gun. Then she shoved a tissue under my nose.

"I can't blow my nose with my hands tied," I objected.

"If you think I'm gonna untie you, you've got another think coming," she said.

"Are we going to the canal company?" I asked.

"Can't you shut her up?" Randy asked irritably.

"Just drive, asshole," she replied.

"Who you calling an asshole, bitch?"

"Why are we going to the canal company?" I persisted.

"If you don't shut up, I'll knock you senseless," she said. "Or maybe I'll just shoot you now and be done with it."

"Oh, yeah, right," Randy snarled. "Just shoot her. Like you did your cousin and his wife. What was that all about?"

She'd killed her cousin and his wife? Who the hell were they?

"Use your head, dummy. We would have had to share the money. Marty didn't do all that insider trading for nothing, you know. Now that the SEC's caught up with him, he'd have had to use it all to pay the fines."

Oh my God, her cousin was Marty Dubois—alias Mortimer Duke.

"No, he wouldn't," Randy argued. "They stood to get three times that much from suing the hospital. Not to mention that they still owe us all that money you loaned them when Marty lost his job and couldn't get another one. You think we'll ever see that money now?"

So that's it, I thought. Brenda and Morty had borrowed it from someone other than a bank.

Also, since I'd proved that my cardiac puncture hadn't killed Beulah, the only thing left to sue for was the premature release of Beulah's body to the morgue, and I knew now that Carole had done that. Should I mention it? Carole might conk me on the head with the butt of her gun, but she and Randy were apparently already at odds with each other. Maybe I could use that to my advantage.

United we stand, divided we fall.

"No, they didn't," I piped up. "That suit's not going anywhere. You were seen, Carole. You released Beulah's body to the morgue. There was no wrongdoing on the hospital's part."

"You idiot!" Randy erupted. "Can't you do anything right?"

"Don't you talk to me like that," she shot back. "How about Beulah and Dwayne? I made that look like an accident, didn't I?"

"Yeah, but Beulah wasn't dead," he snapped. "How do you think I felt when I hauled her car out of the canal? I thought you'd killed her. How the hell did she manage to drag Dwayne's body out to the car and put it in the trunk? Did you even check for a pulse?"

"Are you kidding? There was blood all over the floor. I would have had to step in it."

"Oh, right. Footprints. Big fucking deal."

"You never give me credit for anything," she complained.

"Oh, really? It's your fault we're in this fix in the first place."

"How do you figure?"

"If you weren't such a jewelry junkie, I wouldn't have had to start embezzling in the first place."

"Oh yeah?"

"Yeah. Every birthday. Every Christmas. Every time I hit you. Every time your Uncle Leo was right there with something he knew you couldn't resist—and nothing under five grand a pop."

Every time he hit her? Christ on a crutch.

"Oh, yeah, you're so pussy-whipped," she jeered. "You're the pussy. You couldn't even look at Beulah's body without getting sick to your stomach."

"Fuck you, Carole. You're a castrating bitch."

The car stopped. Apparently we'd arrived at our destination. I tried to roll over and sit up. "Are we at the canal company?" I asked.

Carole pushed me back down. "Never you mind. You don't need to know."

Randy got out of the car, leaving the engine running, and opened the back door. "Out."

Carole got out, still holding the gun on me. "You get out too."

"I can't," I protested. "I can't get up without using my hands."

"Oh, for God's sake." She reached in and dragged me out of the car by my collar. She needed both hands. I'm heavier than I look. I was hoping she'd have to drop the gun, so I went completely limp, trying to make it as difficult as I could for her to hold onto it and me at the same time, but no dice. She retained her grip on the dratted thing. I landed on the ground, which was not concrete but dirt. I rolled over and sat up. We weren't at the canal company. There were no buildings in sight. The pitch darkness was broken only by the Subaru's headlights and interior lights, and in their light I could see the reflection on water.

We were at the canal.

Uh-oh.

And there was the excavator, sitting right next to us, just waiting.

I realized what they had in store for me.

Beulah's rescue in reverse.

"Okay," Randy said. "On your feet, Doctor." He reached down and unceremoniously jerked me to my feet. "Start walking."

"Where?" I asked.

Randy didn't answer. He had hold of my collar and pushed me roughly around the front of my car to the passenger side. He tried to open the door, but it was locked.

"Fuck! How do you unlock this thing?"

"With the key," I said.

The key was in the ignition, out of reach.

"Carole!" Randy called. "Unlock the goddam doors!" To me he said, "You would have to have one of those fucking smart-ass cars."

My Subaru had one of those systems where all the doors automatically lock when the car is put in gear. "Yeah, so assholes like you can't hijack my car," I said.

Carole punched a button on the driver's door, and the locks clicked open. Randy opened the door and shoved me rudely inside. "Shut up, bitch." He slammed the door and walked back to Carole, who, to my utter astonishment, turned the gun on him.

"Get in the driver's seat," she ordered. "Come on, move!"

Randy objected. "What the hell do you think you're doing?"

She jammed the gun into his ribs. "Pussy-whipped, huh? I'll show you pussy-whipped." She jabbed him again. "Move!"

He stepped back, looking at his wife with a perplexed expression. "Look, what's this all about? I thought we agreed that the doc needs to die."

"Oh, we did, we did," she agreed. "But so do you."

"Damn it, Carole, this is no time for jokes."

"Get in the driver's seat," she commanded. "Move!"

He turned and faced her. "Or what? You'll shoot me? That won't look good."

"You won't be around to care. Now get in."

"The hell I will!"

In a lightning fast motion, she pushed him in and shot him—right in the middle of his forehead. The back of his head blew off and splattered all over me. The bullet whanged past my head and blew a hole in the window behind me. His lifeless body fell into the driver's seat, and his ruined head dropped into my lap. I stared in disbelief. "Carole, what the hell is wrong with you? Get him off me!"

She reached in, grabbed Randy's collar, and pulled him upright. Then she picked up his feet and tried to push them into the car. She was having a hard time because of the length of his legs. I shook my head, trying to dislodge bone and tissue fragments.

"If you untie my hands, I can help with that," I observed.

"In your dreams." She gave a final mighty shove and got Randy's body arranged more or less upright with his feet inside the car. At least the thing that used to be his head wasn't in my lap anymore. "It's gonna look like you two were having an affair and I caught you."

"Won't it look funny if they find me with my hands tied behind me?" I asked.

"By that time, I'll be long gone," she said and slammed the door. She walked over to the excavator and climbed in. I heard her start up the engine. The excavator's lights came on, and they were much higher and brighter than the Subaru's.

The vertical arm began to move.

I watched, mesmerized, as she raised it to a horizontal position above the cab and then slowly swiveled it out to the side toward my car. Gradually, she moved the scoop into place and dropped it right on top of us. I watched as the thumb and bucket clamped down on the car and began to lift it.

She was going to pick us up and drop us into the canal. Randy wouldn't care, because he was already dead, but I sure as hell cared. I was not about to let her drown me without a fight.

The car began to rise. With my hands tied, I couldn't open the door and jump out. Even if I could, I didn't see how I could swim to shore or climb out. It might be possible if my hands were tied in front of me instead of in back, so I shifted myself around until I could get my hands under my bottom, and then under my thighs. Then I bent my knees until I could get my hands under my feet—one foot, then the other—and then, voila! My hands were now tied in front of me. Luckily, the cable tie was loose enough to allow me to do that, although it did cut cruelly into my wrists. And thanks to aerobics, I was pretty limber for someone pushing fifty.

The car continued to rise. It looked like a good six feet off the ground now. I pressed the door handle down. The door clicked open but didn't move. The excavator thumb held it firmly in place.

The car kept rising. We had to be at least ten feet off the ground, maybe more. Maybe when Carole got the car out over the water and dropped it, I could push the door open and jump. The car stopped rising and began to move sideways toward the canal.

I had to get the cable tie off my hands. It was loose, but not loose enough for me to work one hand out. I turned on the interior lights and flipped open the center console. Maybe, just maybe ... aha! A pair of nail clippers. That should do it. It took me several tries to get them into a position where they'd cut the cable tie, but finally I did it. The cable tie fell away, and I was free.

The car was moving with excruciating slowness. It would do Carole no good, I reasoned, to drop us too close to the edge of the water. It would be too easy to find the car. If Carole wanted to make sure we weren't found until the water was turned off in the fall, she'd have to drop us way out in the middle of the canal.

I waited. We were past the water's edge now. I waited just a few seconds more. I tensed. Any minute now, the thumb would loosen its grip, and I could push the door open and jump. Any minute now ...

I wondered if my phone connection was still open. If so, could Hal still hear me? He'd need to know where to find me. "Hal, if you're listening, I'm in my car with Randy's dead body, and Carole is about to drop us in the Low Line Canal. Turn right off Washington and keep going until you see an excavator."

We were out over the water now. I heard a creak, and suddenly the car dropped. I pushed on the door. It opened. The car hit the water, carrying me under.

That's it for phone communication, I thought inconsequentially.

It was like déjà vu all over again, all my muscles cramping in the excruciatingly cold water. This time I wasn't wearing a heavy wool coat and heavy boots. I had put on a light windbreaker and sneakers to go to the hospital, expecting to go right home after I was done and not spend any significant length of time outdoors in the cold.

I swam upward until my head broke the water. I took a huge breath and resubmerged, hoping Carole hadn't been looking. Below me, the Subaru's lights were still on. Above me, the excavator's lights shone out onto the water. But the current was swift and had already carried me out of their path. Underwater, I swam toward the light, coming up for air two more times, and eventually reached the side of the canal.

By that time, I could no longer see the Subaru's lights. Either I was too far away, or they'd gone out. I was in the shadow of a large rock. The side of the canal here was slanted, not straight up and down like it had been where Beulah's car had gone in. I climbed out of the water, being careful to stay behind the rock. The wind bit through my wet clothes—more déjà vu.

From my vantage point, I had a clear view of the excavator. Carole was in the process of returning the arm to its upright position. Next to it was the dark shape of a pickup truck: a black Toyota Tundra perhaps—Randy's. Carole's Camry was probably back at the hospital.

I shivered violently. I couldn't stay where I was. I had to either get out of my clothes or out of the wind. The only good thing about being wet was that the water had probably rinsed off the blood and tissue fragments of what had once been Randy's head.

Carole couldn't possibly see me from where she was, not unless she turned the excavator around and pointed the headlights at me. I could hear the engine still running, and I could see Carole's silhouette in the interior lights of the cab.

Perhaps she was running the engine for warmth. I envied her.

With the engine running, she wouldn't be able to hear me if I sneaked up on her. But she would see me if I got close enough. Luckily, my clothes were dark-colored. That would help me stay invisible.

What to do, what to do …

I was so cold I could hardly think.

The Tundra stood between me and the excavator. Maybe I could make it that far without being seen. Carole wasn't expecting anybody else to be moving—certainly not me, and certainly not from this direction. She probably wasn't even looking this way. I took a deep breath and sprinted.

I reached the Tundra without any problem, but then I realized that even if it was unlocked I couldn't open the door without the interior lights coming on and giving my position away.

Cautiously I raised my head and peered through the Tundra's windows. I saw Carole open the door of the excavator cab and scramble out, leaving the engine running and the lights on. She jumped down and began walking.

Shit.

But wait. She wasn't walking toward the Tundra. She was walking toward the bank of the canal—maybe to gloat about her clever plan, or maybe to watch the bubbles rise, or maybe to make sure nothing else did. In any case she wasn't looking my way.

I could see her clearly in the bright light, and she didn't appear to be carrying her gun either. Maybe it was in a pocket, but maybe she'd left it in the cab. Or maybe she was out of ammunition. Maybe that was why she hadn't shot me when she'd shot Randy. Maybe I didn't need to worry about the gun.

On the other hand, she might have stashed more ammo in the cab of the excavator and reloaded. I couldn't take the chance.

I tiptoed around the dark side of the Tundra. Carole stood on the shore, looking out toward the water.

From watching Carole, I'd learned that the door to the cab was on the other side, and that there were steps and a handrail leading up to it. So I crept around the dark side of the excavator and looked again. Carole was still standing in the same place. The cab door was open. The interior lights illuminated the path she must have taken to get down to the ground, and without wasting another nanosecond, I climbed up and into the cab. Finally, I was out of the wind. It was much warmer in the cab, though not as warm as it would have been if Carole hadn't left the door open.

Quit bitching, Toni. You can't have everything.

Carole's gun lay on the seat. I grabbed it and put it in my pocket.

There was no place to hide in the cab. It was just big enough for one person to sit and operate the controls, and the back of the seat was right up against the rear wall. Furthermore, the entire cab was clear on all sides for all-around visibility. With the interior lights on, I was a sitting duck.

These thoughts flew through my brain in just the time it took for me to vacate the cab and reach the ground, and not a minute too soon. From behind the tank treads, I saw Carole turn away from the canal and begin walking back.

Carole climbed back into the cab just long enough to see that her gun was gone. "What the fuck?" I heard her say, and then, "I could have sworn I left it here. Maybe I dropped it." Then she jumped down from the cab and stood still, looking around her with a flashlight. If she turned her head in my direction, she might see me. I kept still and crouched down behind the tank treads.

But I was in luck. She started retracing her steps toward the canal. If she'd turned back toward me, it would've been harder to take her unawares.

I wished I didn't have to do this. I wished that help would come. Maybe the cell phone thing hadn't worked. But Carole was bigger than me. In hand-to-hand combat, she could probably take me two falls out of three.

I'd have to take her in one—and then keep her under control until help arrived. If help didn't arrive, I'd have to subdue her, throw her into the back of the Tundra, and drive her to the police station myself. There were two problems with that. She would be too heavy for me to lift her into the truck bed, and I didn't have anything to tie her up with.

Or did I?

Hadn't I seen a rope in the cab?

Quickly, I climbed back up. There it was, neatly coiled on the floor under the seat. I grabbed it and jumped down. Carole was almost to the bank of the canal now. This was it, now or never. With the gun in one hand and the rope in the other, I ran silently at her and hurled my full weight at her back.

She went down heavily, the wind knocked out of her. I sat on her and tied her hands behind her. Then I swiveled around and tied her feet together. Finally, I tied her hands to her feet and pulled the rope tight enough that she couldn't even struggle.

I stood up and surveyed my handiwork, noticing that we were a mere two feet from the canal bank. Carole had her wind back by then and began screaming invective at me.

"Shut up, or I'll throw you in the canal," I said.

"You're not strong enough, you fucking little twerp," she yelled.

"Really?" I said, and I pulled upward on the rope that held her hands and feet together. She screamed in pain. I let go. She was silent.

"That's better," I said.

"What are you gonna do to me?" she whimpered.

I began to stroll slowly around her, staying just out of reach, casually waving the gun in her general direction. "Oh, now, what am I going to do. Let me see. I could drag you over to the Tundra and throw you in the back and take you to the sheriff. Or, since I'm such a fucking little twerp, I could just leave you here and take the Tundra and go to the sheriff by myself. Or I could throw you in the canal. What'll it be? Door number one, door number two, or door number three?"

Carole began to cry.

"None of the above? Dear me, what a shame. Those are the only choices you have. There's no door number four, you know. Or is there? Well, whattaya know. You're in luck. I think door number four has just arrived."

26

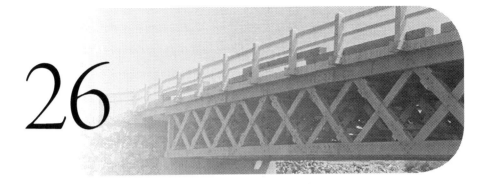

LIGHTS APPEARED DOWN THE ROAD, looking unearthly in clouds of dust.

The rescue vehicles appeared one by one—first the police car and then the sheriff, followed by the fire engine, the ambulance, and the tow truck. They pulled up and stopped, throwing up even more dust and nearly obscuring the excavator. Out of the gloom came several male figures, all running in our direction.

Nigel saw me first. "There she is, by Jove!" he called out.

Hal reached me first, catching me in his arms and lifting me off my feet. He held me tight, wet as I was. "Thank heavens you did that thing with the phone," he said into my ear. "We heard everything right up until you went into the water."

I hugged him tight. "I've never been so glad to see anybody in my life."

Nigel came up to us. "I say, old girl, we thought you were still in the canal. How'd you manage to escape?"

I told him.

"Blimey!" was all he said.

Sheriff Bob Barton took charge of Carole. "Holy cow, Doc. How'd you learn to hogtie like that?" Experimentally, he tested the rope. Carole screamed.

"Just got lucky," I said. "This is her gun. Sorry about the fingerprints."

He took it, fished an evidence bag out of his pocket, and placed the gun in it. "That's all right. I doubt we'll need them."

Pete came up and said, "Toni, you need to get into the ambulance now."

"I don't need any ambulance," I objected. "I'm perfectly all right." But I was shivering violently, and my teeth were chattering, probably as much from reaction setting in as cold, and Pete didn't believe me. What a surprise.

"You're hypothermic," he said. "You need to go get checked out."

"Yes, you do," Hal said. "I'll ride with you, and Pete and Bernie will be right behind us."

"What about Carole?"

"She's riding with the sheriff."

So I capitulated. At least it'd be out of the wind and warm.

Bernie was waiting for me, talking to the paramedics. I recognized one of them as the one who'd taught me two years ago how to treat cyanide poisoning in the field. He recognized me too. "Hey, Doc," he greeted me. "Don't you know better than to go swimming in the canal?" Then he got a good look at me in the interior lights of the ambulance. "What's all this stuff in your hair?"

"Pieces of Randy Schofield's head," I said.

Bernie turned abruptly and walked away very fast into the darkness, where I heard him retching. But the paramedic was made of sterner stuff. "How'd that happen?"

I told him, and as I did so, I thought I heard a faint "Oy gevalt!" from the front seat.

By the time we reached the hospital, I'd been changed out of my wet clothes into a (dry) hospital gown and wrapped in a (dry) warm blanket, and I had an IV running in one arm. They'd put a nasal cannula on me too, for oxygen, which I didn't think I'd need, until they told me that the pulse oximeter on my finger said that my pO2 was eighty-six. They also told me that my body temperature was ninety-two.

I asked if they'd used a low-temp thermometer.

The paramedic grinned and said, "Hell, yes. Doc Martin would never let us hear the end of it if we didn't."

❧

My stint in the emergency room was much more pleasant than the last one had been. I was allowed to change into scrubs and was wrapped in a Bair Hugger, while prewarmed, 5 percent dextrose in saline ran into my veins. I was snug and warm while my body temperature slowly returned to normal, and I didn't have to vomit at all.

It was just the opposite, in fact. I was allowed to drink water, soda, and coffee. The latter made me a little nervous, because I'd once heard a story where sixteen men had been rescued from the ocean in a severely hypothermic state and had been given hot coffee. Every one of them had dropped dead. But I sipped it, slowly, and when I did not die, I finished it.

Hal sat behind me on a stool, trying to pick the bits of bone and brain out of my hair. It was so curly and so tangled that he was having a tough job of it. "First thing we're doing when we get home," he vowed, "is wash your hair. This is disgusting."

I couldn't have agreed more. In the warm cubicle, I was beginning to smell it. What's the point of having a cold if you can still smell?

The doctor came into my cubicle to check on my progress. It wasn't Dave. I guessed the poor man had to sleep sometime. It was a resident in the family practice program sponsored by the University of Washington in the various hospitals of the Cascade system.

"We've got some antibiotics running into that IV," he said. "Who knows what nasty little critters are swimming around in the canals these days?"

I couldn't have said it better myself.

"If you start coughing or running a fever," he continued, "come back in. It might mean you're developing pneumonia."

"I have a cold," I told him. "I'm already coughing."

"Toni," said my long-suffering husband, "don't argue with the man."

I sighed.

I was discharged at dawn, my temperature and pO2 normal. Pete and Bernie had run Hal and Nigel home in the cruiser so that Hal could get his Cherokee and come back for me. Hal had spent the whole time with me in the ER, but Nigel had gone gratefully home to bed. "Not as young as I used to be," he'd remarked. "Fiona's right. I should leave the heroics to the young Turks from now on." He'd waved tiredly and left without another word.

True to his word, the first thing Hal did was send me upstairs to shower and wash my hair, something I was only too glad to do. The smell of decomposing human remains had become quite strong, and Killer and Geraldine were all over me, but Mum screwed up her face and held her nose as I walked by. I still wore the hospital scrubs, as my clothes had been deemed unsalvageable. The judicious application of conditioner enabled me to comb the last of Randy's pieces-parts out of my hair. Removing them from the drain, however, was another matter entirely. In the hospital, disposing of human remains was routine, but what do you do with human remains in your own home?

I put them in a baggie and carried them out to the trash bin in the garage.

∞

Pete and Bernie came back after breakfast to update us.

"Search and rescue recovered your car," Pete told me, "but I don't think you want it back. The water did a lot of damage. I expect your insurance company will declare it a total loss."

I agreed. I didn't really want it back. A man had been killed in it, and the blood and tissue splattered all over the interior would never completely come out. That smell would always be there.

"But they found another car down there," Bernie said. "Care to guess whose it was?"

"A black Escalade," I guessed, "belonging to Brenda and Morty Duke. Were their bodies in it?"

"They were," he said. "They'd both been shot in the forehead, just like Randy."

"What happens to the money?" I asked. "And the jewelry?"

"I have no idea," he said. "I guess it depends on whether they wrote wills or not. Elliott would be the one to ask about that. By the way, that was a clever thing you did with the phone. We heard the whole thing."

"You heard it?" I asked surprised. "How'd you do that?"

"When I heard you say 'Randy, is that you' and mention a gun," Hal said, "I called Pete on the landline. He told me to record it."

"How?" I asked.

Pete pulled out his cell and showed me the app. "I told him to download that app, and it worked a treat. Show her," he said to Hal, and Hal obliged.

Randy's and Carole's voices came through strong and clear. I shuddered when I heard Carole's voice saying, "If you don't shut up, I'll knock you senseless. Or maybe I'll just shoot you now and be done with it." And then Randy's, saying, "Oh, yeah, right. Just shoot her. Like you did your cousin and his wife. What was that all about?"

"That's enough," I said. "I'm getting creeped out here."

"So am I," Mum said.

Hal turned it off.

"One thing I don't get," Bernie said, "is why Beulah put her husband in the trunk of her car and drove to the canal in the first place."

"My guess is that she regained consciousness and saw Dwayne's dead body and thought she'd killed him," I said, "and the only thing she could think to do was to get rid of the *corpus delicti* by dumping it in the canal."

"But why right next to the bridge?" Bernie argued. "Somebody driving by would be bound to see her."

"Someone did see her," Hal said.

"Maybe that wasn't what she was planning to do," I said. "Maybe she was planning to take the body down the access road to a place where there were no bridges or houses around. I'm guessing she lost consciousness right about when she made the turn onto the access road and then went into the canal instead."

"She might have been heading for the same place Carole and Randy took you," Pete said. "That's about as far away from civilization as you can get."

"Well, now we know the whole story, thanks to you two," Pete said.

"Except for who killed Bobby," Hal said.

"I guess we'll never know for sure," I said, "but I suspect it was Carole. Randy was too squeamish."

"And by the way," Pete said, "the footprint in your backyard matched Randy's boots, and the orange fabric matched his hunting vest, just as we thought."

"What about the truck Dwayne had his accident in?" I asked.

"It was totaled," Pete said, "and sold for salvage. Pieces of it have been installed in any number of other vehicles, so there's no way now to tell if it was tampered with or not."

"We don't exactly need to know that anyway," Bernie said. "Randy's dead, and we've got Carole in custody with plenty to charge her on. End of story."

"How's Nigel doing?" I asked Mum. "He looked pretty tired when I saw him last."

"He was," said my mother. "His bum was dragging when he got home. Reaction setting in, no doubt. I gave him a brandy before he went to bed, and it seemed to help. I hope he's learned his lesson," she added. "Honestly, you two. Always thinking you can be heroes and never get hurt. A lot of codswallop, in my opinion."

"Was it really that bad, Mum?" I asked.

She laughed. "That bad? It was worse than bad with Nigel and Hal strutting around like roosters, seeing who could crow the loudest."

Nigel, who had just come downstairs in his bathrobe and slippers, objected. "Fiona, would you give over?" he said severely. "We did nothing of the sort." He sounded highly offended, but his lips twitched, so I knew he was trying not to laugh.

"Oh, it was classic," Pete said. "Bernie and I came over here to listen to that recording, and then we were about to go, when Hal insisted on going too."

"And then," said my mother, "that fool of a husband of mine decides he wants to go too. 'I say, old chap,' he says, 'aren't you forgetting something? I too am an officer of the law.' 'Nigel Henry Gray,' I said, 'you'll do nothing of the kind. You're forgetting that not only are you out of your jurisdiction, but you're retired. You're too old for such nonsense, and you've just had prostate surgery.'"

"And then," Hal said, "Nigel says, 'P'r'aps that's true, dear girl, but I can still handle a gun.'"

Nigel chuckled. "I say, old chap, very good imitation, eh what? Had you thought of going on the stage?"

"I said, 'Nigel Henry Gray, you're not going anywhere,'" Mum continued. "'What do you expect me to do while you're gallivanting about with a gun—sit idly by and worry that you'll get yourself shot? Not a bloody chance in hell.'"

"I don't blame you," Hal told her. "How do you think I felt all those times Toni got herself into trouble? At least this time she had some backup."

"I'm not sure that isn't worse, as far as Mum is concerned," I said. "All of us could have been shot."

"That's true," Mum said. "That's exactly what I thought."

"Well, then Fiona decided to go too," Hal said. "It took all four of us to convince her that somebody needed to stay with Bambi and Little Toni, and finally she gave in."

"So away we went," Nigel said grandly, "once more into the breach, dear friends, for Merrie England and Saint George!"

"Yes, dear," Mum said. "With all your guns."

"Wait a minute," I said. "Did all of you have guns?"

"Certainly," Hal said. "Even me."

Wonderful, I thought. A family affair, with guns. What could possibly go wrong there?

As Mum would say, it's a good job no one actually had to shoot one.

EPILOGUE

ANOTHER WEEK HAD PASSED, AND it was Friday again.

Jodi and Elliott had come to dinner, along with Pete, Bambi, and Little Toni. "What's that wonderful smell?" Bambi asked.

"Fiona is cooking a standing rib roast," Hal said.

"With Yorkshire pudding?" I asked hopefully.

"Of course with Yorkshire pudding," Mum said.

Hal brought me a scotch of noble proportions. "You can drink it all," he said. "Nobody is going to call you to do an autopsy today."

"I should hope not," I said. "I'm not on call. And now that they've recovered my Subaru and the Dukes' Escalade, Mikey's going to have three autopsies this weekend."

"Paybacks are a bitch," Hal agreed.

"Oh, I'll probably go in and help him," I said. "But not tonight."

"Speaking of your Subaru, did you get your new car yet?" Jodi asked.

The insurance company had indeed declared my Subaru a total loss, and I had replaced it with a new Subaru. This one was a lovely shade of cobalt blue.

"I get to pick it up tomorrow," I told her.

Nigel raised his glass to me. "Here's to the lady of the hour," he said. "P'r'aps you should consider joining the ranks of law enforcement, eh what?"

"They can't afford her," Hal said.

I looked around at my little family with affection and realized how lucky I was to have all this love and support in my life. I raised my glass to Nigel and everybody else. "L'chaim!"

Little Toni, sitting in my lap, reached for my glass. I held it out of her reach. "Not yet, baby girl. You've got about twenty years to go."

My granddaughter didn't like that and let everybody know it with an earsplitting squall. "Here, sweetie," I said, "here's your apple juice. It tastes a lot better than scotch, really."

Little Toni wasn't having any truck with that, and she batted the sippy cup away.

I stuck my finger in my scotch and touched it to her lips. Greedily she sucked on it, made a face, and screamed. This time she accepted the sippy cup and let me have my scotch all to myself.

"Did you just give her *scotch*?" Bambi asked in disbelief.

"Yes, and now she knows she doesn't like it," I said.

"I did the same thing with Antoinette," my mother said. "Worked like a charm."

"So what's gonna happen to all that money?" Bambi asked.

"Good question," Elliott said. "In a perfect world, the money Randy embezzled from the canal company should be returned to it, plus interest. But Morty had all that money in a Lehman Brothers account in Leo's name, and now it's in a bank in the Caymans under Leo's name. On paper, it belongs to Leo, and there's no paper trail connecting it to Randy and Carole. Legally, the canal company has no claim to it."

"What's Leo going to do with it?" asked Hal.

"Buy jewels, I expect," Elliott said. "Of course, anything that was in Morty's account will come to his daughter, Crystal."

"What happens to Marlin Schofield's money," I asked, "now that both his sons are dead?"

"I believe it goes to charity," Elliott said, "although I'm not sure which charities he wants it to go to."

"Do you suppose," I speculated, "he could use some of it to establish a scholarship fund for Crystal?"

"For Crystal? Why?"

"So she can go to medical school. That's what she wants to do, and she can't afford it."

"I could ask Ray to go talk to him about it," Pete offered.

"Okay," Elliott said. "Let me know. If he wants to do that, I'd be happy to help set it up."

"How did you know about that, kitten?" Mum asked. "Did Crystal tell you?"

"She told the world," I said, "in her blog."

"Do you think her parents knew?" Bambi asked.

"I doubt it," I said, "but her aunt Beulah would be very proud."

Little Toni stood up in my lap and wound her tiny arms around my neck. "Wuv Bubbie," she said.

Praise for *Murder under the Microscope*

"*Murder under the Microscope* is an exemplary first novel."

—*The US Review of Books*

"A very fast-paced read that will hold your attention. The author, Jane Bennett Munro, MD, like the main character, Toni Day, is a pathologist. This fact lends quite a bit of credibility to the novel, and I enjoyed the inside look into the day-to-day life of a person in this profession. This "realness" definitely added to the story in a positive way, as it would have been very difficult for an "outsider" to this profession to write this book in such a believable and compelling manner."

—*Rebecca's Reads*

"A page-turning romp through the intrigue in a small Idaho town that rivals Twin Peaks for strange goings-on."

—New York BookFest

"I found this to be a real thought-provoking novel, with twists and turns on every page. I was hooked from page one. The characters and the setting were superb."

—Blogger for *Rebecca's Reads*

"I hope that this book is the first of a long series."

—Pathologist, Indiana

"*Awesome* medical/forensic mystery! Must read! Grabs your attention from the first page. You walk/read right into a murder mystery that keeps you guessing until the last page."

—Blogger for *Rebecca's Reads*

"There's nothing like someone who really knows the ins and outs of the investigative process pouring that experience into a book, and Jane Munro does a fantastic job with *Murder under the Microscope!*"

—Blogger for *Rebecca's Reads*

Praise for *Too Much Blood*

"Munro's writing is entertaining, believable, and fast-paced. She takes you into the autopsy room, shows the fragility of the characters, and makes the readers feel they are inside the story. Readers will definitely be looking forward to solving more cases with this character."

—*The US Review of Books*

"Exceptional realism that only comes from personal, hands-on experience. Munro writes with captivating flair, and her story line is believable and realistic."

—*Rebecca's Reads*

"Riveting and action packed, this book will take you on a mind-blowing journey of a lifetime!"

—*iUniverse*

"Toni is a very likable character, well written and three-dimensional. I rated *Too Much Blood* five out of five kitties. I give it my highest recommendation to anyone who enjoys medical murder mysteries."

—*JaneReads.blogspot.com*

Praise for *Grievous Bodily Harm*

"Sassy pathologist Toni Day shines in this modern-day mystery of corporate shenanigans and hospital politics ... A smart, enjoyable summer read."

—Kirkus Reviews

"Munro's story is a roller coaster ride of suspense and intrigue, with twists and turns that will entertain a lover of mysteries and forensic crime novels for hours."

—The US Review of Books

"This book was a thoroughly enjoyable book that kept me guessing throughout the entire thing. I actually enjoyed this book *more* than *Too Much Blood*, and for that reason, this book gets a full five stars from me. I cannot wait to see what the author writes next."

—GoodReads

"This is a book that you should read if you like mystery, murder, and mayhem. Who doesn't like a combination of those three? The author didn't fail to deliver another fantastic book."

—Gayle Pace, author of May a Rainbow Shine Down on You

"Now that I have read this novel, I cannot wait to read others in the Toni Day mystery series. I give this a five-star rating and suggest you get a copy for yourself in e-book or paperback!"

—Miki Hope

"The author brilliantly shares her expertise in forensic pathology, allowing readers inside the room during the autopsy, and sharing her expertise and knowledge.

—Fran Lewis, BookPleasures.com

"This book is one adventure after another ..."

—Rebecca's Reads